"What the hell is going on?" Leon asked.

"Flora arrives in Stillwater and...what? Someone decides he, or she, doesn't like the way she looks or the color of her lipstick? So they kill her receptionist and two of her patients, while also running a social media campaign to drive her out of town?"

"And then try to drive me off the road as I was on my way here." Flora pointed to her dented car with the bumper hanging off.

"What?" Leon's already elevated stress levels kept on going.

"Did you get the registration details?" Laurie was already flipping to a clean page in her notepad.

"No. I was too busy trying to stay alive."

"Damn it, Flora. You could have been killed."

"I could have been killed if I'd stayed on that road and taken my chances with that SUV. This way, I had a fighting chance of getting to Eve's place." She turned to Laurie. "But Leon is right. It looks like someone took one look at me and decided they wanted me out of Stillwater so bad it was worth killing for."

* * *

Be sure to check out all the books in the Sons of Stillwater miniseries!

* * *

If you're on Twitter, tell us what you think of Harlequin Romantic Suspense! #harlequinromsuspense

Dear Reader,

Family in the Crosshairs is the fourth book in the Sons of Stillwater series. Thank you for joining me on this latest adventure to Stillwater, Wyoming!

It's a beautiful place. Cradled low in the embrace of a towering mountain range, the town has been largely untouched by time and retains its historic buildings and Western charm. Doctor Leon Sinclair has clawed his way back from heartache to earn a position of respect in the town where he was born. When out-of-town medic Flora Monroe starts work at a shiny new medical center, Leon feels his job and status are at risk.

Not long after her arrival in Stillwater, Flora and her twin sons are threatened and the only person she can turn to is the starchy doctor who clearly resents her. As the danger grows, so do the feelings between the rival doctors. But can they put aside their conflict and save their new family?

I loved the intricacies of this story. Leon is such a complex character, and after everything that happened to him, it would have been easy for him to be downtrodden. I'm very proud of him! I hope you'll enjoy his story and the way he and Flora grow together.

I'd love to hear from you and find out what you think of Leon and Flora's story. You can contact me at:

Website: www.JaneGodmanAuthor.com
Twitter: @JaneGodman
Facebook: Jane Godman Author

Happy reading!

Jane

FAMILY IN THE CROSSHAIRS

Jane Godman

HARLEQUIN
ROMANTIC
SUSPENSE

HARLEQUIN®
ROMANTIC SUSPENSE™

Recycling programs
for this product may
not exist in your area.

ISBN-13: 978-1-335-62674-5

Family in the Crosshairs

Copyright © 2020 by Amanda Anders

All rights reserved. No part of this book may be used or reproduced in
any manner whatsoever without written permission except in the case of
brief quotations embodied in critical articles and reviews.

This is a work of fiction. Names, characters, places and incidents
are either the product of the author's imagination or are used fictitiously.
Any resemblance to actual persons, living or dead, businesses,
companies, events or locales is entirely coincidental.

This edition published by arrangement with Harlequin Books S.A.

For questions and comments about the quality of this book,
please contact us at CustomerService@Harlequin.com.

Harlequin Enterprises ULC
22 Adelaide St. West, 40th Floor
Toronto, Ontario M5H 4E3, Canada
www.Harlequin.com

Printed in U.S.A.

Jane Godman is a 2019 Romantic Novelists' Award and National Readers' Choice Award winner and double Daphne du Maurier Award finalist. She writes thrillers for Harlequin Romantic Suspense and also writes paranormal romance. When she isn't reading or writing romance, Jane enjoys cooking, spending time with her family and watching the antics of her dogs, Gravy and Vera.

Books by Jane Godman

Harlequin Romantic Suspense

Sons of Stillwater

Covert Kisses
The Soldier's Seduction
Secret Baby, Second Chance
Family in the Crosshairs

The Coltons of Mustang Valley

Colton Manhunt

Colton 911

Colton 911: Family Under Fire

The Coltons of Roaring Springs

Colton's Secret Bodyguard

The Coltons of Red Ridge

Colton and the Single Mom

Visit the Author Profile page at Harlequin.com for more titles.

As always, this book is for my lovely husband, Stewart, who is gone but never forgotten. We don't say "goodbye."

Chapter 1

The body that came crashing out of the trees and charging toward Flora Monroe was large and furry. Her initial thought, an accompaniment to panic, was that if she survived this attack, she would be having strong words with the author of the Stillwater Trail public information booklet. The one that stated bears didn't stray this far south.

Before turning to flee, she took a moment to register that the creature heading her way was more donkey-shaped than bear-shaped. Then she wasted a precious few seconds wondering if there was any way her first few weeks in a new town and at a new job could get any worse. First, there had been the break-in at her home, then the receptionist at the medical center where she worked had quit after only a few hours, throwing the administration system into chaos. Now this.

As she broke into a run, the animal raised up on its hind legs and knocked her to the ground. Flora's rear end hit the grass, the breath left her lungs in a single, dramatic rush, and the *thing* licked her face.

"Get off me, you monster." From her sprawling position, she shoved at the creature. Closer inspection revealed it to be a huge dog. Pushing had no effect. She'd have more luck trying to move one of the mountains on the Stillwater Trail. Her attacker appeared to believe they were engaged in a game. Wagging its tail in delight, it increased its efforts to smother her in sloppy kisses.

"Tiny." *Tiny? Seriously?* The voice was a man's, but Flora couldn't see the speaker on account of the large canine planted on her chest. "Come here."

Tiny ignored him.

"Come. Here. *Now.*"

Tiny looked over his shoulder, heaving a reluctant sigh before turning back to give Flora one last lick. Sitting beside his master, he gazed up at him with adoration, suddenly a model of obedience. As he looked from his owner to his victim and back again, Flora observed his expression held all the triumph and delight of a dog who had dug up a juicy bone, or found a new chew toy. The comparison did nothing to improve her mood.

Furiously pulling her rucked-up sundress down around her thighs—fairly sure it was too late to avoid Tiny's owner getting an eyeful of her white lace underwear—Flora sat up…and almost groaned out loud. Of course. The pain of a few scratches couldn't compare to the humiliation that set her face on fire. The way this day was going, it had to be *him*. The good-looking doctor who worked at the Main Street Clinic. Where Flora was viewed as the enemy.

Last time she'd seen him, Leon Sinclair had been professionally smart in black pants and a crisp blue button-down shirt that clung lovingly to his biceps. Now he was sweaty and mussed up in jogging pants and a T-shirt so faded it was impossible to read the logo. Both looks worked equally well for him.

"You called that thing *Tiny*?" It was the most scathing, spur-of-the-moment comment she could come up with.

"In my defense, he was tiny when I adopted him." He reached out a hand. "Are you okay?"

She let him help her up, huffing out a breath as she did. "Yes, but it's no thanks to your dog."

Did his lips just twitch? She'd seen him around town a few times, but, until now, his facial muscles had never relaxed into anything that came close to a smile. "My dog apologizes, and so do I. He's just a puppy."

"Are you sure?" She eyed the half dog, half buffalo combination in disbelief. "What breed is he?"

"Closest I can tell, he's a cross between an Irish Wolfhound and Great Dane, and he's ten months old, so I guess he's at the phase where he's learning not to be a puppy."

"He needs to try harder." She rubbed her sore backside reminiscently, blushing as she became aware of the way his eyes followed her hand as it skimmed her buttocks.

"I'm not trying to make excuses for Tiny's bad manners, but we don't often encounter other people out here on our evening run. I guess the excitement was too much for him." His gaze swept over her. "You don't look like you're planning on doing any hiking." She was wearing a short cotton dress, light-weight sweater, and high-top sneakers.

"No, I'm not here for my daily exercise," she confirmed.

It was early evening, and they were at the point where the road became a narrow track before it led on to the Stillwater Trail, the main tourist route. During the day, the lower levels were popular with walkers. Higher up, the going got tough and only serious hikers and hunters ventured that way. This was lake and mountain country. The route started out in the town itself, leading upward from Stillwater Lake, passing the smaller lakes known as Tenderness and Wilderness before winding onward until it reached the highest point in the county, the treacherous mountain known as the Devil's Peak.

"I'm looking for Joy Valeski's house."

"Joy lives over there." Leon pointed along the track in the direction from which he'd come. "We're neighbors, although our houses aren't exactly close. Out here, we have a long way to go to borrow a cup of sugar." He studied Flora's face. "Is everything okay?"

"I'm one of the doctors at the new Ryerson Medical Center. Joy is my patient." She cast a glance his way to see how that went down. His nod was tight-jawed. Clearly, they were still at the raw stage where work was concerned. The whole "this town isn't big enough for two medical practices" thing wasn't going away anytime soon. "She didn't turn up for an appointment today and I haven't been able to contact her. I don't usually stalk a no-show, but Joy has been good to me since I moved to Stillwater. My boys have eaten more meals cooked by her than by me. I thought I'd stop by and see if she needs anything. I drove most of the way and knew I'd have to walk a little way to reach her house."

There was another reason, one she didn't care to discuss with Leon. Since the Ryerson Medical Center had only recently opened, and Flora had moved to Stillwater for her new job, all Flora's patients were new to her. During her initial assessment with Joy, the other woman had divulged some worrying information. As a result, Flora had set up a follow-up meeting between Joy and a colleague so her patient could get a second opinion. Joy had missed that appointment. Since the information she had shared with Flora concerned another doctor and could lead to an allegation of malpractice, the situation was not exactly routine.

She cast a side-long glance in Leon's direction. "Am I right in thinking Joy used to be a client at the Main Street Clinic?"

There was that nod again. It was barely a movement, more a tensing of his muscles. "Before she made the switch to your center, she used to see my colleague, Alan Grayson."

There was more in what he left unsaid than in the words themselves. It seemed Leon's loyalty to his friend and employer at the established Main Street Clinic was as strong as his resentment of Flora. There was already a perception that the new medical center would poach clients from the traditional firm.

When she had relocated from her post as a family doctor in Denver to her new job, Flora had known there would be challenges. The trustees of the new center had anticipated there might be hostility from existing clinics. The RMC's new facility was part of the Mountain States Health Group, a not-for-profit health care organization with a network of nineteen hospitals and forty-eight clinics across Montana, Wyoming, and Colorado. It offered enhanced and localized services for which locals previously had to go farther and pay more.

Keen to settle into her role as one of the medical practitioners at the RMC, Flora had done some informal research on the area, so she already knew the Main Street Clinic had problems. Dr. Alan Grayson, who had started the practice over thirty years ago, was winding down his career. One doctor at the Main Street Clinic had been unwell for several months and another was on maternity leave. The generally held opinion was that the clinic would be closed altogether if Leon hadn't been single-handedly holding things together.

The Stillwater gossips had told her a few other things about Leon. She knew his wife had died in a car accident a few years ago. There was no shortage of people wanting to tell her what a great doctor he was. A good listener, generous with his time, just plain *nice* to his patients.

The scandal-mongers had told her a few other things, mainly about his past, but she found it hard to believe the hell-raiser they described and this quiet man were the same person.

"Maybe we should both go?" Leon nodded in the direction of Joy's house. "Joy and I have been neighbors for a long time. If there is a problem, I may be able to help."

Flora blinked. Helpfulness from the reserved doctor? That was unexpected. "Thank you."

"Joy is my friend."

The message was clear. *Don't thank me. This is for Joy, not the person who has breezed into town and is threatening my job.*

Then he smiled and the whole world stopped turning for a few heart-stopping seconds. Because, when Leon smiled it was like the sun breaking through storm clouds. Following swiftly after his closed expression, it almost took Flora's breath away.

"Besides, Tiny loves visiting Joy. She gives him cookies."

Tiny barked at the sound of his name. Flora eyed him warily. "I hope she buys catering sizes."

"Don't be mean about my dog." They started to walk along the track. "Or I might not stop him next time he decides to kiss you."

As they headed along the narrow path toward Joy's house, Leon succumbed to temptation and let Flora go ahead of him. There was nothing chivalrous about the impulse.

He'd already noticed her slender curves when he'd seen her around town, putting it down to an annoying lapse of judgment on his part. She was one of the high-powered doctors who were here to save Stillwater from him and the other small-town quacks. That had been the essence of an article in the local newspaper published just before the Ryerson Center had opened.

Although there were two other doctors at the new center, Flora's picture had accompanied the piece. The headline, "Just What Stillwater Ordered," had appeared atop an article about the demise of his own, traditional clinic.

Her appearance should be the last thing on his mind. Instead, it had begun to drift into his thoughts when he was least expecting it. Now, instead of one of her efficient, tight-fitting business suits, Flora was wearing a dress that skimmed her thighs and seemed designed to draw his attention to her perfectly shaped rear and long, slim legs.

Even with her composure ruffled following Tiny's onslaught, she was stunning. Leon saw plenty of different eye colors in his job, but Flora's were the first he'd seen that were such a clear shade of blue. There was no hint of gray in their sapphire depths. Everything else about her made him think of sunshine and laughter. Her smile was a full-on, knee-weakening dose of mischief and fun. Except when she looked his way. Then her expression became wary and confused. And who could blame her?

I confuse myself most of the time.

The red hair that she ruthlessly confined when she was working now fell loose in a long, wavy mass about her shoulders. For an instant, Leon pictured it spilling over a pillow as they…

Whoa! What the hell was going on with him? Was this the inevitable culmination of four years of celibacy? Although why his sex drive should suddenly surface now, when it hadn't bothered to recently, was a mystery. And why did it have to be directed toward *this* woman?

The one who his boss was convinced would be respon-sible for the closure of the Main Street Clinic?

As they walked, Leon threw a ball for Tiny. The dog chased after it each time, bringing it back and dropping it at his owner's feet, his tongue lolling and his tail wag-ging as he waited for the next throw.

Flora shielded her eyes against the sun, watching as Tiny hurtled after his toy. "He may be crazy, but he is quite cute."

"Thanks," Leon said. "I think the running helps and I try to watch what I eat. Although I'm not sure about the crazy part... Oh, wait. You meant the dog?"

Her laughter was delicious. Musical and joyful, it invaded his senses and momentarily pushed aside his cares. It was dangerous as well as infectious. He had a feeling too much of it could be addictive...and he'd fought enough battles with addiction to last a lifetime.

"Next you'll be telling me you trained him to knock women over."

When Tiny returned, Leon rubbed the dog's broad head. "The doctor figured us out. We're going to have to come up with a whole new technique."

Flora's laughter bubbled up again and one hand skimmed the enticing curves of her buttocks in a rem-iniscent gesture. "When flirting leaves bruises, you're doing it wrong."

Leon pitched the ball again and Tiny took off, skim-ming the ground with a speed and agility incredible for his size. "I had a feeling the dog was giving me bad advice."

Leon wasn't usually good at conversation. A severe stutter when he was younger meant talking had once been the worst kind of torture. Although years of speech therapy enabled him to get the issue under control, he was still painfully aware of the slight hesitation that remained. It left him self-conscious around new people. But talking to Flora felt okay. Light and easy. No pressure. He even felt the urge to do more of it.

They drew close to Joy's house and, still carrying his ball, Tiny darted toward the building. When he was out on his evening run, Leon occasionally stopped by and said "Hi" to his neighbor, but he didn't make a habit of it. Although Joy had a heart of gold, she could talk for hours once she got started. No matter how much Leon enjoyed her company, he didn't always want a lengthy analysis of everything that had gone on in Stillwater that day. Joy was one of those people who loved to share the details of town life, but she had gradually realized that Leon preferred privacy. And, since she knew his reasons, she generally respected his wishes.

Tiny often had other ideas. The dog's parentage was doubtful, but whatever his genetics, it was impossible to get him full, and he was always looking for more food. The treats Joy gave him were one attraction, but he also enjoyed the attention she showered on him. Now, he bounded onto the front porch, sure of a warm welcome.

As Leon reached the house with Flora at his side, he was surprised to see Joy's door was closed and her rocking chair—the one she usually occupied on the front porch at this time of day—was empty. This situation clearly unsettled Tiny, who abandoned his ball. Going back and forth from the steps to the door, the dog sniffed the air and whined as though searching for a clue as to Joy's whereabouts.

"He really wants those cookies." Flora's words were light-hearted, but her tone was slightly nervous as though she, too, sensed something off-key about the atmosphere.

Leon could tell there was more to Tiny's behavior than hunger. He kept looking over his shoulder as though urging his master to hurry. The dog was clearly anxious about their neighbor's welfare.

Leon quickened his pace, his heart rate kicking up a notch as Tiny started to scratch at the bottom of the door. When he reached Tiny's side, Leon knocked on the glass panel, then stood back, surveying the house.

"Could she have gone away?" Flora asked.

"Joy has a cat. She rarely goes anywhere, but when she does, she lets me know. I have a key so I can come in and feed Bungee."

"Let me guess. He likes jumping?"

"You have no idea." The fact that Bungee had not appeared yet was another sign that things weren't right. The large ginger cat was generally laid-back, but he hated dogs. Tiny's presence was usually his cue to leap onto the porch in full-on hissing and spitting mode, ready to chase away the intruder.

When Leon knocked again and there was still no answer, Flora tried peering through the glass. Since there was a lace drape on the other side, it was impossible to see anything. "Maybe we should try the door? It may not be locked."

After a brief hesitation—*What if Joy is sitting inside watching TV and she tells me to get the hell out of her house?*—Leon tried the handle. When the door opened, his heart sank even further. He entered the cool interior with Flora at his heels.

"It should have been locked."

Tiny pushed past them, through the neat sitting room and into the kitchen. His single bark held a note of anguish that sent a trickle of ice-cold dread down Leon's spine. Before he stepped foot over the threshold, he already knew whatever he found in the next room wasn't going to be good.

Sure enough, Joy lay on the tiled floor of the small room. As they approached, Tiny lay down, placing his head on his front paws and flattening his ears. Leon didn't need to check her vital signs to know their friend was dead.

He was a doctor. Seeing bodies was a sad part of his routine, but he experienced a moment of deeper sorrow as well as shock as he looked down at the woman he'd liked and considered one of his few friends. Heartbreak had been his constant companion for the last four years. He knew all the forms it could take, knew its viciousness and twists and turns. Just when he thought it had no more surprises for him, pain delighted in finding new ways to sucker punch him. Like now. What he felt when he looked at Joy was nothing in comparison to what he had experienced when his wife, Karen, had died. Didn't even scratch the surface. No, what astonished him was that he was still able to feel fresh grief after he had been turned inside out by it for so long.

A widow in her early sixties, Joy Valeski had to be one of the most popular people in Stillwater. She could be counted on to provide a hot meal in an emergency and a bunch of flowers in times of sickness. If there was a problem, Joy would be there with her sleeves rolled up, digging gardens, raking leaves, collecting newspapers, and providing home-cooked meals. Now, all that goodwill was gone and Leon wasn't the only one who would miss her.

As he squatted close to the body without touching it, it was obvious that his medical expertise would not be required to determine the cause of death. It was immediately and horribly apparent. Joy had been repeatedly stabbed in the neck.

He clenched his teeth together hard, riding the twin emotions of shock and anger. When he spoke, his voice was tight with suppressed emotion. "The medical examiner will c-c—" his stutter hit hard, and he had to force the word out "—confirm the exact cause of death, but the wound on her neck looks particularly deep." He drew Flora's attention to a gaping injury on the right side of her neck. A deep crimson puddle surrounded Joy's upper body, and the sweet, sickly tang of blood filled his nostrils.

Flora placed a shaking hand on his shoulder, leaning closer to get a better look. As she studied the wounds to Joy's neck, she was pale, but composed. "There's bruising to the right side of her head, suggesting that the killer struck her with a blunt object, knocking her unconscious, probably before stabbing her."

Leon nodded. "The lack of defensive injuries to her hands supports your theory that she wasn't conscious when she was stabbed."

Flora reached into her pocket, fumbling slightly as she withdrew her cell phone. "I'll call the police."

"I don't think that will be necessary." Leon nodded

toward the open door. Tiny was scrambling to his feet, his tail wagging in greeting as a dark-haired woman entered the house. She was accompanied by a tall man. "They're already here."

Chapter 2

"I don't understand what's going on." Flora was genuinely confused as the two police officers entered the kitchen and viewed the scene. "We only just found the body."

"I was leaving the office about fifteen minutes ago, when I got a call that there had been a murder at this location." The woman had an air of authority and, instead of answering Flora's question, she looked at Leon as she spoke. "Why are you here?"

"Firstly, I'm not the person you should be speaking to. Dr. Monroe is Joy Valeski's physician and it was her decision to come here. I just happened to accompany her." Flora took a moment to appreciate his professionalism. These people obviously knew each other well and it would have been easy for Leon to allow the police to sideline her. Instead, he was publicly acknowledging her status as the lead medic. "Secondly, maybe some introductions would be useful?"

The woman officer held out her hand to Flora. "Leon is right." She sent a quick smile in his direction. "He usually is. I'm Chief Laurie Delaney of the Stillwater Police. And this is my colleague—"

"Dr. Monroe and I have already met," Detective Joe Nolan said. When his boss raised her brows, he elaborated. "Her house was broken into last week and I attended the scene."

Flora had been in Stillwater for less than a month, but she already knew of the formidable reputation of its police chief. Responsible for capturing a prolific serial killer who had made her one of his targets, Laurie was known for her no-nonsense approach. She was married to Cameron Delaney, the town's former mayor. Cameron now headed up the Stillwater Chamber of Commerce and was one of the trustees of the new medical center where Flora worked.

Laurie's eyes narrowed slightly as she glanced from Flora to the body on the floor and back again. "Your new venture seems to have gotten off to a bad start, Doctor."

Aware of Leon's eyes on her profile, Flora bit back the first answer that rose to her lips. *My new venture is going just fine. It's my luck that seems to be going to pieces.* This wasn't the time or place for an emotional response and she doubted Laurie's words were intended as a criticism of her professional expertise.

"In answer to your question about why we're here, I was concerned because Joy Valeski missed an appointment this afternoon," she said. "Before you ask, no, I don't visit every patient who doesn't show up. But the circumstances of Joy's appointment were unusual, and she'd been good to me since my arrival in town. I thought I'd stop by and see how she was."

"Who made the call to your office?" Leon asked Laurie.

The police chief was frowning as she looked up from the body. "It was anonymous. And it was to my personal cell phone, not to the Stillwater PD."

A shiver ran down Flora's spine. It felt horribly co-incidental that someone was calling Laurie around the same time she and Leon were heading to Joy's house. "But you must know if it was a man or a woman? And surely you can trace the call?"

The frown line between Laurie's brows deepened. "No. That was also strange. He, or she, used voice-changing software. It was like listening to an alien. And the number was withheld. There's no way of knowing who it was."

"The person who made that call went to a lot of trouble to make sure you didn't find out their identity." Leon's words were almost an echo of Flora's thoughts.

Laurie nodded as she got her cell phone out. "Which is why we need to get Dr. Lamb's team here urgently to collect the body."

While Laurie was making the call to the West County Coroner's Office in Elmville, Flora looked down at the body, emotion coming at her in a rush. Three and a half years had passed since her husband, Danny, had been killed, but the same sadness hit her every time she came face-to-face with death. The emotional connection was part of her job, but she was reminded that this was a person. Joy had laughed and loved. She'd had hopes and dreams, too…

"It could take some time for Dr. Lamb to get here, but we can wait on the porch."

Leon's hand under her elbow brought Flora back to the present, his touch drawing her away from the memory of that awful night when she'd waited and waited for Danny to come home. Instead, his colleagues from the narcotics squad had turned up in the cold, gray dawn. Danny and his partner had been following up on a lead, pursuing a drug dealer. One bullet. That was all it had taken to end Flora's hopes and dreams.

When they got outside, Flora drew in a welcome breath of fresh air. She took a seat on the porch steps and Tiny joined her. She took a moment to consider the situation. Sitting down, the dog was taller than her and his bulk took up most of the space, but there was something comforting about his presence. Almost as though he sensed her distress and was trying to ease it.

She reached up a hand to stroke his head, and he turned his whiskery face toward her, licking the inside of her wrist. None of the sloppy, exuberant kisses of earlier. Just that single, comforting touch. Maybe Leon was right, and the oversized puppy was trying to find a way to grow up.

Looking up, she found Leon was watching her. His expression was hard to read. It could have been concern. There might even have been a hint of sympathy in the troubled depths of his eyes. If that was the case, it meant the Stillwater gossips had been hard at work and he knew her story.

"It never gets any easier, does it?" The gentle note

in his voice put her off balance. It was as if he really did understand what she was going through. Flora was grateful for the warmth and understanding she saw in his eyes. At the same time, she saw a reflection of her own pain in his gaze.

"It's always hard when a patient dies and we ask ourselves if we could have done more." Flora searched for the right words of comfort for both of them. "But loss is harder for those of us who are already experiencing feelings of bereavement. It's piling fresh hurt on top of existing pain."

Leon's eyelids fluttered briefly, telling her she had struck a chord within him. It was clear that he had as many emotional burdens to carry as she did. Flora wasn't sure she wanted to know any more than that. What she wanted was to get on with her job and make a new home for herself and her boys. The thought served as a reminder...

"I have to make a call. I was expecting to be done here by now." She reached into her pocket for her cell phone. "I need to call the daycare center to explain why I've been delayed."

"Ah, yes," Leon said. "I've heard about the new arrivals who've been taking Daisy's Daycare by storm."

Flora groaned. "Are you trying to tell me my boys already have a *reputation*?"

That slight twitching of Leon's lips was more pronounced this time. It was almost as if his smile muscles didn't get much use and they needed to warm up before going for the real thing. In another situation, it might have provoked her into wanting to make him use them more often. But Leon was the one who'd drawn up the professional battle lines. He was the one who'd made it clear they were on opposing sides. Flora had no idea why, particularly as the trustees of the Ryerson Center had offered his boss a lucrative partnership.

Before he could respond, Detective Joe Nolan, who had come out onto the porch without her hearing him, laughed. "Two little whirlwinds, that's what they were when I came out to your place to investigate your break-in. How old are they?"

"Almost three."

Joe shook his head. "Mine are eight and six. I don't know how you do it with two of them so small. And you all on your own—" He broke off, his expression becoming a mask of confusion. Clearly, he *had* heard her story and didn't know how to react.

"I've never known it any other way." Flora had never quite gotten the hang of this widowhood thing and how to spare other people second-hand embarrassment over mentioning her dead husband.

She saved either of them need for further comment by making her call to Daisy Cain at the daycare center, explaining the situation. Finding Daisy's Daycare had taken away one of the biggest headaches involved in making the move to a new town. And she liked Daisy. It was too soon to say she was becoming a friend, but Flora felt comfortable with her.

"Not a problem. My staff and I have a few other late pick-ups today," Daisy assured her. "Everything's fine."

"Is that fine as in 'fine,' or fine as in 'that's what we tell the anxious parents'?" Flora asked.

Daisy laughed. "I've dealt with twins before, but I've never seen anything like the way your two work as a tag team. While one gets your attention, the other one is behind your back stirring up something else."

"Welcome to my world," Flora sighed. "I'll be with you as soon as I can."

Laurie emerged from the house as Flora ended her call. "Bad news. Dr. Lamb has just been called out to attend an unexpected death and his assistant is on vacation. We could be here for a while."

As she spoke, tires crunched on the track outside. The vehicle that came into view was a coroner's wagon with the West County Medical Examiner logo on its side. When it halted, the man who climbed out of the passenger seat walked straight toward the house.

"Chief Delaney." Dr. William Lamb was tall and gray-haired with a stern attitude. Flora recognized him, having driven over to Elmville to introduce herself to him in her first week in the job. "I came as soon as I could."

Laurie regarded him with a bemused expression. "Dr. Lamb. I just finished calling your office." Elmville was over an hour's drive from Stillwater. "But they told me you were out dealing with another case."

He frowned. "I don't know what you're talking about. When you and I spoke earlier, I put everything else on hold, so I could meet you here as you requested."

Laurie looked even more confused. "Dr. Lamb, I haven't spoken to you in person today."

He shoved his hands in his pockets, glaring down at her with an expression that Flora imagined would send any other police officer running for the hills. "Of course you have. You called me and gave me this address. Told me you had a stabbing case and asked me to come right over."

* * *

"I'm going to get some lunch." Leon paused in the act of picking up his jacket from the coat hook behind the door. The look on Tegan Jackson's face told its own story. "I'm *not* going to get some lunch?"

The receptionist shook her head. "I just got off the phone with Daisy at the daycare center. She's got a kid with his arm stuck under the outdoor play equipment."

"Sounds like a job for the fire service." Even as he voiced his doubts, Leon was returning to his office for his bag.

"They're on their way, but Daisy is worried the kid may have broken his arm. He could need some pain relief while they cut him out."

Daisy's Daycare was at the opposite end of Main Street from the clinic, but it was a long road. That, the thought of a child in pain, together with the possibility that he might have to take the boy to the emergency room if his parents weren't around, or didn't have transport, factored into Leon's thinking as he drove the short distance.

The morning had been a quiet one, which was just as well because his mind insisted on replaying the events of the previous evening.

Dr. Lamb had taken Joy's body away in the coroner's wagon, promising a speedy investigation. There hadn't been anything more to do. After the police had gone, Leon had secured Joy's house, feeling that pang of sorrow again for the woman who had been almost a friend. As he was leaving, Bungee had emerged from the undergrowth and, scooping the fluffy ginger tom cat under one arm, he'd taken him home with him. He had no real expectation that the cat would stay, but it felt like one final thing he could do for Joy.

Flora had accepted the offer of a lift to the daycare center from Laurie. Leon had watched her as they drove away. He could have kept his eyes on Laurie or Joe Nolan, but, for some reason, all his attention had been focused on Flora. She'd had quite the introduction to a new town and the impact was plain. Her face was pale and, when she lifted that glorious mass of hair back from her neck with one hand as the police cruiser drove away, he could see her trying to process what was going on.

Because what the hell *was* going on? If someone knew Joy had been stabbed, why all the mystery of the strange calls to the police and the medical examiner? The answer seemed obvious, but it still left too many unanswered questions. Had the person making the calls murdered Joy? If so, why would he, or she, be in such a hurry to let them know about the death? It was as if the killer, or someone linked to them, was determined to flaunt their crimes.

Leon had spent the morning puzzling over those questions in between seeing patients. He also devoted a considerable amount of time to wondering how Flora was bearing up. Finding an excuse to call her had taken a strong grip on his imagination and he was annoyed with himself. He didn't do this. Didn't do other people. Didn't do caring. Not anymore.

When you've been responsible for the death of your wife and your unborn child...well, I guess you're allowed to say to hell with the rest of the world.

Within a few minutes, thoughts about the previous

day were put to one side as he pulled up outside the low-level, white-painted daycare building with its brightly colored railings. He winced as he left his car and the sound of screaming greeted him. If the decibel level was any indication, a nasty injury awaited him. He followed the noise around to the rear of the center.

One of the daycare assistants unlocked the gate to admit him, and he took in the situation with a swift glance. A child was lying on the ground with his arm wedged under the climbing frame. A woman sat beside him, rubbing his back and talking quietly to him. The screams weren't coming from the kid who was stuck. Another boy, identical to the one who was trapped, had his arms wrapped around the woman's neck. This child was the source of the high-pitched wailing.

Daisy stood nearby, watching the scene with a blank expression that Leon could only attribute to panic. Her staff, apparently taking their cue from the boss, also seemed to be in shock. They wandered around helplessly. The other kids were either crying or dashing about overexcitedly.

Leon took charge. He loosened the screaming boy's grip on the woman's neck and, keeping hold of his hand, took him to Daisy. "Get this little guy away from here. Make sure he can still see his mom and his brother so he knows they're okay, but distract him."

"Cookies will do it." Now she had emerged from under the stranglehold, his suspicions proved correct. It was Flora. She spoke directly to her clinging son. "Mommy will be right here with Stevie. He's going to be just fine, Frankie."

Her son's cooperation hung in the balance briefly, but he looked up at Daisy, the tears suspended. "Cookies?"

"Cookies." Daisy seemed to regain some of her composure. "The ones you like with the chocolate chips."

Leon glanced over his shoulder as he knelt beside the climbing frame. "Maybe you could get the other kids out of the way as well?"

Daisy nodded, signaling to her staff. The whole group followed her inside.

"Thank you." Flora gave a relieved sigh. "Stevie's staying very calm, but the noise and the audience weren't helping."

Leon observed that she'd removed her light-weight jacket and slipped it under Stevie's head so the rough surface of the play area wasn't too uncomfortable against his skin.

"Do you want me to deal with this?" The daycare center always called him if there was a medical problem, but this was an unusual situation. Flora was a doctor herself and more than capable of caring for her son.

"Oh, yes." Now he got a closer look, he could see she wasn't quite as calm as he'd thought at first glance. She was doing that remarkable mom-thing of keeping it together for Stevie's sake. "I would never try to treat my own kids. Not for anything big. The nerves get in the way, you know?"

"Then let's take a look at Stevie, shall we?" He had to lie at an awkward angle with his face up close to the little boy's to be able to feel his way along the trapped arm. Huge blue eyes, just like Flora's, regarded him with interest. "My name is Dr. Leon. How are you doing, buddy?"

Stevie's lower lip wobbled. "I'm stuck."

"So you are." Leon turned his head to look at Flora. "I have no idea how he managed to do this. It must have taken some force to jam his arm under this bar."

"That was what I thought." When she stopped biting it, her own lower lip trembled slightly. "Daisy said no one saw what happened. The only thing I can think is that he must have slipped and pushed his hand under as he fell."

Leon turned back to Stevie. "However you did it, I don't think you've broken anything." Fire chief Andy Mellor and his colleague Rick Morris approached at that moment and he spoke directly to them. "I'm going to need you to cut through the bar on either side of his arm so we can release him."

He made a move to shift out of the way to allow the firefighters to get in close with their hydraulic cutting equipment, but the fingers of Stevie's free hand clutched the front of his shirt.

"Dr. Leon, stay here." His protective instincts were roused by the boy's pale, determined features, which made him think of Flora and the way she'd dealt with Joy's death. The boy had clearly inherited his fighting spirit from his mother.

"Is that okay?" Leon asked.

Andy nodded. "We can work around you."

Stevie was regarding the huge cutting shears nervously, so Leon decided to distract him. "Do you like ice cream?"

The blue eyes swiveled away from the firefighters and fixed hopefully on Leon's face. "I like choclit best.

Frankie likes 'anilla." The contemptuous tone told its own story of his regard for Frankie's preference.

"How about we get some ice cream once your arm is free?" He had to raise his voice above the noise of the cutters.

"Frankie too?" Leon nodded. "And Mommy?"

"We'll all go." He wasn't sure how Flora would feel about that plan, but it was taking Stevie's mind off the cutting operation and that was all that mattered.

The giant shears cut through the bar like a hot knife through butter and Stevie was scrambling free a minute later. Flora caught him up into a hug, ruffling his curls, and the boy made a protesting noise as he squirmed in her embrace. Andy and Rick departed, having assured Leon they would tell Daisy to get the equipment checked before the kids used it again.

"I'm going to need to get another look at that arm." Leon didn't think there was any real damage, but he wanted to be sure.

Stevie stood still, watching Leon with interest as he checked the arm for signs of a break. Although the tender skin was red, there was no sign of swelling or severe bruising and Stevie could bend his arm and grasp Leon's fingers without pain.

"We'll get a cold compress from Daisy, but I don't think there's any other treatment he needs."

"Thank you." Flora's sigh of relief seemed to reverberate right through her slender body. "When I saw him lying there…"

"It must have been a shock, but he's fine."

"Ice cream."

Leon looked down at Stevie as the little boy pulled

on the knee of his pants. It was a bittersweet reminder
of the family he'd lost. The twins were nearly three and
the child he and Karen had been expecting would have
been about a year older.

"Oh, hey, you really don't have to—" Flora's bright
curls tumbled as she shook her head "—I can take them
to the Ice Creamery."

"Dr. Leon come, too." The grip on Leon's leg tightened.

"I did make him a promise. And I'd like it…if you
don't mind?"

*I don't do closeness. I don't do caring. How's that
working out for you?*

Leon was aware he was coming across more like a
shy teenager on a first date than a professional doing
his job. Or a man who kept a lock on his heart.

"You may have no choice. They can be pretty determined." Flora looked from her toddler's upturned face
to Leon's with a smile. "It's a family trait."

He'd told himself her smile couldn't have the sort of
impact he remembered. He was wrong. It wasn't just the
way it lit up her face. It was the message it gave. Flora's
smile inspired happiness and, once she got started, she
was generous with it. That expression was the most beautiful thing Leon had seen in quite some time.

He wanted to see more of it. As Stevie wrapped
plump arms around his knee, it looked like he was going
to get his wish…with a side order of ice cream.

Chapter 3

Since the Ice Creamery was just a block away, Leon left his car at the daycare center and they walked. Frankie, once he had been assured that his twin was okay, became jealous of the attention his brother was getting from this interesting new acquaintance. He was determined to make up for lost time. As a result, Leon had a twin clamped to each hand.

"Call me later and let me know how he is." Flora had thought Daisy's pale face and worried manner had been out of proportion to the incident.

"He's really fine. Look at him." Flora had attempted to reassure her as they'd left.

"Just call me. Please?"

"I'm surprised at the way it affected her. Little kids have accidents all the time," Flora commented to Leon as they walked along the sidewalk.

"They do, and Daisy usually deals with them calmly. She may be worrying about repercussions, even a possible lawsuit."

"Really?" She gave the matter some thought. "It was just a typical kid thing. No one was to blame."

"Since we both commented on the effort Stevie must have put into getting stuck, I expect Daisy will be relieved to hear you say that." They reached the ice-cream parlor and Flora held the door open so Leon could walk through sideways without letting go of the twins. "Some parents might suggest there was a supervision issue."

That aspect hadn't occurred to her but, now Leon had raised it, the prospect bothered her more than she liked. She handed her boys, her most precious parts of herself, over each day, trusting they would be safe in the care of Daisy and her staff. Was it possible Stevie hadn't been watched carefully enough?

She was conscious of Leon's gaze on her profile. "Daisy has been doing that job a long time. Almost ten years. I've never heard of a problem at the center." His voice was reassuring.

Flora relaxed a little. "Stevie is like a whirlwind. They both are. I guess all it takes is for the adult in charge to look away at the wrong moment." Even so, she would double-check with Daisy about supervision when she next spoke to her.

They found a booth and sat down, the twins causing a distraction from more serious matters with their insistence that they both needed to sit next to Dr. Leon. It was a strange sensation. Normally Flora was the person they fought over. Now she was a spectator as, one on each side of him, they vied for Leon's attention. He handled it well, with a combination of gentleness and firm good humor.

"Do you have children?" The words slipped out before she stopped to consider whether they were intrusive.

The question brought an abrupt end to his smiles. As he looked up from the twins' chatter, she thought his eyes were the most intense she had ever seen them. They were dark green, reminding her of lake water in the early evening light. In that instant, their depths appeared to hold a world of pain and secrets.

"No."

That curt negative was clearly all the response she was going to get. No additional information, no sense of how he felt about the question, no change in his facial expression.

Then he smiled, his mood changing swiftly. "I'm informed that Stevie likes 'choclit' and Frankie likes 'anilla."

"And Mommy likes scotch," Frankie said.

"He means butterscotch sauce. I'm not an alcoholic." Flora's cheeks flamed as she realized what she'd said. "I didn't mean..."

She was still floundering helplessly when the waitress came to take their order. Lapsing into silence, she watched as Leon assured the twins they could have both sprinkles and syrup. He also chatted to the young waitress about how her grandmother was doing after her operation. It was as if he was going out of his way to demonstrate how to make polite conversation. Flora wanted to put her head in her hands and groan. She had just ricocheted right off the scale of tactlessness and now she had to find a way to make amends.

The waitress brought coloring pencils and dinosaur pictures for the twins. For once, they bent their heads over their task, both determined to do their best picture for Dr. Leon.

Flora launched straight into her apology. "I'm sorry. I shouldn't have said that."

"Why not? You aren't an alcoholic. I am. Well, if we're going to be precise about terminology, I have PTSD that caused a drinking problem. I'm now in recovery from the disease." She hated that she had triggered discussion of this battle. "Please don't worry that my patients are in danger. Or anyone else." His gaze went to the twins. "I've been sober for two years and I plan on staying that way. But my past is no secret. I'm sure the Stillwater scandal-stirrers have shared every fascinating detail."

The tone was brave, if self-mocking. But his half-smile and the hurt in his eyes…they were both prompting her in the same, unexpected direction. She wanted to move around the table and hug him. To try to take away some of the pain. Instead, she settled for a light touch on his wrist. Just the brush of her fingertips against his flesh caused a wildfire reaction, almost a jolt of static electricity, except this was internal. Starting deep inside and zinging along her nerve endings, it was raw, breathtaking, and unlike anything she had ever felt before.

Probably just as well I decided against the hug.

Leon's indrawn breath told her the contact had affected him in the same way. Self-consciously, Flora withdrew her hand. This day was taking a series of unexpected turns. "I try not to listen to gossip. I know how much damage it can do."

Leon raised a brow. "That sounds like you're speaking from experience."

"Our stories may be different, but they have both taken place under the glare of the public spotlight." She regretted the words immediately. It was a long way from opening her heart, but it felt like too much. Cutting her gaze away from his, she fell silent. She still wasn't comfortable talking about what had happened. Somehow, it felt like a betrayal to Danny.

Flora was glad when any further conversation was brought to a halt as the waitress arrived with their order. By the time Flora had tucked serviettes into the front of the twins' T-shirts, given reminders about the use of spoons instead of hands and warned Leon that he might want to get out of the firing line of food projectiles, she felt ready to change the topic.

"I spoke with Dr. Lamb earlier. He is sending the autopsy report to the Ryerson Center. That should speed up the process."

Leon maintained eye contact while holding on to Frankie's wrist as he tried to launch a spoonful of ice cream in the direction of his twin. "Is there any service your center can't provide?"

Although there was a trace of bitterness, she sensed a genuine interest behind the question. She contemplated the best way to answer it, which was not an easy task when Leon was sitting opposite her looking so delicious.

Even the blob of vanilla ice cream in the center of his blue tie couldn't detract from the fact that he was easily the most handsome man she had ever seen. His looks had a bad boy edge at odds with his obvious desire to hide away and not draw attention to himself. Flora wanted to tell him it was never going to happen. With a face like that? *Get used to it, Doctor. You are always going to attract attention.* But she guessed he probably already knew that. It made her wonder all over again at his story.

Wavy hair a dark, golden shade that could probably still just be called blond; angular, chiseled features; a perfect mouth with lips that looked like they had been made for kissing… She pulled herself back from the edge of that highly dangerous thought only to get lost in his eyes. They were mesmerizing, drawing her in and holding her in their depths.

Focus. He had asked a serious question. "As you know, we aren't equipped for major surgery—"

"As I know? Why would I know anything about what you do?"

Nature, as well as giving him so many gifts in the looks department, had also endowed Leon with an incredible voice. Warm, deep and rich. It was like warm honey poured over cream. Although it was the perfect doctor's voice—soothing and reassuring—the things it was doing to Flora's heart rate were definitely *not* medicinal.

She realized an answer was required, but she was bewildered by the question. "Because of the partnership the Ryerson Center trustees suggested to Dr. Grayson. I know it was a disappointment to them that he didn't think a merger between the two clinics was a good idea…" Leon was staring at her as if she had two heads. "You don't know what I'm talking about."

"No. This is the first I've heard of it."

"Ah." On the contrary, Alan Grayson had said he talked about the merger with his colleagues and staff, but they were against the idea. "Then it's probably not something I should discuss further now."

There was an uncomfortable silence as Flora tried to gauge the impact of her words on Leon. It was impossible. His expression was closed, those dark eyes shuttered. The only giveaway was the deepened crease at the corner of his mouth.

After a moment or two, he nodded at her untouched ice cream. "You should eat that. It may not contain any scotch, but it's really quite good."

So she did. Ice cream for lunch, the company of a handsome man and her twins' laughter. For a brief half hour, she allowed herself to enjoy those things and put thoughts of a stabbing, mysterious calls and the strange behavior of Leon's boss to the back of her mind.

When they left the ice-cream parlor, Leon needed to go back to the daycare center for his car. When Flora headed the same way, Stevie clung to her, shaking his head.

"Stay with Mommy."

Deciding he had been more troubled by his accident than she had realized, she decided to take the boys with her.

"I'm working from home on paperwork today. I'm sure he'd be fine going back to daycare, but I'll keep them with me for the afternoon."

"These incidents can be more of a shock for the parent than thc child," Leon said. "Try not to worry. Stevie will soon forget all about it."

Since the twins had started chasing each other in and out of the decorative hedge bordering the Ice Creamery, it seemed likely Leon would be proved right.

They went their separate ways and Flora walked the short distance down Main Street toward the intersection with Lake Drive. She followed the road along the edge of Stillwater Lake, keeping her attention on the twins. A sense of pride gripped her as she approached the pretty, cream-and-blue painted house with its small porch and huge, protective trees lining the lot. *Our place.* The street was quiet, and she had a good view of it as she walked along the sidewalk with a child at each side. Even so, it wasn't until she got up close that she could tell something was wrong.

She slowed her stride, but it was too late to shield the boys from the sight of the destruction awaiting them.

Frankie noticed it first. "My garden…broken?"

He was right. When they first moved in, Flora had bought two large wooden planters, placing one to each side of the front step. Under her supervision, the boys had taken responsibility for their own garden, planting herbs and tending to them each day. Now, the contents of the wooden boxes were scattered across the white-painted boards of the porch. Each of the plants they had taken such pleasure in caring for now lay twisted and crushed as though a heel had ground it underfoot.

As she sank down onto the top step, clutching her sobbing twins to her, the scents of ruined herbs and disturbed earth filled Flora's nostrils. But it wasn't the physical scene that was strongest. Whoever had caused the damage had left something more behind, something sour and malignant.

This emotion had come her way once before. It had been present in the courtroom on the day they sentenced Danny's killer. It was at its most overpowering when the drug dealer's girlfriend had screamed threats of revenge at Flora as they took her lover away to the cells.

It was hatred.

"Why would a doctor go uninvited to a patient's house?" Tegan Jackson cast a furtive look over her shoulder as she spoke into her cell phone. "Joy didn't show for an appointment. Next thing, she's lying dead on her kitchen floor. It's all over town…"

Leon cleared his throat as he approached the desk and the receptionist gave a little start before hurriedly ending her call.

"That conversation had better not be what I think it was." He nodded in the direction of Tegan's cell. "Whilst you work for this clinic, you will not repeat malicious gossip about another medical professional, do you understand, particularly when the implication of what you're saying is that Dr. Monroe is a murderer?"

Tegan hung her head, her expression miserable. "But it must be true. Even Dr. Grayson was talking about how Dr. Monroe out at the Ryerson Center—"

Stifling the curse that rose to his lips, Leon made his way along the corridor to the office of the Main Street Clinic's senior partner. These days, Alan Grayson rarely scheduled any appointments with patients before noon. Leon couldn't remember the last time he had seen his colleague in the morning, usually the busiest part of the day. Although it was Thursday, Alan hadn't put in an appearance yet that week. His absences were becoming longer and more frequent. The thought, like so many to do with the Main Street Clinic's senior partner these days, troubled him, and Leon paused, considering what it could mean.

Leon had returned to Stillwater four years ago. He had spent the first twelve months trying to drink his hometown dry. *Damn near succeeded, too.* The second year had been a desperate fight to get sober. Years three and four had been about attending AA meetings, getting his life back on track and remaining in recovery.

When he looked back on what had helped him reach the point he was at now, there were two people without whom he wouldn't have made it. One was Bryce Delaney, Laurie's brother-in-law. Leon and Bryce were both veterans of the war in Afghanistan. Bryce had been an explosive ordnance disposal specialist, while Leon had been an army doctor. Bryce's career had been brought to an end by a roadside bomb. Leon had been given a medical discharge for mental health reasons. He had retained his medical license to practice because his issues had never placed his patients at risk. Although they had manifested themselves in a search for oblivion at the bottom of a bottle, his mental health problems had been triggered by the death of his wife in a car crash.

Bryce had been there whenever Leon needed him. Still was. Recognizing post-traumatic stress disorder through his own problems, Bryce had been the person to get Leon into rehab and counseling. For a long time, he had also been the only person in Stillwater who had believed Leon could get sober. Back then, even Leon himself hadn't been convinced, which made Bryce's faith in him even more remarkable.

The other person who had gotten him here—and kept him here—was Alan Grayson.

Initially, Leon had owed his job at the Main Street Clinic to the fact that his return to sobriety had coincided with a series of misfortunes, or life changes, for other doctors at the practice. Faced with a recruitment crisis, Alan had taken a brave decision and approached Leon with a job offer. It had started out as a short-term position. To everyone's surprise, Leon had repaid Alan's faith in him. He was good at his job and popular with his patients and maintained his sobriety. He had quickly become an indispensable member of the team.

Even at the start of his employment at the Main Street Clinic, Leon could tell Alan was struggling with personal problems. A man of enormous charisma, he was getting by on a professional reputation that was outdated. The once-thriving clinic was barely surviving. Out of loyalty to the man who had picked him up from rock bottom and given him a chance when no one else would, Leon did everything he could to keep things going. It was a thankless task when the person in charge seemed to be sinking deeper into his own mountain of cares with each passing day. His impression was that the problems were financial and he wished Alan would confide in him, but they didn't have that sort of relationship.

Yesterday, when Flora had dropped the bombshell news that Alan had been offered a way out, Leon hadn't known how to react. At first glance, it had sounded like the ideal way to solve their problems, yet she'd said Alan had turned it down. No matter how hard he had tried, Leon hadn't been able to come up with a good reason for the decision. Setting aside the gratitude and respect he felt for Alan, he and his colleagues were entitled to some answers about why their boss hadn't at least discussed an option that impacted their future.

As for the rumor he had just heard Tegan discussing… Leon knew what small towns were like. He had grown up in Stillwater and had been the subject of scandal-mongers more than once. While he hadn't welcomed the Ryerson Center, the thought of Flora being the receiving end of that sort of vicious lie made him burn with anger. The image of her face rose before him and he fought the instinct to charge down Main Street giving the true version of events about Joy's death to anyone who would listen.

The idea that Alan would promote such a story had him even more concerned. It couldn't be true. Tegan must have gotten it wrong. Their boss was going through a tough time lately, but Leon had always thought of him as an honorable man. Holding on to that thought, he knocked on Alan's door.

When he didn't get the customary response to enter, he waited a few moments before trying again. Deciding Alan must be taking a call, he went back to Tegan's desk.

"Can you ask Alan to let me know when he's free to see me?"

She fiddled with some papers. "Dr. Grayson isn't here."

"Pardon?"

"He's gone." Her lip wobbled. "He cleared out his office on Tuesday. He came in early and left before you got here."

Leon ran a hand through his hair as he tried to process what she was saying. Gone? As in...*gone?* "And it didn't occur to you to share this with me until now?"

She hung her head. "Dr. Grayson told me not to say anything until you asked where he was. He told me to reassure you that he still owns the practice, but he won't be coming back to Stillwater anytime soon."

Leon was trying to process that information. Alongside picturing his already bulging workload expanding even further, he was trying to work out how Alan had managed to spread any information about Flora's alleged role in Joy's death. Leon and Flora had found her body on Monday evening and, according to Tegan, Alan had cleared out his office early the following day. It seemed like too much of a coincidence that he was also casting suspicion on Flora at the same time.

His thoughts were interrupted as the phone on Tegan's desk rang. Taking a deep breath, she answered it with her customary sing-song greeting. "Main Street Clinic. How may I help?" Covering the mouthpiece with her hand, she looked up at Leon. "It's for you. It's Chief Delaney."

Chapter 4

Stillwater City Hall was a majestic structure housing the mayor's office, the police department, the Clarence Delaney Memorial Hall and other municipal services. Flora gave her name to the clerk at the front desk and was escorted up a wide staircase to Chief Delaney's office.

As she approached, the door opened, and a tall, dark-haired man stepped out of the room. Flora had met him only once before, but Cameron Delaney was unmistakable. As a trustee at the new medical facility, he'd been one of the interviewers when she'd applied for the job at the Ryerson Center. Cameron had asked her about the challenges of moving from a big city to a smaller town. Looking back, she guessed neither of them could have anticipated anything that had been thrown her way so far.

Cameron greeted her with a smile, his perceptive eyes scanning her face. "I hear your first few weeks in Stillwater have been eventful."

"You could say that."

"Look, my sister-in-law is having an awareness day at the weekend for the animal sanctuary she runs. Why don't you bring your kids along? It'll be fun for them and you'll get a chance to relax away from the pressures of work."

After the whispering behind hands she'd encountered over the last few days, the friendliness in his eyes was like a breath of fresh air. "I'd like that."

They both turned at the sound of footsteps and Flora's heart gave a glad little bound as Leon approached.

For the last three and a half years her heart had felt like a molten weight in her chest, and now all of a sudden it was *bounding*? It was hard to explain, but, as Flora met Leon's gaze, the exchange that passed between them made the world feel a little bit lighter. Some of the tension that had been holding her spine rigid eased and she even managed a smile.

After a quick greeting to Leon, Cameron departed. Flora didn't have time to say anything before Laurie emerged from her office.

"Oh good, you're both here. I thought, since you were together when you found the body, I could bring you up to speed with the investigation and ask you some questions at the same time." Her keen eyes went from Leon's face to Flora's. "But that's up to you."

"Works for me."

As Leon spoke, Flora noticed that he seemed distracted. The flash of intuition startled and scared her at the same time. She barely knew this man. How could she already be so in tune with him that she could read his moods? It didn't matter how, or why. She *was*. And that was the scary part. With everything else going on in her life, she could do without this connection to someone who clearly had so much emotional baggage he was staggering under its weight.

"It's fine with me, too."

That was another thing. Every nerve in her body was on high alert. Since her arrival in Stillwater, her house had been broken into and her garden had now been vandalized. Both incidents had been reported to the police, but also, her medical center's receptionist had quit on the first day without giving a reason, one of her patients had been murdered and a nasty smear campaign had started up implying that Flora was responsible for Joy's death. Trusting a stranger, particularly one who might be antagonistic toward her, probably wasn't the smartest thing she could do right now. But she did trust Leon. Not only that, but she also felt safe with him. A self-confessed recovering alcoholic and hell-raiser with a world of hurt in his eyes.

What does that say about my judgment?

As a doctor she had witnessed the nightmare ways in which drugs and alcohol could destroy lives. Involvement with an addict, even one in recovery? As far as she was concerned, that could endanger a life.

Why was she even having these thoughts? Yes, she trusted Leon. That didn't mean she was contemplating a relationship with him. She could enjoy his company while keeping her distance emotionally.

Laurie took a seat at her desk, indicating the two

chairs opposite. She had several pages of type written notes in front of her, to which she occasionally referred.

"Dr. Lamb completed the autopsy yesterday. His full report will be available in a few days, but the main thing we need to know is that Joy Valeski *was* murdered. Having seen the body, I don't think any of us were in any doubt about that. She was in good health, apart from a few minor complaints typical of a woman of her age."

"Was she unconscious when she was stabbed?" Leon asked.

"Yes. She was hit over the head with a blunt object. Dr. Lamb thinks we're looking for something similar to a baseball bat." Laurie flipped through her notes. "Joy was lying on her side when the killer slashed at her neck with one of her own kitchen knives. The blade, which we found under the table, was about seven inches long. It severed her jugular vein and carotid arteries. The autopsy report confirms that, although there were twelve other stab wounds, that was the injury that caused her death." Laurie sent a sympathetic look in Flora's direction. "I'm aware that there has been some vindictive gossip directed at you following Joy's death. I know police inquiries aren't going to help the situation."

Flora thought of the kindly woman who, on her first visit to the Ryerson Center, had brought home-baked cookies and a recipe for apple pie. Dealing with the gossip wasn't pleasant, but the truth would come out… eventually. "I want to help you catch the person who did this."

Laurie nodded approvingly. "Is there anything you can tell me about Joy Valeski that might shed any light on this inquiry?"

"I only met her a few times. She brought my family homemade meals when we arrived in Stillwater, and when she switched to my care we had an initial consultation to review her treatment and medication." Flora thought back to that meeting, casting a glance in Leon's direction. This wasn't going to be easy. In the brief time she had known him, his loyalty to the man he worked for at the Main Street Clinic was all-too-apparent. Nevertheless, she had information that could be relevant. She took a deep breath. "Joy told me she felt she had received unnecessary or inappropriate treatment from Dr. Grayson over a period of several years."

She felt the weight of Leon's gaze in the silence that followed. Laurie made a few notes before looking up. "Did you find anything to support that claim?"

"She was being treated for Crohn's disease, and my initial assessment suggested she didn't have that condition. Because of that, I made some changes to her medication," Flora said. "I also asked a colleague to see her and provide a second opinion. That was the appointment she missed."

Laurie pursed her lips. "Had Joy made a formal complaint against Dr. Grayson?"

Flora risked another glance in Leon's direction. His expression was unreadable. "She told me she was considering it. I said I couldn't advise her."

"Leon?" Laurie turned to him. "Do you have anything to add?"

"Not on this subject." His voice was normal, apart from his usual slight hesitation, but Flora noticed a residual tightness in the fine muscles around his eyes. "Joy Valeski wasn't my patient and, although she was a friend, we never discussed her medical care. But there is something you should know about Alan Grayson, something that may be relevant to your investigation."

Laurie gave him a sympathetic glance. "Anything you can tell me, no matter how minor, may be helpful."

"I don't think this is m-minor." Leon's voice had a hollow note to it and the way he stumbled over the word gave away his discomfort. Flora experienced a fierce desire to grasp his hand. "Alan hasn't seen any patients since last week and I found out this morning that he emptied his office on Tuesday. I have no idea when, or even *if*, he plans to return."

Laurie concentrated on her task as she made a few more notes. "He's not answering calls, but obviously, I'll stop by Dr. Grayson's house as a starting point. We don't have any evidence other than Tegan's word that he's left town and has confirmed that he doesn't intend to return. I will need to look into Joy's claim that Dr. Grayson was providing her with unnecessary treatment. Depending on my findings, I may extend my scrutiny to other patients. With Dr. Grayson effectively missing, you are now the only doctor at the Main Street Clinic, Leon. I'm relying on your cooperation in this matter."

He nodded. "You have it. Of course."

She turned to Flora. "While this issue with Dr. Grayson seems to have opened up one line of inquiry, I can't ignore the way you have been targeted since your arrival in Stillwater, Dr. Monroe. Can you think of anyone who might have a grudge against you?"

An image flashed into Flora's mind. The bland courtroom. The solemn expression on the judge's face as he said the words. *Life sentence.* The venom in the eyes of Danny's killer as he turned to look at Flora. The screams and curses from him and his girlfriend as the prisoner was led away to the cells.

"Only one, but I don't know why she would surface again now when I haven't heard from her for years." Her hands twisted nervously as she spoke, and she clasped them together, forcing herself to remain calm. "My husband, Danny, was a police officer with the Denver PD. He was murdered by a drug dealer he had been tracking for some time. When the killer was sentenced, his girlfriend stood up in the courtroom and threatened me. She said Danny had ruined her life and she would do the same to me. Her name was Luella French. She went missing after that and I never heard from her again."

Just talking about it brought it all back and she drew in a long breath, forcing the pictures out of her head, willing the good memories to take their place. Danny, her high school sweetheart. His big grin and his loud laugh. The day she told him about her pregnancy. Their light-hearted squabble about whether, if it was a boy, it would be Francis after his father, or Steven after hers. He never knew it was twins…

Flora was aware of Leon's eyes on her and she turned her head slightly to look from him. Although he didn't smile, there was a slight softening in his expression that told her he knew what she was feeling. And…*how?* He was a stranger, yet he could look at her that way and ease some of her hurt. She didn't know whether to be glad or start running as fast as she could in the opposite direction.

Since Laurie was talking, she didn't have time to

do either. "I'll have her checked out. We'll look as well at other angles such as whether Joy had any enemies."

"You're talking about Stillwater's most popular resident," Leon reminded her.

"Everyone is hiding something," Laurie said. "It's my job to find out who has a secret so big Joy Valeski had to die for it."

The meeting ended soon after that and Leon accompanied Flora as she walked down the stairs. "How's Stevie?"

She was glad for the normality of the question. "Although his arm is fine, getting him back to daycare wasn't easy. He's normally my little tough guy, but the incident seems to have bothered him and he got quite tearful when I took him back. That affected Frankie as well, of course, so it wasn't a happy return to Daisy's center."

"Not what you needed with everything else that's going on." He held the door open for her and they stepped out into the sunlight.

"They come first. Always. My goodness—" She caught a glimpse of his muscled forearm and stared at it in shock. "I'm sorry, but those scratches look bad."

"Ah." He rubbed his arm with a reminiscent grin. "I got in the way of one of Tiny and Bungee's disagreements."

She stopped by her car. "You took Joy's cat home with you?"

"He had nowhere else to go."

"That was a nice thing to do." She brushed her fingertips against his uninjured arm as she spoke, unable to resist the temptation to touch him. The brief contact reverberated through her. She lifted her gaze to Leon's face and saw an answering darkening in his eyes.

I want more than a light touch. A delicious shiver tracked its way down her spine at the thought. So much for keeping her distance.

"It's a habit I need to get out of." A smile tugged the corners of his mouth upward. "Remind me to tell you sometime how I hooked up with Tiny."

Flora laughed, nodding at the marks on his arms. "If Bungee wasn't vicious, I'd consider offering to take him off your hands. A pet would be just the thing to help the boys settle in."

"Bungee's okay. He just hates dogs. And Tiny's reaction to Bungee has been the same as it was when he first saw you."

Flora raised her brows in a question. "He knocks him over and tries to suffocate him?"

Leon nodded. "Pretty much. Tiny loves everyone. He thinks Bungee feels the same way about him. All Tiny wants to do is kiss him, which provokes the cat into a state of hissing fury within seconds."

"My sympathies are all with Bungee," Flora said.

"The house has been like a war zone since Bungee moved in." When she laughed, he shook his head. "Seriously. It's like living in a cartoon."

"I'm not promising anything, but why don't I bring the boys over to meet Bungee this evening and we'll take it from there?"

"Sounds like a plan. I'd invite you to dinner, but there's just one problem." He appeared so different when the conversation was light-hearted. That intensity in his eyes lifted and it was as if, for a few brief moments, he forgot to be sad.

"You mean we would have to stop your dog from smothering my boys between courses?"

He choked back a laugh. "Between us we should be able to protect them from any excessive outbursts of affection. No, I can't invite you to dinner because I'm a horrible cook."

There was a hesitant invitation in those words. He was batting the initiative over to her. Flora took a moment to think about it. Common sense told her getting in any deeper would be a mistake. She looked into Leon's eyes and decided common sense was overrated. There was no question of getting in deeper. It was only dinner, for heaven's sake, and they would be chaperoned by two boys, a cat, and a Tiny.

"I, on the other hand, receive high praise for my 'getti and meatballs from two notable connoisseurs."

His smile told her that was the answer he had been hoping for. "You supply the food and I'll provide the drinks. Non-alcoholic, of course. It's a…" He paused, and she knew he was searching for the right word. *Date?* Too much and too soon. For both of them. "Deal."

She watched him walk away toward his own car, a tall, broad-shouldered figure. The square of grass in front of the city hall was bordered by bright flower beds and the scent wafted toward her on the late-morning breeze. Sunlight filtered through the poplar trees and dappled the sidewalk. It was a lovely morning in a beautiful town and she felt the same stirring of excitement she had experienced when she first came to Stillwater.

This was her fresh start, the place where she could

put bad memories behind her and allow her boys to grow and thrive. Even so, her excitement had been tarnished right from the start by the over-the-top article in the Stillwater *Sentinel* determined to save Stillwater from outdated medical practices. Flora had contacted the newspaper's editor and complained about the tone of the report. She had been horrified at the criticism of local medics that was included in that article and the implication that she was behind it.

His response had been a half-hearted apology. The reporter had been overenthusiastic, he had explained. These days it was hard to get decent staff. The guy who wrote that article had left town one day without even bothering to hand in his resignation.

Despite the bad experiences, she had a job and a home here, a new life to carve out. She told herself her feelings about this place hadn't deepened when she met Leon. How could they? Flora had no idea what he was carrying inside all that emotional baggage, and she wasn't equipped to help him unpack.

I'm carrying too many bags of my own. And she had her boys to think of, as well as the hundred and one other things that had come hurtling her way since she made this move.

Sighing, she turned to open her car door, only noticing at the last minute the deep gouges in the paintwork all along the driver's side.

It wouldn't exactly be easy to concentrate on her afternoon appointments, but Flora knew she would have to force herself to focus away from the most recent act of vandalism. Life hadn't been easy since Danny's death. Alone, pregnant, and grief-stricken, then coping with newborn twins…it would have been easy to cave under the pressure. But she'd held it together, returning to work part-time when the twins were six months old and full-time just before their first birthday.

It was her approach to life. Sleeves up. Head down. Plow on.

And maybe it had been her way of trying to ignore the gaping hole in her chest where her heart used to be. She'd learned the hard way that grief wouldn't be pushed aside. Her get-on-with-it attitude had only delayed the process. Out of nowhere, it had sucker punched her, surfacing one day as an intense pain, accompanied by an irrational fear for the safety of her boys.

She'd tried to ride it out. Drawing on her medical training, she gave herself the same advice she'd have given one of her patients. *Grief is a cycle. It has to run its course. Your fears are part of the process.* It didn't matter what she told herself. The idea of getting out of the city where Danny had died became fixed in her mind. She had started to think small town. *Safe town.*

Although Flora had family in the Denver area, her parents were dead. Her father had died when she was just out of her teens, and her mother had succumbed to a brief, violent illness a few years ago. Danny had had no close family, so it wasn't as if she would be taking the boys away from their grandparents by moving.

Those thoughts had been barely formed when she'd seen the advertisement for the position in Stillwater. Now, she parked her car near the Ryerson Center and got out. As she gazed up at the beautiful modern structure that had been designed to fit into its surroundings on the edge of the Ryerson River, doubt hit her for the first time.

Safe town? Are you sure about that?

"Oh, my goodness. What happened to your car?" A woman had approached the building on foot from the river path.

Although recent events told her she should be cautious, this woman's sympathetic expression drew a slight smile from Flora in response. "I guess it lost a fight with someone's keys."

She tried to keep her voice light, but it didn't quite work. From the measuring glance the other woman gave her, Flora was fairly sure she'd given away some of her hurt and frustration.

"I'm just on my way inside to register as a new patient. I'm new in town, and my own car had an argument with the gatepost the first day I arrived. I found a guy in town who did a great job of fixing it. I could give you his number."

Was it wrong to want to hug a stranger? Flora settled for a genuine smile this time. "That would be wonderful. I'm new in town myself and I was dreading that whole performance of trying to find someone reliable to do a paint job." They walked up the steps together. "I'm Flora Monroe, by the way."

"Then you're the doctor I'm here to see. I've heard a lot about you already." The woman at her side caught sight of Flora's expression and halted in her tracks. "I'm sorry. Did I say something wrong?"

Flora shook her head, annoyed that, even for that split second, she'd let the whisperers get to her. "No."

She held open the glass door and let her companion pass through ahead of her. "Welcome to the Ryerson Center."

The lobby of the center had a domed roof that caught the sunlight and bounced its rays off a floor-to-ceiling colored glass model of a strand of DNA. The effect was both beautiful and dramatic.

The new patient gazed around her with wide eyes. "Wow."

"I think that's the effect the designer was hoping for." Flora stepped behind the reception desk. "Now, let me take some details."

"I'm Eve Sloane and I don't mean to sound critical, but when you've invested in a lobby this eye-catching wouldn't it be wise to also employ a receptionist? First impressions are about more than aesthetics."

Flora sighed. "Tell me about it. Unfortunately, our receptionist quit on the day the center opened. We're advertising the post next week. In the meantime, everyone lends a hand with the front-desk duties."

"I might be able to…um…help you out with that."

Flora looked up sharply from the computer screen. "I'm going to need you to tell me more."

"Well, I've never worked in a medical center, but I have been employed in a number of hotels and offices in administration. I could step in until you get someone permanent."

While it sounded like a dream offer, there was a lot to think about. Recent events had made Flora wary. Three years was a long time and, while this woman didn't look like Luella French, she had learned to be vigilant. Luella could have ditched the spiky blue hairstyle and done something about the tattoos since the last time Flora had seen her. She might even have lost about fifty pounds in weight, but Flora didn't think she could have grown six inches.

Flora's personal situation wasn't the only reason to approach this stranger's offer with caution, however. Medical center employees had access to patients' private information. Even if Flora had the authority to employ a new receptionist then and there, she wouldn't have done so without putting some checks in place.

"Look, I can see the idea is about as popular as a porcupine on a waterbed—"

"No." Flora couldn't help laughing at the image. "But I'm going to need references, then I'll have to talk to the center's trustees."

"Okay. In the meantime, why don't I give you my details and then we can take it from there?" The woman held out her hand with a smile. "You've got my name."

"Well, Eve Sloane, why don't we start with a little role-play?" Flora frowned at the blank computer screen as she spoke. "You be the receptionist and I'll be the new patient. Where would you start?"

"Maybe by doing this?" Eve leaned across the desk and turned the power switch on.

"Congratulations. You just passed the first test." Flora huffed out a frustrated sigh. "My brain seems to be working against me right now. As you can see, your services are definitely required."

"I can start whenever you need me." There was something behind those words. It wasn't quite desperation, but Flora sensed Eve had a story to tell.

Don't we all?

"I'll be in touch as soon as I can, but it won't be today."

The words burst out, proving a new truth Flora hadn't realized until that minute. It *could* be today, but that would mean canceling dinner so she could talk to the trustees about this new appointment. She needed a new receptionist…but she wanted to spend time with Leon more.

Chapter 5

An hour later, the mild optimism generated by Flora's meeting with Eve was bursting like a bubble on a pin. Eve's own appointment was to treat a minor, long-standing ailment. Then, at first sight, there was nothing about Lilith Bronson's sweet, pleasant face to cause any disquiet. The acid reflux that had been bothering the patient after Eve was easily solved with a recommendation for an over-the-counter antacid. It was the last question that did it.

"Is there anything else I can do for you today?"

Flora always thought of that question as the "real reason." Most times, her patients walked through the door with a minor ailment. Sore throat. Bad cough. Nasty rash. Can't sleep. They went through the routine of dealing with those problems. Then she asked that question and—not always, but often—the "real reason" surfaced. Unexplained lump. No sex drive. Depression.

She could tell straight away that Lilith had a "real reason."

"I don't know where to start." Lilith's hands twisted together in her lap.

"Mrs. Bronson, there is nothing you could tell me that I won't have heard before." While she supposed it wasn't strictly true, it was the message Flora liked to give, particularly to her older female patients.

It worked like a charm on Lilith, who sat up straighter in her chair, determination giving her features a previously unsuspected strength. "You think so?" Even though she had clearly been gearing up to this moment, her voice shook. "What if I tell you about a doctor who deliberately misdiagnosed me so he could make a profit from my treatment? Is that something you've heard before?"

Well, yes. Actually, it's something I've heard very recently.

Taken by surprise, Flora remained silent for a moment. Although she kept her eyes on the computer monitor in front of her, she didn't need to check the details of Lilith's medical history. With a feeling of déjà vu and a sinking heart, she reviewed what she knew. Lilith was a widow in her mid-sixties. Before making the move to the Ryerson Center, she had been a patient at the Main Street Clinic. Where she'd been treated by Dr. Alan Grayson.

She drew a steadying breath. Lilith had come to her for help. Even though most of the facts were right there on the screen, she couldn't betray to the woman sitting beside her desk that this story sounded horribly familiar.

"I'm going to make some notes about what you tell me," she explained as she drew a pad and pen toward her. "But this will be unlike our other conversations. When you talk to me about your medical conditions, everything you say is confidential. If you reveal something now that leads me to believe a crime has been committed, I will not be able to keep that information to myself and I may have to inform the police."

Lilith nodded. "Joy said that was what you'd told her."

Flora had been in the process of writing the date, but she paused. "You've already talked about this before you came to me?"

Lilith's eyes filled with tears. "Joy Valeski was my friend." She hitched in a breath as the tears spilled over. "Yes, I spoke to her. We confided in each other. And now… I'm scared."

I'm scared, too.

For a second, Flora's thoughts veered in Leon's direction. She was a professional and her job threw her into unexpected situations every day. Okay, so this was totally out of the ordinary, but that didn't explain why she was experiencing a sharp rush of sensation, an urge to have him at her side. She'd been alone for so long, so why would she need someone else's support now? And why would that someone else be Leon? She didn't have time for an in-depth analysis of this inconvenient surge of emotion.

Determinedly pushing her own feelings below the

surface, she plowed on. "How about you tell me the whole story and then we'll discuss what we do next?"

"Okay." Lilith clasped her hands tightly in her lap. "Ten years ago, I was suffering pain in my right wrist. I went to Dr. Grayson and he diagnosed rheumatoid arthritis. From that day on, I had every drug and therapy you can name. Seems like every time something new came on the market, I was the lucky person who got to try it."

Flora could hear the slightly bitter note in the other woman's voice as she said the word "lucky."

"How did Dr. Grayson make his diagnosis?" she asked.

"Uh, he just looked at my wrist."

Flora made some notes. "How did your wrist look at that time? Was there any swelling or redness?"

"Well, that was the thing," Lilith said. "There was nothing to see. Just the pain. And it was particularly bad when I was working. Before I retired, I was a computer operator and some days it would be so bad, I could barely use the keyboard or operate the mouse."

"And how does your wrist feel now?" Flora asked.

"Fine." Lilith demonstrated by extending her arm and rotating her wrist. "No pain at all. Dr. Grayson told me that's because the medication and treatments were working."

Flora conducted a thorough examination of Lilith's wrist. When she moved on to the other hand and began to also check the joints of her fingers, Lilith laughed. "It's my *right* wrist that's the problem, remember?"

Flora jotted down a few more notes. She didn't have time to complete a diagnosis and she was reluctant to

jump to conclusions. Even so, her instincts were telling her that, ten years ago, Alan Grayson had misdiagnosed a straightforward case of repetitive strain injury
as rheumatoid arthritis, a chronic autoimmune disease.
Even without Joy Valeski's case, this was ringing alarm
bells. Alan Grayson might be guilty of either negligence or fraud.

"Tell me about the conversation you had with Joy."

"Joy and I have been friends for years. We were
the founders of the Stillwater Dozen—" She broke off
when Flora raised an inquiring brow. "It's a baking club.
You know the saying 'a baker's dozen'? The club meets
every Thursday at the Clarence Delaney Hall. We each
bring along something we've made. We have a tasting
session and trade recipes. I don't know how the conversation started, but Joy and I got talking about money.
Specifically, we discussed how we never had any. One
thing led to another, and we realized how much of our
income we were giving to Dr. Grayson by seeing him,
even with insurance."

Flora sat back in her chair. Although she had her own
reservations about Alan Grayson, she wasn't ready to
share them just yet. "It's a big step from knowing you
both spend a lot on medical care to suspecting a professional of malpractice."

"It sure is and I don't want you to think we reached
that conclusion lightly." Lilith clasped her hands beneath her chin and Flora noticed again the ease with
which she moved that wrist joint. "But Dr. Grayson kept
warning us against researching our disorders. He was
really passionate about it. Joy had spent a long time believing she was suffering from Crohn's disease. Then

she met someone who had irritable bowel syndrome. The symptoms were similar, but, when she asked Dr. Grayson if there could have been a mistake in her diagnosis, his reaction shocked her. He was furious and refused to listen to what she was saying. But what made her suspicious was that she felt he was nervous."

Flora knew the rest of the story. "Was that when Joy stopped taking her medication?"

"I did try to talk her out of it, but she could be very strong-willed once she made a decision," Lilith said. "And, of course, she found it didn't make any difference."

"So, when this center opened, she decided to contact me."

"Within days of doing that, she was dead." Lilith choked back a sob. "I want to do the right thing…but I don't want to be next."

Flora focused on maintaining a professional manner to reassure the other woman. Even so, she was alarmed at what she was hearing.

When Joy had come to her—on the very day the Ryerson Center had opened—Flora had been concerned by what she had heard. But the leap from concern to accusing someone of malpractice was a big one. That was why she had arranged for Joy to see one of her colleagues. A second opinion would either validate or contradict her own findings. In a way, Flora had been hoping for an opposing view. Because confirmation of what she believed meant she had walked right into a huge scandal on day one of her new job.

She hadn't gone to the police with Joy's initial, unconfirmed fears about Alan Grayson. Besides, malpractice was generally dealt with through the civil courts. The problem had gotten bigger, of course, for different reasons, ones she could never have foreseen. Instead of a malpractice investigation, she had become embroiled in a murder inquiry.

Now, having taken down the details of Lilith's story, she knew a different approach was needed this time. Leaning forward, she gripped Lilith's hand. "We need to speak to Chief Delaney."

Leon had been born in Stillwater. When he left at eighteen, he had taken a career path that had allowed him very few opportunities to return. College, followed by medical school, then entry into the army as a military doctor.

He and Karen had met when they were in college. They married while Leon was in medical school and she was working as a librarian. Since Karen had no family of her own, the wedding had been a low-key affair, just the two of them and a few friends. The summer after the wedding had been the first time Karen had visited Stillwater. Leon's parents were still alive back then and the week they'd spent together stood out as a sweet, shining memory of his family and his hometown.

Now, his parents were both dead. His father had been carried off by a heart attack six weeks after that visit with Karen. Five months later, his mother had suffered a stroke. Leon had been racing to be at her side when he got the call informing him that a second stroke had killed her. Karen's second and third visits to Wyoming had been to hold his hand at his parents' funerals. In that time, Stillwater had started to feel like someone else's hometown.

Then the unthinkable had happened. On a snowy

New Year's Eve four years ago, on his return from duty in Afghanistan, he had booked a surprise week-end break in the luxury mountain hotel where Karen had always wanted to stay. Leon blamed himself for the tragic chain of events that had followed. He had decided it was okay to drive in the snow. He had been the one who'd decided to take the steep mountain pass instead of the longer route through the valley. He had been the person at the wheel when the out-of-control truck had come toward them. If his reflexes had been faster...

No one had been to blame for what had happened on that icy patch of road. The other driver had not been drunk or reckless. It had just been an awful accident.

Karen, who'd been five months pregnant, had been killed instantly. Leon had escaped with minor injuries. Physically, at least. Unable to cope with the guilt and grief, he had commenced a downward spiral into depression that manifested itself in bouts of binge drinking. Given a medical discharge from the army for mental health reasons, he'd been able to keep his license to practice medicine because he had never been negligent in the performance of his professional duties.

With nowhere else to go, he had returned to the place he had once thought of as home. As he'd moved his few belongings into the house his grandparents had built and his parents had left him, Leon had thought about that word. *Home*. Like so many other things, it had become meaningless to him the day they'd placed Karen and their unborn child in that casket.

Family. Warmth. Companionship. Fun. Laughter... *Love*.

He'd lost them all, along with any concept of who

he was. But that was okay because he hated who he was. The stammer that had plagued him as a child had returned, becoming so bad he had barely been able to make himself understood. The weight had dropped off him until he'd resembled a walking skeleton. His long hair and beard had turned him into the sort of person people side-eyed before crossing the street to avoid.

Leon hadn't cared. He hadn't seen Stillwater as the small Wyoming town where he'd been raised. Where everyone knew each other's name and business. Back then, he'd only viewed it as the place he'd come to die.

Yeah, couldn't even get that right, could I?

Now, he stood on his porch and tried to observe his house through another person's eyes. How would Flora see this place when she arrived?

He took a moment to compare their situations. So alike in many ways and yet, at a certain point in time, they'd diverged. Flora had known the heartache of burying a partner. But the path she'd taken since was sunnier. It would be easy to say that was for her boys, and they clearly played their part in her choices. Leon gave a shrug. Possibly it just came down to personality.

The house itself was compact. A neat, two-floor, log-framed square with a wraparound porch. Leon's mother had described it as "three bedrooms in the middle of nowhere." He smiled at the memory of her standing in the big family kitchen, serving up wholesome food along with equally sensible advice.

But the surroundings made the building special. The Stillwater Trail and surrounding mountains rose protectively to the rear, but at the front and to the sides, as far as the eye could see, the land was Leon's. A barn, two sheds, and the play area that his father had built for him when he was a child were located in a paddock to the right. To the left, also fenced off, was Bobcat Creek, the tumbling brook where Leon's father used to take him fishing.

What would Flora think? He shielded his eyes against the early evening sunlight and watched a vehicle kicking up dirt as it approached along the drive. He was about to find out.

Since he'd spent most of the afternoon with his hand hovering over his cell phone as he rehearsed his reasons for calling off their dinner plans, the rush of pure joy he felt as Flora stepped out of the car almost bowled him over.

Perhaps he should have canceled, after all. She felt like a danger to the equilibrium he worked so hard to maintain. But it felt good. A high that was as natural as the one Flora's smile gave him. Now, that had to be worth the risk. A little loosening of the rigid hold he kept on his emotions. Just this once.

When she stepped from the car, Flora turned a full circle, her eyes wide. As he watched her, Leon had no need of his earlier question. He could see her thoughts reflected on her face before she spoke, and his throat tightened. For a long time, he had taken this place for granted. For so long it had been just somewhere to eat and sleep. The land useful only because it gave him privacy, open spaces for Tiny to run off his excess energy, and wildlife spotting opportunities during the long, sleepless nights. Now, Leon really could see it through Flora's eyes and it transformed once again into the unique, welcoming home of his childhood.

"It's beautiful." Her face shone with pleasure. "I would never tire of looking at those views." She cast a nervous glance around. "Where's Tiny?"

Before Leon could answer, a frustrated volley of howls rent the air. "In the dog run." Leon jerked a thumb in that direction. "I thought it might be best if his first introduction to the twins took place with a fence between them. As you can hear, he's not happy about the situation."

"Oh, dear." Flora bit back a smile. "I don't want to blight your dog's life."

"Blight away." He moved toward the rear of the car. "He's in disgrace. Tiny has had a thing about one of the bushes that grows around the back of the house. After eating the leaves for months and making himself sick, he finally dug the whole thing up while I was at work and left it on the porch. Roots, soil, branches…but no leaves. Oh, no. He'd eaten every last one of them."

When he'd arrived home to find the porch decorated with mangled horticulture and dog vomit, Leon hadn't been amused. While he'd cleaned up, Tiny had watched him with a guilty expression and the occasional sorrowful belch. Now, Flora's gurgle of laughter made him see the funny side of what had happened.

"Is he okay?"

He nodded. "Not only is he okay, he sneaked indoors and stole Bungee's dinner while I was disposing of the mess. Which could have been the plan all along."

As they opened the car doors, he was greeted with cries of delight. "Dr. Leon!"

"Hey, guys." He studied the twin closest to him. "No, it's no good. I can't tell them apart."

"Frankie has a freckle beside his right eye." Since both twins were squirming to be released, it wasn't exactly helpful. "Get ready to move fast."

As they each freed a twin from the restraints of their car seats and set them on the ground, Leon realized what her instruction meant. With a speed that had to be seen to be believed, the two little boys took off across the grass in opposite directions. Leon managed to catch the child nearest to him with an effort and returned to where Flora was holding the other by his hand.

"Do they always do that?" he asked.

"Always. They think it's funny. Almost as soon as they could walk, they worked out that I can't catch them both—"

She was interrupted by the twin at her side. "Pony!" He pointed toward the paddock where Tiny was hurling himself against the fence. The yowls were becoming increasingly more frustrated.

"I think we should get the introductions out of the way before Tiny wins his battle with the fence," Leon said.

Any concerns he had that the twins might be fearful of approaching Tiny scattered on the summer breeze as the two little figures darted toward the fenced-in area with cries of delight. As they approached the dog, they drew closer together and stepped up to the fence holding hands.

"Pony?" Stevie viewed Tiny doubtfully.

Frankie shook his head. "Big doggie."

The "big doggie" thrust his nose through a gap in the wooden slats and the twins squealed in delight as he licked their fingers.

"Shall I let him out?" Leon asked.

When Flora nodded her agreement, he undid the latch on the gate and waited for Tiny to come bounding out. To his surprise, the oversized canine stepped carefully through the opening. Once he was on the other side, Tiny regarded the two little boys with an expression that Leon could only describe as wonder. His gaze went from them to Leon and back again as though inquiring whether the children were real. Then, as the twins rushed forward to pet him, he sat down, his big body quivering with pleasure.

"I think they'll be okay." Leon went to stand beside Flora, who was watching her sons as they hugged and stroked the huge dog.

"Okay?" She turned her head and gave him that smile again. The one that loosened something inside him and, just for a moment or two, took him back to a time before the scars, dents, and damage. "I may never get them to leave. Shall I start dinner?"

"Good idea." They moved toward the house. Tiny, with the twins vying to get closest to him, trotted alongside them. "Then you can meet Bungee and tell me about the rest of your day."

He was watching her face as he spoke, and he had never seen anyone's expression change so fast. Flora went from carefree and smiling to chalk-faced and shaken in a heartbeat. He might be out of practice when it came to conversation, but Leon knew nothing he'd said had killed the mood so spectacularly.

Clearly, something else must have happened since he'd seen Flora earlier in the day. If it involved one of her patients, she was bound by confidentiality and would be unable to reveal the details. It was obvious that whatever had happened was bad news. Leon had never considered himself to be an intuitive person, but recent events had given him a sixth sense. All he knew was what his gut feeling was telling him.

If he was right, the stricken look in her eyes was connected to her job. Worse, it was linked to Joy Valeski's death. And that meant a whole world more trouble was coming their way.

Chapter 6

The evening at Leon's house was exactly what Flora needed to take her mind off her meeting with Lilith Bronson and her subsequent phone conversation with Laurie Delaney. The police chief had listened carefully to the facts, asked a few incisive questions then arranged to come by Lilith's house later that afternoon. Although Flora had offered to be there, Laurie hadn't seen the need for an extra presence in the meeting.

"I know Lilith Bronson. I don't think she'll be nervous about speaking to me. Sometimes an interview works best if I'm alone with the witness," Laurie had said. "I'll stop by your office tomorrow in case there's any additional information I need."

Now, having eaten dinner, she and Leon were sitting on the porch, watching the twins playing on the grass with Tiny. The oversized dog, so boisterous when Flora first encountered him, had turned into a gentle giant where the children were concerned. Darting out of their way as the twins chased him, he let them catch up to him, then lay down as Stevie and Frankie tumbled onto the ground with him.

It was briefly difficult to decipher the tangle of human and canine limbs as they rolled on the ground. Then, the threesome jumped up and started the game all over again.

"It's cardio for toddlers and canines," Leon laughed. It was the first time Flora had seen him really laugh. This side-splitting, eye-watering hilarity that couldn't be controlled. The joy made him look younger. "We could market it as a new sport."

"You have a point," Flora agreed. "It's like wrestling but with shrieking instead of grunting."

"I'd back your boys against a professional wrestler any day," Leon said. "They don't know the meaning of fear."

As he spoke, the twins, working as a team, hurled themselves on top of Tiny, pinning him down. The dog lay still for a moment, then got to his feet with the two boys still on his back. As he ran toward the house, they clung on like tiny, determined rodeo riders.

Flora sighed. "I know. It's a worry sometimes."

As she spoke, Bungee, who had remained aloof during dinner, appeared. The cat was a macho, strutting ball of ginger fluff. Pausing in front of Flora, he favored her with an unblinking green stare before leaping gracefully onto her lap. After kneading her legs for a few seconds with sharp claws, he curled up in a tight circle and purred like a motorbike engine.

"He tried that once with me," Leon said. "It lasted about thirty seconds. Then Tiny thought it looked fun and tried to join in. It didn't end well."

"He seems harmless." Flora stroked the cat's velvet head and the purring reached a crescendo. "But I can see how him and Tiny together wouldn't work out. If it will help, I'll take him."

"I have a feeling Stevie and Frankie would rather you took Tiny." Leon turned his head to look at her as he spoke, and his smile made her heart soar.

The anxiety that had held her in a vise had slowly loosened its grip until it was now a nagging doubt. But it wasn't minor, and it wasn't going away anytime soon. More than anything, she wanted to confide in Leon. That wasn't possible for a number of reasons. The first, and most important, one was that Lilith was her patient. Any information they discussed concerning the other woman's medical condition was confidential. The second reason was that she knew how close Leon was to Alan Grayson. Until she had concrete evidence that malpractice had taken place, she didn't want to speculate about his friend's role. And that led her on to a whole host of other reasons. Joy Valeski's murder might have nothing to do with what she and Lilith had discussed today. Her imagination could be working overtime without reason.

She pushed the dark thoughts aside and returned Leon's smile. "And I get the feeling you and Tiny are inseparable."

"I could be persuaded some days. Like when he plays

in the creek, then decides the best way to dry off is to roll on my bed." His gaze became searching and, when he spoke, his speech impediment was more pronounced. "You look more relaxed than when you arrived. Bad day?"

She took a moment to drink in the mood. The beautiful setting and the warm summer evening. Her boys playing happily with the big, goofy dog. The soothing presence of the cat on her knee. And the unfamiliar, but welcome, comfort generated by having someone who cared how her day had gone.

"After I left you in the parking lot of city hall…" She frowned at the memory. It seemed longer than just a few hours ago. "I found out someone had scratched my car."

"Deliberately?" When she nodded, Leon's expression went from shocked to angry. "You told Laurie, right?"

"Yes." The truth was, she hadn't thought much about the damage to her car in the aftermath of her conversation with Lilith. "But then something else came up. Something I can't discuss with you."

He ran a hand through his hair in a gesture of frustration. "This is crazy. I'm a doctor as well. I took an oath. I know that confidentiality must be at the center of the relationship between a patient and their healthcare provider, but how can I support you if I don't know what's going on with this patient of yours?"

Flora blinked hard, but the action didn't take away the hard, bright sting at the back of her eyes. Leon couldn't know what those words meant to her. Since Danny's death she'd resigned herself to being alone. If she had stopped to think about it, she'd have said she was okay with that. *Just me and my boys.* Now, all of a sudden, it felt like maybe she needed more.

Someone died. The image of Joy's bloodied and brutalized body doused her emotions like ice water. It was only natural that having another person to share what she was dealing with would feel good. The fact that the other person had broad, muscular shoulders, just right for sharing burdens and maybe resting her head on at the end of a long, hard day? Well, yes. She had to admit that helped.

Leaning closer to Leon's chair, Flora placed her hand over his. She intended it to be a fleeting contact. Just enough to reassure them both. Instead, the warmth of his skin on hers acted like static electricity, setting off a chain reaction through her whole body. From the way his eyes widened, she could see it had affected Leon the same way. Heat fogged her brain and her heart commenced a dangerous new beat.

Careful not to let him see how the touch affected her, she withdrew her hand and searched for an insignificant comment. "Laurie is taking care of it and, on a lighter note, I think I've finally found a receptionist."

"Call me old-fashioned, but I'd have thought that, in a center like yours, having someone to do the admin would be an essential." His smile was teasing. "Maybe even before you opened."

She pulled a face at him, liking the way they had slipped into this easy, comfortable way of communicating. "We had someone. She worked the morning of her first day, went out for lunch, and never came back."

"Boy, you must be a tough boss." Leon shook his head.

Flora choked back a laugh. "There are three doctors

at the Ryerson Center, remember? And, once you get to know us, we are all quite nice."

"Did your receptionist give any reason for her abrupt departure?" he asked.

"When she didn't return after lunch, one of my colleagues called her. He said she told him there was a family emergency and she had to leave town immediately," Flora said. "We haven't heard from her since."

"Is she from Stillwater? I know most people around here."

"Her name is Jennifer Webster, but she isn't from around here. We joked about both being newbies and getting to know the town together. It was sad that she had to leave so suddenly. She seemed fiercely efficient. Actually, she was just fierce. Even her clothes, like her bright yellow scarf that was a bit harsh on the eyes. That first day was so busy and then…" Flora trailed off, aware that she was talking to cover up a sudden discomfort. Her feelings of unease were growing stronger, but she wasn't sure why. Although the sun was still shining, she felt like a dark cloud had descended. "You don't think…"

He took her hand, clearly trying to recapture a mood that had been destroyed. "I think it wouldn't hurt to talk to Laurie about Jennifer and the damage to your car."

Flora returned the clasp of his fingers, grateful for the comfort generated by his touch. "She said she'd call by the center tomorrow."

Leon wasn't looking at her. Instead, his eyes were fixed on the rough dirt drive that led to the house. "You might not need to wait that long." He nodded, drawing her attention to the vehicle that was approaching. "That's Cameron Delaney's car."

Leon resisted the temptation to place his arm around Flora's shoulders as they walked down the porch steps. At the same time, Cameron's car pulled up in front of the house and he and Laurie exited the vehicle. In what looked like a pre-arranged movement, Cameron went over to the twins while Laurie walked toward the house.

"How did you know I was here?" Leon suspected he was the only person who would be able to hear the wobble in Flora's voice. It was because he was listening for it.

"I didn't," Laurie said. "But when you weren't at home, I decided to come out here and see if Leon had any idea where you might be."

Flora's eyes were on the twins. Cameron had squatted beside them and was patting Tiny. The two boys appeared to be competing to tell him all about their game. "Is this about Lilith?"

"I'm sorry, Flora. There's no easy way to say this." Laurie's expression was solemn. "Lilith Bronson is dead."

Leon moved quickly. As Flora swayed toward him, he caught hold of her upper arms, steadying her and holding her against his chest. Guiding her back up the steps, he eased her down into the chair she had just vacated.

Although her face was pale, she seemed to have regained some of her composure. Keeping a tight grip on his hand, she looked up at Laurie. "Was she...?"

"Stabbed," Laurie stated bluntly. "Obviously there

will need to be a full autopsy, but the circumstances of her murder appear to be almost identical to those of Joy Valeski's."

"Both women confided in me right before they were killed." Flora's face paled.

Leon dropped on one knee beside her chair. Turning his head, he looked up at Laurie. "Can you get her a glass of water, please?" Laurie went into the house and he placed his hands on Flora's knees. "You don't need me to tell you what to do."

She gave him a glimmer of a smile. "I'm not going to faint."

He ducked his head, getting a better look at her face. "Sure about that?"

"I think so." She straightened. "It was just a shock to hear it that way."

"That was my fault." Laurie returned. She grimaced as she handed Flora a glass of water. "I'm sorry. Police officers and diplomacy, it's not our strong point."

"I don't think there was any way you could deliver news like that and it wouldn't be disturbing." Flora took a sip of water. "Who found the body?"

"I did." Laurie pulled another chair over and took a seat. "Joe Nolan and I called out to see Lilith about two hours ago, just as I told you we would. I knew she was expecting us, so I was surprised when we couldn't get an answer. Joe went around to the back of the house to check things out. The kitchen door was wide open, and we went inside."

"That means she must have been killed soon after she left my office." Flora seemed calmer now and Leon returned to his own seat, drawing the chair closer to hers. She smiled in acknowledgment of the gesture.

"Her conversation with you will be an important part of our investigation." Laurie turned her head as her husband joined them.

"The dog is a better babysitter than I could ever be," Cameron said to Flora. "I think we're safe to talk without your boys overhearing." He shook his head. "I'm sorry your introduction to Stillwater has been so gruesome."

"Obviously the main concern is these poor women. But I'm also worried about the impact on the Ryerson Center. It's possible I was the last person to see both Joy and Lilith alive." Flora managed a grim smile. "It's not the sort of publicity you and the other trustees were hoping for."

"You weren't the last person to see them alive," Leon said. "The murderer was."

Flora gave him a grateful look before turning to Laurie. "Can we talk freely in front of Leon? Although Lilith spoke to me as a patient to a doctor, what she told me impacts on the Main Street Clinic and if her murder is similar to Joy's…"

"Of course," Laurie said. "I've already made Cameron aware of the details of what's been happening to you, Flora. By which I mean, the vandalism to your house, garden, and car. Even though he isn't directly involved. If the Ryerson Center, or you as one of its employees, is being targeted, then sharing information becomes more important than protecting confidentiality."

"I know Lilith was one of Alan Grayson's patients." Leon had an uncomfortable feeling about where this was heading. "And that she'd recently made the move to the Ryerson Center. I think I can guess the rest."

There was a brief interruption as the twins bounded up the steps. "Drink, Mommy." Leon was fascinated by the way they could speak in unison. "Please."

"Let me do it," Cameron said. "I'm the person who is least involved and I already know most of the story."

"There's juice in the fridge," Leon said. "And some leftover chocolate cake."

"Cake!" The suggestion acted like a magic charm on the twins, who followed Cameron into the house. Tiny, who usually responded with similar enthusiasm to one of his favorite words, flopped onto the grass with the appearance of a creature who had been drained of all energy.

Flora waited until the boys had gone. When she spoke, it was directly to Leon. "I've already given Laurie this information, so I'm summarizing to bring you up to speed. Lilith came to see me this afternoon. It was the first time we'd met. The information she gave me was almost the same as what Joy had told me. Lilith believed Alan had misdiagnosed her for financial gain because patients would have to receive continuous medical treatment and then would have to keep coming back and paying his center. Or the drug companies would pay the practice to diagnose people with a condition and prescribe their meds."

"I'm still struggling with this." Leon shook his head. "This is not the man I knew."

"It's early days in the investigation," Laurie said. "But I'm getting a picture of a man whose debts were out of control. One line of inquiry I'm pursuing is a possible gambling addiction."

"It's quite a jump from a poker game or the racetrack to murder." Leon was trying and failing to picture his friend, Alan, as the person who had stabbed two kind older women.

"Of course it is. And that's why we're looking at this from every angle." Laurie's voice was firm and reassuring. "But right now, I'm interested in the fact that both women spoke to Flora. You said they had discussed the treatment they were getting from Alan Grayson?"

Flora nodded. "That's what Lilith said. They were good friends and they'd shared their suspicions that he was treating them for illnesses they didn't have. And he actively discouraged them from doing further research on those conditions."

"But they didn't confront him?" Leon asked.

"According to Lilith, Joy did. His reaction made her trust him even less. Soon after that, she came to me," Flora explained. "And Alan would have known about that, since it involved the transfer of her records to the Ryerson Center. Maybe he killed her because he suspected she had disclosed his malpractice to someone else?"

"Perhaps so. Except…" Laurie appeared lost in thought for a moment. "If that was the case, wouldn't it have made sense to kill her as soon as she made the decision to switch doctors? Once she'd spoken to you, it was almost too late. There was another witness."

Flora shrugged. "Who knows what was going through his mind? He probably panicked."

Leon looked out across the familiar landscape. His

grandfather had known what he was doing when he built the house in this precise location. At this time of the evening, dying sunlight softened the craggy face of the Devil's Peak. Puffs of cloud broke up the endless blue of the sky and a golden glow gave the landscape a peaceful hue.

The conversation had lurched him out of his comfort zone and he took a moment to examine how that made him feel. One thing was for sure. He had no desire to crawl away and hide, or head for the nearest bar. He felt calm and in control.

Leon looked at Flora's face. Listened to the childish laughter from the kitchen. When he spoke, he was surprised at the lack of hesitation in his speech.

"What Laurie is saying concerns me for a whole other reason." Both women turned to him with inquiring expressions. "If Alan Grayson is your number one suspect in these murders, then Flora is a material witness. That means she and the twins need protection."

"You're sure you don't want me to follow you as you drive home?" Cameron asked Flora as he helped her to strap the sleepy twins into their safety seats.

"Thank you, but Leon is going to put Bungee in a cat carrier and bring him, together with all his belongings, to my place."

She smiled across at where Leon and Laurie were deep in conversation on the porch. She knew he was forcefully outlining his thoughts about how the Stillwater Police Department should have an officer at her side, and one watching the twins, until the criminal was caught. Even though Laurie was offering a scaled-down version of that plan, Flora's own preference—a panic button inside her house, an alert on her cell linked to the PD call center, an officer checking the house every hour during the night—his concern felt good, like a warm blanket draped around her shoulders on a cold day.

Flora moved away from her vehicle to continue the conversation out of range of the twins' sharp ears. "He thinks I don't know it's an excuse to check out my place in case there's a serial killer hiding under one of the beds."

"You're very calm about it."

"No. I don't think calm is the first word that comes to mind when I try to describe how I'm feeling. But I can't see how having strong hysterics will help the situation." She looked across at the car, where two curly heads were beginning to nod. Her whole world was right there. Everything had gone crazy, but Stevie and Frankie were the reason she had to hold it together and believe it would all be okay.

She dragged her attention back to Cameron. "By the way, I met someone today who may be able to fill in until we advertise for a receptionist."

He listened in silence as she told him about Eve Sloane. When she finished, he asked a single, probing question. "And you felt comfortable around her, even with what's been going on?"

Flora gave it some thought. After Danny's death and Luella French's threats, her urge for self-preservation was razor-sharp. She didn't give her trust easily, preferring to keep her distance and weigh other people up instead of getting close. Yet, over the last few days, when her senses should have been on their highest alert, she had allowed two people to slip inside her defenses.

One of those people was Leon, whose past should have had her running in the opposite direction instead of wanting to rest her head on one of his broad shoulders. The other was Eve Sloane, who Flora had instinctively liked. Taking risks with her children's safety wasn't an option, but she didn't believe she was wrong. About either Leon or Eve.

"Yes." Her reply to Cameron was confident. "And her references checked out. The only unusual thing is that she seems to have traveled around a lot. But that's not exactly a crime."

"If you're happy with her, that's good enough for me," Cameron said. "I'll check with the other trustees, but my suggestion will be to hold off on advertising the position. Let's give Eve a trial. If she works out, she can stay. Right now, the center needs stability."

His words acted like a release valve, easing some of the pressure Flora was feeling. It was one less thing to worry about, and she was grateful for his support. "I'll let her know tomorrow."

"Take care of yourself." He made a move toward his own car, then turned back again. "Oh, and I'll see you on Saturday at two."

Flora's brow furrowed. "You will?"

"Awareness Day at the animal sanctuary. Trust me. You'll love it and your little whirlwinds will have a great day out." With a wave of his hand, he went to join Laurie, who was waiting beside their car.

"Everything okay?" Leon called across from where he was loading his own vehicle.

Since he was holding a cat carrier that was making some remarkable high-pitched noises, she decided against confiding that Cameron's invitation had aroused discomfort. The truth was that she was unsure about her reception among the townspeople of Stillwater. She was the new-in-town doctor who was the last person to have seen two of her murdered patients alive. It wasn't the best recommendation for the Ryerson Center, or the way Flora wanted to be introduced to new people.

At the same time, Cameron was right. The twins *would* love to see all the animals.

"Meet you at my place," she replied, keeping her inner debate to herself.

It was only when she got behind the wheel that she realized she'd forgotten to talk to Laurie about Jennifer Webster, the receptionist who had worked for half a day before quitting her job. She made a mental note to call the police chief in the morning.

Chapter 7

Bungee began his introduction to his new home by staging a protest and refusing to leave his cat carrier. Flora suggested they leave him in the kitchen with the door to his crate open while they got Stevie and Frankie into bed.

The layout of the house was open, with a small porch, a large family room, and stairs leading off the kitchen.

"As you can see, I wasn't expecting company." Flora turned to look at Leon with a laughing expression as she indicated the toy-strewn floor of the family room. They each carried a sleeping twin as they carefully navigated the hazards. "The plan was to tidy up once we got home from your place."

He followed her up the stairs and into a bedroom containing two small beds with dinosaur pictures on the quilts and an abundance of cuddly toys. The twins didn't stir as Flora undressed them, changed them into pajamas, and tucked them in. Leon watched her face as she bent to kiss them. He was surprised by the warm glow her expression triggered deep in his chest.

Since Karen's death, he had shut himself off from images of family life. He didn't begrudge other people their happiness, but it was usually too painful to view it up close. Although seeing Flora with her boys reminded him of what he'd lost, being with them didn't bring an overwhelming rush of grief and pain. Instead, he was surprised to find he enjoyed spending time in their company. It was impossible not to be drawn to Stevie and Frankie, and watching Flora engage with them was like listening to the notes of an old, familiar song.

Somehow, the trauma of losing his wife had made him shut out the memories of his own happy childhood. This little family brought them back. Incomplete snippets that came together to make a patchwork quilt of sights, sounds, scents, and tastes. Warm milk and cookies. The smell of his grandmother's button box. Shouting himself hoarse at the football game. Watching the moths dance in the golden light of the porch.

Life goes on. He looked up to find Flora's gaze on his face. *If you let it.*

"I suppose you get tired of people asking how you do it?" he asked, after she had switched the baby monitor on and carefully closed the door. "Work full time in such a demanding job and take care of twins, I mean."

Flora led the way back downstairs. "I'm a mom and a doctor." She led the way through to the kitchen. "I don't know any other way to do this. But I'm no superhero." She turned to smile at him as she reached into the fridge and brought out a plastic box containing left-over chicken. "My boys are my life, and they *rule* my life. They are a pair of miniature dictators."

She fascinated him. They had both been through tragedy, but they had dealt with it in completely different ways. Everything about Flora, like her name, was vibrant and alive, the opposite of how Leon felt most days.

"They do everything together, but they also fight *all the time*," Flora continued. "Their new word is 'want.' As soon as they hear something, they want it, even if they don't know what it is. And one wants anything the other twin has. Including me. Although I have two knees, they both want to sit on the same one. I sometimes wonder if it would have been different—"

She knelt on the floor, concentrating on her task as she placed a few pieces of meat beside the cat carrier. When she looked up, the smile was back, but it was just a little too bright.

"Having two parents would obviously have been easier. On all of us." She managed a laugh. "Or maybe not. They'd probably have been fighting over who got to sit next to daddy at dinner time."

"It must have been hard." Leon looked away briefly as Bungee emerged and ate the pieces of chicken.

"You find ways to deal with it." Her gaze was steady on his profile. "But you already know that."

"My way was at the bottom of a bottle."

"Mine might have been the same if I hadn't been pregnant," Flora said. "Now, I see flashes of them growing up and it scares and enchants me at the same time. I actually overhear them having their own sweet, independent conversations and I think about the things that will soon come our way." Her lip quivered, but she got it under control. "So, no matter how tired I am at the end of each day, I try to savor every minute because I know they won't be my tiny warriors forever."

In that instant, the urge to go to her and wrap his arms around her was almost overwhelming. Almost. *Because, let's be realistic here, no one wants a hug from the guy who's damaged goods.*

"I think it's clear where your tiny warriors get their fighting spirit." He injected a note of levity into his voice and was pleased to see her expression lighten correspondingly.

"You think?" She sighed. "Maybe I should use some of that fighting spirit to tackle the toy massacre in the other room."

As she spoke, Bungee decided to live up to his name. Leaping onto the counter, he sprang from there onto the top of one of the wall cupboards and settled down to view the scene below him with apparent disgust.

"He's at home already," Leon said. "Come on, I'll help you tidy up."

"You really don't have to."

"I want to. By the way…" He paused as they entered the family room. "On the subject of warriors, did the twins overcome their fear of the daycare center?"

Flora sighed. "It's the strangest thing, but I don't think they did. Not completely. They still seem reluctant to go." She lifted the lid of a large toy box and began to pile playthings into it. "Stevie's accident must have affected them more than I realized."

"You're sure nothing else has happened to upset them?" Leon asked.

"I spoke to Daisy about it, but she can't think of anything." If they ever gave out medals for toy-tidying, Flora would be standing on the highest podium in first place. She whirled around the room in double time, leaving him feeling slightly breathless. "She reassured me that they're quite happy once they get there, and she's asked all the staff to keep a close eye on them just to be sure."

Leon knelt to restore toy cars to their place in a brightly colored garage. He also picked up a pad of paper and a pen that had been dropped close to the safety screen that guarded the fireplace. "Do these go into the toy box?"

"No." She clicked her tongue in exasperation. "Frankie has a thing about taking them out of my work bag. Although—" She broke off, looking around her with a frown.

"Is there a problem?"

"Yes." Flora's movements slowed, and she stared across the room, concern stamping itself onto her face. She pointed to the items in his hand. "I used that pad and pen in work this afternoon to record my conversation with Lilith Bronson. When I left the Ryerson Center, I collected the boys from daycare, and came straight home. I placed my bag in the closet in the porch. Then we got ready and came out to your place." She swallowed hard. "The boys didn't have an opportunity to get into my bag."

Leon placed the pad and pen down on a coffee table. "Let's check it out."

Flora moved to his side, her hand automatically sliding into his. Leon took a moment to be pleased with his own reactions. Calm and decisive. Was it the situation or the woman at his side that had triggered the return of those personality traits? He didn't have time for any in-depth self-analysis.

When they stepped into the small square porch, Leon flicked on the light. There was a closet to the right of the front door and Flora let go of his hand to open it. Reaching inside, she emerged holding a leather bag that looked like a cross between a tote and a briefcase.

Her expression had softened and was more puzzled than fearful. "I still don't understand how those little mischief-makers found the time to get away from me." She opened the zipper as she spoke. "I'm even more surprised that they could reach this door handle—oh!"

Although Leon couldn't see into the bag, the reason for the exclamation became clear as she dropped it onto the floor and its contents spilled out. Among them was a scarf. It was vivid yellow and styled to look like a strip of crime-scene tape.

"Is that the same as the one you described as belonging to Jennifer Webster?" Leon asked.

"Yes." Flora's complexion paled.

His shocked brain had latched onto the most trivial detail. The color of the scarf, not how it had gotten into her bag. "I can see why you didn't like it. You didn't mention the bloodstains."

She moved closer, clutching hold of his arm and leaning against him. "There weren't any bloodstains when I last saw Jennifer wearing it."

"The kitchen window has been pried open," Leon said as he came back into the family room. He and Detective Joe Nolan had completed a thorough check of the whole property. "You would only have noticed it when you opened the window and realized the catch was loose. Joe has gone back to his patrol car. Even though he doesn't think the intruder will return, he said he wants to watch the house from the rear."

Flora huddled farther into the sofa, clutching her coffee cup a little tighter. The unthinkable was true. Someone had been inside her house. *Twice.* The place she had taken possession of with such pride a few short weeks ago, the dream home for which she had such plans, the safe haven where her boys were sleeping upstairs…

She choked back the panicky gasp that rose to her lips. "Even if we set aside all the other questions for the time being, how could the person who broke in here have known that my bag would be in that closet?"

Laurie looked up from her task of labeling an evidence bag. "It was probably a lucky chance. The intruder wanted to plant the scarf to make a big impact. Once inside the house, he, or she, would have looked around for somewhere to place it. The closet might have seemed obvious. You'd probably look there regularly. When he—I'm going with he, even though none of us have any idea about this person's identity—saw your bag, he could have come up with the plan to put it in there. He wanted you to find it tonight, so he put your pad and pen in the family room, knowing you'd immediately be suspicious about how they got there."

No one had touched the scarf until Laurie had arrived. Donning a pair of disposable gloves, she had placed it in the evidence bag. Flora had seen enough bloodstains to be sure she knew what she was looking at. What remained to be seen was whether the blood was human and, if it was, to whom it belonged. *Jennifer?* She tried to stop her mind from jumping several steps ahead.

Leon took the seat next to her on the sofa, not quite touching her, but comforting her with his presence. He seemed to know what she was thinking. In other circumstances, she might wonder how this had happened. How could two people who were each struggling with their own emotional issues have developed a close bond in such a short time? With everything that was going on, she didn't bother to question it. She was just glad to have him there.

"What happens now?" he asked Laurie.

"Now, we try to find Jennifer Webster." She held up the evidence bag. "And I get this sent off for analysis."

"Okay. That answers my question as far as the investigation is concerned." Through her shock and fear, Flora noticed how authoritative Leon's clipped tones sounded. It was almost as if he had never had a speech problem. "Now tell me what you're going to do about protecting Flora."

Stillwater's police chief was not the sort of person who backed down when confronted with a stern green gaze. Even so, Flora caught a hint of unease in Laurie's reply. "I wish there was more I could offer, but, right now, we're looking at vandalism, a break-in when Flora first moved in and now a bizarre follow-up. It just doesn't meet the threshold for any more police resources." She offered a helpless shrug. "I'm sorry."

Flora could sense Leon keeping his anger and frustration in check. "Are you saying that Flora, or the twins, have to get hurt before you can step up your official involvement?"

"We have an alert on Flora's cell phone and on her number at the Ryerson Center. I have a patrol car driving past here every hour and we're installing a panic button," Laurie said. She picked up her notebook, which she'd placed on the arm of her chair, and flipped through a few pages. "I know we've been over this, but is there anything else you can think of that might help the investigation?"

Flora shook her head. "I gave you the notes from my conversation with Lilith Bronson."

Laurie appeared lost in thought for a moment or two. "I'm confused." Flora got the impression they were words the police chief rarely used. "If Alan Grayson was the person who killed Joy Valeski and Lilith Bronson, these attacks on you don't make any sense." She sent an apologetic glance from Flora to Leon. "What I mean is…why not just kill you as well?"

"Damn it, Laurie," Leon muttered.

"No. I understand," Flora said. "I don't like it, but I know what you mean. Are you suggesting that the person who killed the two women is not the same person who is harassing me?"

"It's too early to suggest anything." Flora figured it was a typical police officer's response. "Until today's incident, I would have said you were the victim of some unpleasant, but low-level, targeted attacks…possibly stalking." Laurie's gaze fell on the evidence bag. "But the scarf changes everything."

"Because it sends a different message," Leon said.

"Exactly." Laurie nodded. "Whether it's true or not,

the person who left that scarf here wants Flora to think that Jennifer Webster has been harmed, even killed. But to give that message, the criminal had to know something very important."

Flora shivered slightly. "He had to know that Jennifer had one of those scarves."

"And that there was a link between you and Jennifer, however brief." Leon picked up on the same train of thought. "He had to know you would instantly recognize the scarf. Which means he saw you together while she was wearing it."

"Not necessarily," Laurie said. "The scarf is very distinctive. Jennifer was wearing it the last time she was with Flora. So the killer must have seen Jennifer on that day. Anyone who saw Jennifer would remember it. If she's dead, and her killer wanted to leave Flora a message to let her know that, something like the scarf would be the obvious thing."

"Do you always see the sinister side, Laurie?" Leon achieved a wry smile from the chief.

"It's my job." She looked up from the note she was scribbling. "I've been involved in several murder cases. You start to think like a killer." She got to her feet. "Right now, I don't know what to think. We don't know if the person who left that scarf is the same person who killed Joy and Lilith. I might speak to Jennifer Webster tomorrow and find her scarf was stolen the day she left Stillwater. The lab results could come back and show the stains are pig blood."

"None of that would change the fact that someone has been in my house. That was intended to frighten me, and it succeeded." Flora wrapped her arms around herself. "I don't know how I'll ever sleep again."

Even though Luella French had made threats against her three years ago, she had learned to push the anxiety to the back of her mind. Luella hadn't acted on her warnings, and Flora had been able to get on with her life. Although Luella's behavior had troubled her, in the cold light of day, she could reason it had been the result of grief and anger.

But this *was* real. Her mind insisted on replaying stories she had heard in the news of violent stalkers. Her head whirled, seeking a reason, a person. Anything. Anyone. Something she had said, or done, must have triggered this. It was like stumbling around in the maze of her own mind, constantly coming up against a dead end.

The physician in her was conscious of the way her body was responding to an overload of anxiety. Heart pounding, chest heaving, skin clammy, eyes wide. Every time she tried to get her stress levels under control, the same thought intruded.

My boys are upstairs.

A large, warm hand closed over hers. Gratefully, she looked up into Leon's eyes and felt her breathing begin to return to normal.

"You don't need to worry about tonight." His voice was soothing, taking away some of her cares even before he offered a solution. "Because I'm going to be right here on your sofa."

When Laurie had gone, Leon did a final check of the doors and windows, making sure the house was secure. Reaching the kitchen, he double-checked the repairs he and Joe had made. Once he was certain the window was safe, he stared out into the darkness beyond his own reflection.

Earlier today, when they had eaten dinner at his house, or while the twins were tumbling on the grass with Tiny, a malignant presence had entered this pleasant family home. That person wanted to scare Flora, maybe to hurt her. Or worse. The knowledge made him feel angry and helpless. But it made him *feel*. Although he didn't want her and the boys to be in danger, he was shocked at the depth of his new ability to experience emotion.

In the short space of time since he had met Flora, he had been catapulted out of the half-life in which his only close relationship had been with an oversized pup with an insatiable appetite. While this was not the way he'd have chosen to have his sensitivities restored to normality, it was incredible to feel alive again. It was also scary. Like white-water rafting while blindfolded. He had no idea where this was going, or even if it was leading anywhere.

Add in a serial killer and a stalker, who may or may not be the same person…

A bump against the back of his calves startled him and he looked down. Bungee made a sound somewhere between a meow and a growl and nudged him again. Leon bent and scooped him up. "I guess you and me both have some adjusting to do, don't we?"

He scratched behind the cat's ears and the room was filled with a sound similar to a helicopter preparing for take-off.

"Talking to the cat?" He looked up to see Flora leaning against the door frame. "I guess it has been quite a day." She came closer and ran her own hand along Bungee's back. The cat closed his eyes with an expression of ecstasy. "On the subject of animals, what's happening with Tiny while you're here?"

"Ah." He smiled down at her. "I was wondering when you'd ask that."

Although she put her hands on her hips, her own mouth curved upward in return. "Spill."

"I want you to bear in mind that he *is* house-trained."

She clapped a hand to her head. "Oh, dear Lord. This house is so small. How will we fit him in?"

"Don't worry. I'm joking. I gave Joe Nolan the key to my place. He's going to stop by, pick up Tiny, and take him to his favorite place."

"The all-you-can-eat buffet?" Her smile reached parts of him that had been long frozen, warming and reviving them.

He laughed, enjoying the easy familiarity and pleased to see her looking more relaxed. "Almost. I sent a message to Steffi Delaney at the animal sanctuary and asked her to take him."

Flora's smooth brow furrowed. "I don't want to disrupt your dog's life."

"You haven't met Steffi, so you have no idea how much Tiny will enjoy spending time with her and the other animals. He may never come home."

She sighed. "The truth is, I don't feel like I've gotten to know *anyone* here in Stillwater. Since we arrived, our time has been taken up with settling into the house, work, and daycare." Her hand flapped in a helpless gesture. "And then all of this…"

"I was born in Stillwater, and I know most of the people here, but I don't have many friends," Leon said. "In fact, Steffi and her husband, Bryce, are probably the only ones. Bryce helped me pick up the pieces when… when I left the army. And Steffi had a difficult time before they were married. I guess the three of us have some things in common."

If Flora noticed his hesitation, she didn't show it. He'd been about to say "when Karen died," but he wasn't ready to go there. Not yet. Even though it was the closest he'd come to talking about his wife, he still couldn't cross that line.

"But you *do* have friends."

"So do you." Emotion gave Leon's voice a gruff edge. "You have me."

He saw an answering glow in Flora's eyes. As she rose on the tips of her toes to kiss his cheek, Leon stooped to place Bungee on the floor. In the confusion, their lips met. Or maybe that was the plan all along.

He remained still, savoring the softness of her mouth on his. This was a moment he had never even dreamed of. Until now, he would have said that kissing another woman was the ultimate betrayal. Instead, his torn heart felt…easier. Not healed. He couldn't go that far. But there wasn't any guilt. The painful memories didn't intrude. There was Flora. And, in that instant, she was *everything*.

He slid his hands up her back, drawing her closer, and she responded by pressing her body tight to his. When her lips parted, warmth flooded through him. It was a slow, sweet kiss. A long embrace in which they took the time to explore and taste each other. When urgency started to take over, and things heated up, they broke apart.

"I think…" Flora's cheeks were flushed, her eyes sparkling.

"I know." Leon briefly rested his forehead against hers.

Too much. Too soon. The words didn't need to be spoken out loud. Two broken hearts. Two damaged souls. Two lives destroyed by loss and pain. One kiss couldn't fix that. Going beyond that? It was tempting. But it would be madness. Delicious madness.

Even so, when their lips had met, and time had stood still, Leon had caught a glimpse of something he had never dreamed he would see again. He had seen hope.

"I put a blanket and some pillows on the sofa." Flora was clearly striving for a return to normality.

Leon glanced at the clock over the cooker. "It's past midnight. We should try and get some sleep."

She moved to the door, then turned back. "Thank you."

The smile in her eyes almost had him crossing the room to take her into his arms again. "What for?"

"Being here. Everything."

Heat shimmered in the air, fiercer than before, and Leon clenched his fists at his sides. There was already so much going on, acting on this would be a mistake. He was almost certain of that.

He tried for a lighter note. "Maybe Tiny knew what he was doing when he knocked you over?"

Flora rolled her eyes. "If he leaves his next victim unconscious, I don't think you should rely on that as a defense."

Leon watched as she left the room. Before he followed her, he reached for the pull-cord and closed the blind, shutting out the inky darkness beyond the window.

Chapter 8

After two hours of trying to clear her head and force herself to fall sleep, Flora sat up. Switching on the light beside her bed, she opened the drawer of her bedside locker and fumbled inside for the bestseller she kept there. Her fingers closed around another object and she paused for a moment before withdrawing it.

She clasped the locket in her hand for a moment, feeling its familiar weight. When she opened it, her chest tightened painfully. That picture of Danny had been taken on their wedding day. In it, he was smiling into the camera in that clear, unself-conscious way he'd had. More than ever, he reminded her of the twins.

Were we ever that young?

Six years. It felt like a lifetime ago. She smiled as

she touched the picture with one fingertip. So much had happened since that day. *Face it. It was a lifetime ago.*

Just after Danny's death, she would cling to this picture. Overwhelmed by grief, she'd tried bargaining. Five minutes. That was all she needed with him. Just enough time to have him back so she could tell him everything that was in her heart and hear him say it would all be okay. That was in the early days when she'd wondered how she was going to keep going, when even taking her next breath seemed pointless.

Then the twins had come along, and sorrow had been forced to take a back seat. Flora wasn't sure if time healed all wounds, but the memories became kinder. The occasions when she could remember him with a smile instead of tears became more frequent. Missing him was like riding a roller coaster. Some days her heart hurt so much all she could do was get by. There were other times when she almost felt normal.

Now, she was looking at Danny differently. And maybe that was because she had been lying awake, unable to catch hold of sleep, partly because of the killings and the break-in, but also because of the man who was downstairs on her sofa.

There had been many imagined early-hours-of-the-morning conversations with Danny. In her head, she'd tell him about the milestones in the twins' lives. Teething, ailments, those memorable toilet training weeks. She would ask his advice on a range of decisions. Should she buy a new car or give the old one another six months? Was she doing the right thing with the move to Wyoming?

As time had gone by, his voice had faded from her

mind. While that saddened her, she was still able to maintain those silent dialogs, mainly because she was able to predict Danny's response.

Let go or be dragged.

It was his saying. His mantra. The least Zen person she had ever known had somehow taken a distinctly meditative approach to life. And that was what she heard in those late-night chats. When Stevie's biting phase coincided with Frankie's high-pitched screeching? *Let it go, babe. Don't be dragged.* That male colleague in Denver who stepped across the sarcasm line and became downright insulting? *Let go...*

Until now, she hadn't shared the details of the current situation with him in one of her imaginary talks. Honesty compelled her to assess the reason. Was it because even Danny wouldn't be able to apply his usual slogan to a double murder or the overt threats to Flora's own safety? Or was it because the attacks had started at the same time that she'd met Leon?

She closed her eyes, unable to prevent a single tear from escaping and tracing its way down her cheek. This was too hard. Three and a half years ago, she had vowed that her boys would always come first. That would never change. But Flora was a realist. She had predicted that this day would come.

She touched a finger to her lips, a slight shiver running through her as she relived the sensation of Leon's lips on hers. Yes. She had anticipated that one day she was likely to feel attracted to another man. What she could never have foreseen was the speed or intensity of her connection to Leon.

She had heard Leon described by the town gossips as

an alcoholic. Even if that wasn't true, his post-traumatic stress disorder had led to a drinking problem that had, at one time, been out of control. Clearly, his life was back on track these days. He held down a responsible job, had a good home, took care of himself. Actually— a flare of heat started deep and low inside her as she recalled the hard, muscled body that had been pressed against hers a few hours ago—he took *very good* care of himself. But one look into his eyes was enough to confirm that his emotional issues were still close to the surface. She worried that those would prove too much to deal with, between the threats on her life, her job, and her boys. She felt like she was straddling two pathways. One was taking her along the road to a new love with Leon. And that was everything she wanted right now. But, at the same time, she was being pulled further away from her responsibilities. Her boys. Her job. Her new home. Her head and her heart were at war. And she wasn't sure which was winning.

The answer was simple. She couldn't. *Shouldn't.* She owed it to the twins, to Danny... Most of all, she owed it to herself. Her heart was too damaged, too fragile, for her to contemplate putting it under that sort of strain, to try to heal someone else's heart on top of everything else. Unfortunately, her body had woken up with other ideas. It had decided the only man who could set it on fire was Leon Sinclair.

Another tear followed the first. Because Flora had never contemplated this moment. The one in which she would look at Danny's picture and apply her husband's own words to *him*.

Let go. She heard Danny's voice clearly this time and the tears flowed fast in response.

But what should she be letting go of? What would drag her down? The past? Or this wonderful, new, *crazy* feeling? The one telling her that the right man for her now was actually the wrong man?

Flora closed the locket with a click that sounded overly loud in the quiet house. Holding it against her heart for a moment or two, she drew in a deep breath. She would never truly let go of Danny. He was her first love and he would always be with her as she watched Stevie and Frankie grow. But something had changed—*she* was changing—and, although it hurt, it felt like time to start a new chapter. Would Leon be there when she turned the pages? That remained to be seen.

As she turned to replace the locket in the drawer, another noise caught her attention. There was no mistaking the sound of footsteps on the gravel drive. *At 3:00 a.m.*

A cold hand of fear clutched her heart. After sliding out of bed, she slipped on her sneakers and was heading for the door when she heard glass breaking downstairs.

As Flora ran for the boys' room, she almost collided with Leon, who'd reached the top of the stairs at the same instant. He was fully dressed and wide awake.

"What's happening?" she asked, as she darted into the twins' bedroom.

"Fire on the porch." He wrapped Frankie in his quilt as Flora did the same with Stevie. "We need to get these two out through the kitchen and as far from the house as we can."

Each carrying a twin, they hurried down the stairs.

Adrenaline was flooding into Flora's system like she was on an intravenous drip. Delivered direct into her bloodstream, it heightened her senses. Her eyes grabbed every bit of light, showing her flickering flames close to the front door. The fire hadn't fully taken hold, but she could smell the smoke and hear the wooden panels starting to crackle.

As Leon tugged open the door to the backyard, an orange streak ran ahead of them as Bungee made his own break for safety. Feeling like her heart was about to explode out of her chest, Flora drew in a lungful of night air.

Stevie stirred in her arms and she hugged him close. His little, warm body nestled tighter to her and she felt anger kick in to join the fear.

This is no accident...

She could almost feel malevolent eyes watching her. Her spine prickled in anticipation. A series of "what ifs" raced through her mind. The killer had used a knife on Joy and Lilith. What if he'd changed his mind this time? What if he had a gun? The moon was high and bright, illuminating the scene as if it was a film set.

"What if..."

"Not now. Keep low and follow me."

Leon moved fast, ducking low through the yard. Flora stayed close behind him. When she'd bought the house, the yard had been the least appealing element. Its main features were dead grass, weeds, and two bent trees. Over on the far side there was a tumbledown shed, its door held closed with a rusting padlock the size of her fist. With a fence that was close to extinction, it was no one's idea of a beauty spot. Now, she was glad she hadn't begun to renovate it.

"To your left," she whispered. "The gate doesn't lock."

They scurried in that direction. Once they were through the gate, Leon led her into the scrubby sage-brush that grew behind the houses on Lake Drive. The twins had woken up but were still too sleepy to make much noise.

"Mommy?" Stevie poked his head out from inside the quilt. "It's dark."

"I know, sweetie." She tried to get past the panic that was a tight band around her chest and think fast. "It's a game Dr. Leon wants us to play."

"Oh. Like hidey-seek?"

"Yes, but we have to be quiet. No talking." They were climbing a slight incline now. With the trees around them, they could look down on the rear of her house. Although there was no evidence of a fire raging out of control, she could see an orange glow at the front of the building that shouldn't be there.

We should be inside. Asleep and safe in our beds...

"Okay." Stevie called across to his brother. "Frankie, be quiet."

"Shh." Flora looked around her fearfully.

"Don't worry. I think we're alone." Leon moved closer. "My cell phone is in my back pocket. You call 911 while I keep a lookout."

Flora did as he instructed, her fingers shaking as she swiped. Keeping her voice under control with an effort, she gave the details to the dispatcher. "Chief Delaney knows all about this case," she finished. When she ended the call, she handed the phone back to Leon. "I need to sit down."

He helped her to a fallen tree trunk. Sitting next to her, he slid an arm around her shoulders and she leaned gratefully against him.

"Good game, Dr. Leon." Frankie emerged from his quilt, clearly unaware of any danger.

Stevie nodded his agreement. "We play chase next?"

Two hours later, Flora entered the kitchen of Leon's house just as he was pouring coffee into two cups. She wore one of his sweaters over her pink-and-white-striped pajamas and had swapped her sneakers for a pair of his socks. He scanned her face thoughtfully. Although she looked tired and pale, some of the initial shock appeared to have faded.

A fierce desire ripped through him. He wanted to take away the cares from those slender shoulders and ease the worry from her delicate features. It was so intense it took his breath away. As soon as it hit, a sobering thought followed in its wake.

He had no right to feel that way. And he'd already proved worthless as a protector. His wife had died as a result of his inability to care for her. If he failed all over again, would Flora and her boys be the next ones to pay the price? He could not, would not, let that happen.

"They're both asleep." Flora took the coffee from him with a grateful smile. "I can't thank you enough, but we'll be out of your hair tomorrow."

This was his chance. If he couldn't trust himself to shelter Flora and the twins from harm, he should let her go. Leave the job of safeguarding her to the professionals. There was no way he should be thinking about turning his home into a fortress with himself as the gallant defender who would watch over her.

"Stay here."

Her eyes appeared bigger and bluer than ever as she studied him over the top of her cup. "Pardon?"

"I want you and the boys to stay with me until this is over." It was only once the words were out that he knew how much it meant to him. He didn't just want to protect Flora. He *needed* to do it. It had nothing to do with restoring his lost self-esteem. It was about her and Stevie and Frankie. In the short time since he had met them, he had begun to care for all three of them. No matter what happened in the future, he had to be there to get them through this. They would deal with the rest later. "This house is less accessible than yours. Before I left the army, I was a serving officer in Afghanistan. I have the skills to protect you. And, although his judgment might sometimes be questionable, Tiny isn't going to let anyone get close without kicking up a ruckus."

"Leon, I can't let you turn your whole life upside down." He caught a glimpse of tears in Flora's eyes and fought off the temptation to draw her into his arms. That was an angle he hadn't considered. If she agreed, his ability to resist temptation was going to be tested to its outer limits.

"Has it occurred to you that I might welcome the idea of a little chaos?" he asked.

"If that's the case, why didn't you just keep Bungee?" she challenged. "Shut him and Tiny in a room together a few times a day. The effects would be similar to inviting my boys to stay."

Leon took her hand, and his heart ached to feel how much her fingers were trembling.

"Let me do this, Flora." He felt the words getting away from him, the old impediment resurfacing as it always did in times of stress. He took a moment to get it under control. "I need to know you and the boys are safe."

The tears shimmered brighter now, but she blinked them away as she nodded. Her hand twisted beneath his, and he could sense her embarrassment. She sucked in a breath, color flaming in her cheeks. "If we're going to share a house, I think we should talk about that kiss."

He smiled, pleased that they could do this without *too* much awkwardness. "Kissing you was the best thing that's happened to me in a very long time. It can't have escaped your attention that I think you're gorgeous." Although she bent her head over her coffee cup, he noticed the slight upward curve to her lips. He could have continued with a list of all the things he thought about Flora. That she was intelligent, funny, brave, an amazing mom… And where was he going with this? With an effort, he got himself back on track. "But we've both been through so much heartache, and we've been thrust together by danger. Now is probably not the best time to take things further."

He didn't add that there would never be a good time. Flora was smart enough to work it out for herself, if she hadn't already done so. No matter how strong the physical attraction between them might be, she deserved better than damaged goods. And Leon didn't believe his emotional cracks could be repaired.

As soon as he finished speaking, there was a heartbeat, a to-hell-with-it moment, in which he wanted to take the words back. He knew Flora could feel it as well. Maybe it was a signal that this connection between them couldn't be neatly packaged up and put to one side. Whatever it was, it made his pulse race and his blood burn with something that felt a lot like longing.

Reason and emotion were at war inside him. It was as if his body, having discovered how to feel again, was determined to test every sensation, just to be sure they all worked. Desire, anxiety, confusion, fear, nervousness… each vied for supremacy.

Aware that the silence was stretching and becoming tense, he searched for something to say. Before he could think of anything, his cell phone buzzed. As he checked the display, he didn't know whether to feel relieved or annoyed at the interruption.

"It's Andy Mellor," he said to Flora as he prepared to answer it. She raised her brows in a silent question. "The fire chief."

After Flora had called 911, they'd remained in the cover of the trees until the police and fire teams had arrived. When they had emerge, the porch had been ablaze, but the fire didn't seem to have progressed deeper into the house. Joe Nolan, the first police officer on the scene, had taken initial statements from Leon and Flora before approving their plan to remove the twins to Leon's home.

Leon listened now as Andy outlined what had taken place at the house since then. When he ended the call, he relayed the information to Flora.

"The good news is they've found Bungee. One of the fire crew will bring him over in the morning."

"I hadn't thought of that. We'll be back to refereeing the cat and dog situation," Flora said.

"I think the big guy will have been pining for his buddy," Leon said. "When Steffi brings Tiny back, maybe he'll go easy on Bungee for a while. Anyway, Andy said the fire hadn't progressed much beyond the porch. Andy called it an amateur job. In his opinion, the person who did it wasn't well prepared. They broke the glass panel and threw burning rags into the porch. Without an accelerant such as gasoline, it was unlikely to take much of a hold. It did burn the rug and the wooden panels in the porch. The biggest problem is smoke damage."

Flora's shoulders drooped. "So all my new furnishings and decorations…"

"I'm sorry." He hooked an arm around her shoulders as she swayed toward him. To hell with keeping his distance. This was about being a friend, being there when she needed him. "Andy said it didn't look good."

She rested her forehead against his chest and he ran his hand down her spine. After a minute, she looked up. In that instant Leon would have given all he had to take away the pain from the depths of her eyes.

"Those are just things. They can be replaced. I have home insurance." She attempted a smile and almost made it work. "My boys are okay. That's all that matters."

He gave her an encouraging nod. "I know it will be light soon, but maybe we should snatch a few hours' sleep while we can?"

This time the smile was genuine. "Almost light? Welcome to the world of the nearly three-year-olds. They'll soon be wide awake and demanding breakfast."

He laughed. "I guess I need to make some adjustments."

"On that subject, are there any areas of the house you want to keep off limits?"

Leon gave it some thought. "Maybe my study. I don't really use it much, but there are a few things in there I'd like to keep." He tried not to sound too geeky. "When I was a kid, I used to collect comic books. They were my prized possession and some of them are quite valuable."

As a former army officer, Leon had an open carry permit for a gun, which he kept locked away. Even his medical equipment was safely secured.

"Oh, good Lord." Flora looked alarmed. "By all means keep the boys out of there. In fact, I'd recommend a lock on the door."

"I'll do my best to source a lead-lined box," Leon joked.

"Oh, Leon." Flora leaned back, smiling into his eyes. "Lead lining is for amateurs. My two would be all over that in two minutes."

And it was in that moment that everything became clear. He could keep telling himself he was going to resist her and get past this attraction. The truth was, he didn't want to do those things. His life had changed because of Flora. If that meant feeling too much, too soon? At least he could feel again. And that was a hell of a lot better than the alternative.

Chapter 9

"Are you sure you're okay?" Daisy Cain scanned Flora's face as she dropped the boys at the daycare center the following morning. "You look awful."

"Thanks." Flora made an unsuccessful attempt to pry Stevie away from her leg. "That makes me feel *so* much better."

"I'm sorry. I didn't mean to be rude." Daisy drew Flora and the twins away from the other families who were arriving. "I guess it would be more tactful to say you look tired."

"We had a rough night." Flora didn't elaborate. It was possible she didn't need to. She was wearing Leon's sweatpants, cinched in tight at the waist, one of his sweaters, and her own muddy sneakers. The twins were still in their pajamas. If those things weren't enough of a giveaway, the way news traveled in Stillwater, half the town probably already knew about her house fire. The other half would hear before lunch time.

"Can you get Stevie and Frankie a change of clothes?" she asked Daisy.

"Of course. We always keep spares in case of accidents."

Flora wanted to hug Daisy hard when she said those words and didn't follow them up with any questions. Instead, she focused her attention on Stevie, who was pressing his face into her knee. It really hurt her to see him like this. Frankie held on to her hand and regarded his twin with a troubled expression.

Flora squatted to talk to Stevie in a coaxing tone. "Sweetie, this is the way we do things. While Mommy goes to work, you and Frankie get to come here so you can have fun."

"Don't like having fun."

"Would you like to play in the sandbox?" Daisy asked.

Stevie shook his head and huddled closer to Flora.

"This is so hard." Flora wrapped an arm around each twin, drawing them close and feeling the familiar tickle of their curls under her chin. "I have to go to work, but how can I leave them if they aren't happy?" She tried a different approach. "Stevie, I need you to be big and brave."

Stevie turned his head to look at her. "Brave like Dr. Leon?"

Oh, sweet heaven. Was she going to do this? She was homeless, frightened, and exhausted. So, yes, if this was what it took, she would use emotional blackmail to get her kids into daycare. She could feel Daisy's eyes on her face.

Don't judge me. You have no idea what's going on in my life.

"Yes. Dr. Leon wants you to be a brave boy. Then tonight, we can tell him all about it over dinner."

The words acted like a magic spell. Stevie gave a decisive nod. Squaring his shoulders, he took his twin by the hand. "Come on, Frankie. Be brave like Dr. Leon."

Flora watched with a lump in her throat as her little pajama-clad warriors marched toward the sand tray.

"So…um…you and Dr. Sinclair?" Daisy's eyes were bright with curiosity. "The man half the women in Stillwater would vote the nicest doctor in the world?"

Flora got to her feet. "We're friends. That's all."

She liked Daisy a lot, but Flora hadn't been in town long before she'd figured out how things worked. "In confidence" meant something very different in Stillwater. You told one person a secret. With the best of intentions, they would share it with a few more people. Before long, the whole place knew your business.

Her message to Daisy was clear. *Nothing to see here.* Was that true about her and Leon? If it wasn't, she didn't want the town gossips to be the first to know.

When she arrived at the Ryerson Center, she went straight to her locker, where she kept a change of clothes. Donning a navy skirt suit, white blouse, and heels, she felt herself slipping into her professional persona. After securing her hair into a chignon, she went into the morning briefing with her doctor colleagues feeling almost restored to her old self.

Like Flora, Rajiv Laxman and Vivien McAuley were

new in town, having been recruited when the center opened. The Ryerson Center had a unique remit. It provided all the services of a family medical practice, but with ground-breaking laboratories and equipment, its doctors shared their facilities and expertise with others in the wider area.

Although it was early days, there was a vague sense among the trio that things were not moving forward as planned. Maybe that was because the proposed merger with the Main Street Clinic hadn't gone ahead and their workload was heavier than anticipated. Whatever the reason, if they were to open up their resources to other medical professionals in the area, someone needed to be able to get out there and lay the groundwork that was needed for a merger. None of them had the time.

Flora told Rajiv and Vivien of the events of the previous night and explained that she would need to liaise with the police and take care of some personal business during the day. They were shocked and immediately offered to help in any way they could.

Rajiv opened his laptop and accessed the morning's appointments. "We can re-schedule some of these to free up your time."

"I'd appreciate it," Flora said. "I have another important job to do today." She told them about Cameron's approval of her plan to give Eve Sloane a job. "But I've tried calling her and I can't get an answer. She lives out on the Elmville road, close to Eternal Springs. I thought I'd stop by her place—"

"That settles it." Vivien picked Flora's jacket up from the back of her chair and held it out to her. "Raj and I will cover *all* your appointments today. Don't come back here until we have a new receptionist. If you also need to do some shopping for you and the twins while you are out, that's fine by us."

As Flora headed out to the parking lot, she reflected on how complicated her emotional life was getting just lately. A simple gesture from Vivien had almost tipped Flora right over into wild sobs. The situation must be getting to her, as was her hunger, coupled with exhaustion. Although why everything made her long to have Leon's strong arms wrapped around her again was a real mystery.

Heading out of town toward Elmville, taking a road that ran parallel to the Ryerson River, she reflected on Eve's choice of location. Although the area around the waterfall, known as Eternal Springs, was beautiful, Flora didn't think there were any other houses in that remote region. Surrounded by rolling hills and forest, it must be a lonely place to live.

As she approached the left turn that would take her to Eve's house, a silver SUV drew level with her car. Flora spared a glance in the direction of the other vehicle and her heart skipped a beat. Maybe her suspicions were working overtime right now, but the blacked-out windows made her nervous. So did the way the driver was keeping pace with her. The highway was quiet, there was plenty of room to pass. Its presence was like a message...or a warning.

What had she been thinking of, coming out here alone when she knew someone was out to get her? She didn't even have a cell phone. That had been in her bag, the one that had been in the porch closet when her house had been set on fire.

Those thoughts were whirling through her head as she tried to out-maneuver the other car. She tried speeding up to get past it, then dropping back to let it go by. Neither tactic worked. The SUV remained stubbornly at her side. Then, when no other vehicles were around, the driver swung sharply toward her. It was a calculated move. The other car clipped her left front wing and sent her veering toward the edge of the highway.

Flora fought hard to keep control of her vehicle. If she was forced off the highway, she would end up in the deep drainage ditch that ran along the side of the road. Even if she escaped injury, there was no way she would get her car back out again. She was all alone out here, at the mercy of the person behind those blacked-out windows.

Gripping the steering wheel as if her life depended on it—*my life* does *depend on it*—she hit the gas pedal like a woman possessed. Shooting past the other car, she took the left turn like a speeding bullet, crossing the path of an oncoming truck, much to the fury of the driver. The noise of his horn was still blaring in her ears when, panting as though she had just run a marathon, she pulled into Eve's driveway.

"Uh, Dr. Sinclair?" Tegan regarded Leon from the door of his office with the same expression on her face she might wear if she was watching an escaped tiger. It was the look she had worn ever since he had reprimanded her for gossiping about Flora in relation to Joy Valeski's death. When had that been? It felt like another century.

He looked up with a slight frown. The morning appointments had been non-stop, and this was the first break they'd had. He'd been hoping to call Flora, then he'd remembered she no longer had a cell phone. How the hell was he supposed to get through the rest of the day not knowing if she was okay?

"Yes?" He tried to disguise the impatience he was feeling. It wasn't Tegan's fault that work was the last thing on his mind right now.

"I thought you should see this."

She handed him her smart phone and he got the strong impression that she wanted to run away. He glanced at the screen and his gaze became riveted. Tegan had been checking her social media accounts and one platform contained a page entitled "Doctor Death." It was a smear campaign targeted at Flora.

Whoever had set it up had taken the Stillwater *Sentinel* report written just before the Ryerson Center opened. Using the same picture of Flora, and a similar format, the revised article contained allegations ranging from a vague hint that she had been forced to leave Denver because of professional misconduct to a blatant allegation that she was responsible for the deaths of Joy Valeski and Lilith Bronson. The final message was clear: the citizens of Stillwater should get this woman out of their town.

"Do you know who is behind this?" Leon asked.

"No." Tegan shook her head so hard he was surprised she didn't fall over. "I swear. I was just scrolling through and that came up on my timeline. It seems to be aimed at people who live in Stillwater."

He scrubbed a weary hand over his face. If Tegan had seen it, most of the residents of Stillwater probably had as well. He would contact Laurie and she could arrange to get it pulled. He didn't imagine these things happened fast, and, in the meantime, damage was being done to Flora's reputation. Would the police be able to discover who was behind this poison? He wasn't hopeful.

"Thank you for bringing it to my attention. You did the right thing."

Tegan flushed, her hands twisting together nervously. "Dr. Sinclair, is it true that the Main Street Clinic is going to close?"

Leon paused before answering. There had still been no sign of Alan Grayson. Laurie had checked his credit cards and recent transactions showed signs of suspicious activity because he had withdrawn large sums of money. But even if he wasn't implicated in the murders, things weren't looking good for the man who had founded the Main Street Clinic. Before they were killed, both Joy and Lilith had given Flora information that suggested Alan was guilty of malpractice. The longer he remained missing, the more damning it looked.

"I don't know, Tegan. I wish I could give you a better answer, but I don't have any information right now. If I hear any more, I'll let you know."

"It's just—" she sucked in a breath, the next words coming out in a rush "—I heard there's a position at the daycare center. I don't want to leave here, but I have a childcare qualification and…"

Leon almost smiled at the irony. Just as Flora had found herself a receptionist, it looked like he was about to lose his. If Tegan went, the Main Street Clinic would just be Leon.

"If there is another job you want to apply for, you

should take that opportunity. I can't make you any promises about what the future will look like here."

She nodded. "Thank you for being honest."

When Tegan had gone, he reached for the phone on his desk and called the Stillwater Police Department. Chief Delaney and Detective Nolan were both out on police business. Frustrated, he left a message asking one of them to call him back urgently.

His next appointment was with an elderly man named Bradley Warren who pushed the door wide without knocking. Standing in the doorway, he looked Leon up and down with a frown.

"Who are you?"

Leon got to his feet and held out his hand. He had already checked Mr. Warren's file and knew he was one of Alan Grayson's patients. "I'm Dr. Sinclair. I'm afraid Dr. Grayson is unavailable so I'm covering his appointments."

Mr. Warren ignored the hand. Stalking past Leon, he dropped into a chair. "Unavailable? Is that a fancy way of saying 'on the run'?"

"Pardon?" Leon moved to his own side of the desk, trying to decide on the best approach to take with this unconventional character.

Mr. Warren wheezed out a chuckle. "Think you can hide what's going on?" He tapped the side of his nose. "The rest of the town might be fooled, but not me. No, sir. I had it figured right from the start."

"How can I help you today, Mr. Warren?" Leon wasn't sure sticking to the script would work, but he decided to give it a try.

His attempt provoked a fit of laughter so strong Leon

thought he might need to resuscitate his patient. After a moment or two, Mr. Warren managed to get his mirth under control. Wiping his eyes, he pointed a shaking finger at Leon.

"Call me Bulldog, and it's not about how you can help me, doctor. Oh, no. I'm here to talk about how *I* can help *you*."

Feeling as though he had entered an alternate universe, Leon sat back. "Please, explain…er, Bulldog."

"Blood pressure." Bulldog said it as though those two words were the answer to the mysteries of the universe.

"You want me to check your blood pressure?"

"You can check it if you want to. The point is, there's nothing wrong with it." Mr. Warren leaned his forearms on the desk. "But that's not what Dr. Grayson told me. Oh, no. For years, he had me believing I was on the verge of a stroke."

Leon took a moment to consider what he was hearing. The anecdotal evidence against Alan was stacking up hard and fast, but he needed to stay calm and act like this was the first he'd heard of any possible malpractice by his colleague.

"Are you suggesting that Dr. Grayson may have misdiagnosed your condition?"

Bulldog snorted. "Misdiagnosed? He cheated me out of thousands of dollars by misdiagnosing me and prescribing me drugs I didn't need. I found out the truth when my sister-in-law bought herself one of those over-the-counter blood pressure machines. I tried it out and mine was normal. Of course, I told her the thing was a waste of money and she should throw it in the trash. But she argued and said it matched up with the reading her doctor had given her just that morning. So I got myself a second opinion."

"And it differed from Dr. Grayson's?"

"Differed? I found out I was as fit as a thirty-year-old. All that money on drugs, regular check-ups, therapy, dietary advice—" Bulldog broke off, real anger on his face this time. "Every dime went into that crook Grayson's pocket. Then I heard some folks in Dino's Restaurant talking about how the fine doctor had gone missing. I came here today to find out if it was true."

Leon decided there was no point in denying it. "Dr. Grayson has gone away. I'm not sure when he'll be back."

"I guess that letter from my lawyer informing him he was the subject of a malpractice lawsuit scared him right out of town?" Bulldog nodded his satisfaction. "You know what they say. He may be able to run, but he sure as hell won't be able to hide."

When Bulldog had gone, Leon tried calling Laurie again. He got the same message from the police department and his frustration levels kicked up another notch. Although he'd advised Bulldog he would be sharing the details of their conversation with the police, this new information changed everything. If Alan Grayson was already the subject of a malpractice lawsuit, why would he need to kill Joy and Lilith to keep them quiet?

Just as his tension levels approached breaking point, his cell phone buzzed, and he viewed the caller display with relief. "Laurie? I have some new—"

She cut across him without apology. "Do you know where Flora is? I've been trying to reach her and she's not at the Ryerson Center. We've found Jennifer Webster's body."

* * *

"Is that a goat on the roof of your car?" It wasn't an everyday sentence. But Flora's morning had hardly followed a conventional path so far.

"That's Scape. He's my guard goat." Eve came toward her with a smile. "Although we have had the conversation about not climbing onto motor vehicles."

She clapped her hands and the goat blinked his yellow, side-slanted eyes at her. The outcome hung in the balance for a moment. Then, with all the grace of a hoofed ballerina, the little creature jumped down and trotted away.

"Scape?"

"Scape goat," Eve explained. "Plus, he likes to e-*scape*. It's a name with a double meaning."

Flora watched the brown-and-white goat as he wandered around the front yard, examining every item and either head-butting or tasting it. Hawk Farm was every bit as isolated as she'd anticipated. The house was set in a clearing, but around it the foothills of the Stillwater Trail rose steep and sharp, their slopes covered with dense sagebrush and soaring pines.

"I've never known anyone who had a pet goat before."

"If you're thinking about getting one, my advice is simple. Don't," Eve said. "There is an old joke about goats. Take three goats and put them into barrels. When you come back in an hour, one will have gone, one will be dead, and one will be tied up. My experience tells me they're cleverer than that. I think one will be gone, one will have eaten the barrel, and the other will have tied up a human." Her eyes scanned Flora's face. "But I don't think you came here to talk about my crazy pet."

"No, I came to offer you the receptionist job at the Ryerson Center." Flora's voice started to shake. "And, as I was driving out here, someone tried to run me off the road."

"Oh, sweet heaven. While you're in shock, I'm telling stupid stories about goats and barrels." Eve slid an arm around her shoulders and Flora leaned gratefully against her. "Come and sit down. I make a great chamomile tea. It's the best stress reliever."

Ten minutes later, Flora had removed her jacket and was seated on Eve's porch swing, sipping the herbal tea made with honey and lemon and feeling some of the tension ooze out of her. Eve was a good listener and, while Flora couldn't explain all the circumstances, she told the other woman about the house fire and the new development of the dangerous driver.

"I don't pretend to know exactly what you're going through." Eve's brown eyes were sympathetic. "But I've had some personal experience of harassment."

Flora looked up from her drink. "That's why you've moved around so much."

"Yes. I was married for a while. My ex didn't take the breakup well." Eve's gaze cut away from hers, and Flora got the impression she was lost in thoughts of another time and place. Then, with a slight shiver, she dragged herself back to the present. "We need to contact the police about what just happened to you."

"Can I use your phone? My cell was in the house when the fire started. I don't know if it survived."

As Eve went to get a handset from inside the house,

Flora inhaled the aromatic steam from her drink. She couldn't set off for Stillwater in case the maniac who had tried to force her into a ditch was waiting for her to leave Eve's place.

Let's see. How has my day been so far? Well, I need a police escort and it's not yet noon.

Eve returned to the porch and handed Flora the phone before returning to the house. Flora called Laurie's cell phone and the police chief answered immediately. "Flora? I've been trying to reach you all morning. Where are you?"

Startled at the abrupt question, Flora gave a flustered response. "I'm with a friend."

"I'm going to need you to be more specific." There was a hint of exasperation in Laurie's voice.

"Her name is Eve Sloane. The place is called Hawk Farm. It's on the Elmville road, just past the turn for Eternal Springs."

"Stay put. I'm on my way."

Flora started to ask for more information, but she was talking to dead air. What now? A chill swept over her and she gave a little moan. Not her boys. Or Leon…

Eve came out onto the porch, her quick glance assessing the situation. "You've had bad news."

"The police are on their way, but I don't know why."

"I know it's hard, but don't assume the worst." Eve came to sit next to her. "While we're waiting, you can tell me about my new job. What will my hours be? How many people will I be working with? Anything you think I need to know."

Grateful for the common-sense response, Flora started talking about the Ryerson Center. She told Eve about the staff: the three doctors, the nurse, the physiotherapist, the dietitian, and the two lab workers. Eve listened and asked a few questions and, before long, Laurie's car pulled into the drive.

At least one of Flora's fears was put to rest when she saw Leon in the passenger seat. Her first impulse was to hurl herself into his arms. Fighting it with difficulty, she walked toward him as he exited the vehicle.

"What's going on?"

He stepped in close, catching hold of her upper arms. "The twins are okay. The police have found Jennifer Webster's body."

Her hand fluttered to her throat in a helpless gesture. "Oh, dear Lord, no. Where was she?"

Leon looked over his shoulder at Laurie. The police chief gave a single, grim nod, signaling that he was free to speak. "Flora, there's no easy way to say this. Jennifer's body was in your shed."

Chapter 10

Eve tactfully went into the house, so Laurie could speak freely. They pulled three porch chairs close and huddled together. Leon, who had already heard the details, focused on Flora. Although her face was white as a sheet and her grip on his hand was painful, she was holding up well.

Laurie flipped open her notebook. "The fire crew made the discovery. It's routine in arson cases to make a thorough search of the property."

"How did she die?" Flora's voice was tight, as though the effort of talking was straining her vocal cords.

"She was stabbed. The medical examiner will give us more information, but it looked to me like she was killed in the same way as Joy Valeski and Lilith Bronson."

Flora's eyelids fluttered briefly, and she swayed toward Leon. He caught her, holding her tight with an arm around her shoulders. She leaned against him for a moment or two before opening her eyes.

"Was she killed in my shed?"

"I can't give you a definite answer to that question, Flora." Although the words were businesslike, Laurie's expression was sympathetic. "But initial forensic findings suggest she was killed elsewhere. You're both doctors. You know moving a body isn't easy. There are indications that Jennifer was dragged into the shed postmortem."

Flora shook herself like someone surfacing from a bad dream. "No, wait. The padlock on that shed was huge." She held up her clenched fist. "Almost as big as this. The guy who sold me the house couldn't find the key, but I didn't mind. I was glad the shed was secure. Although I didn't let the boys play in the yard on their own, the wooden panels on the shed looked rotten and I didn't want them getting inside."

"Can you remember the last time you noticed the padlock was in place?" Laurie leaned forward slightly, her keen investigative senses clearly on high alert.

"I know for sure it was there yesterday morning." Flora started to speak slowly, speeding up as she gained in confidence. "I was standing at the kitchen window while the twins were eating breakfast and I was mentally planning how I was going to remodel the yard. I remember thinking how ugly the shed was."

"And you're sure this was yesterday?"

"I'm positive." Flora nodded firmly. "Because my pleasant daydream was interrupted by a call from your secretary asking me to come to a meeting."

Leon shook his head. Had that meeting in Laurie's office really only taken place on the previous day?

Laurie tapped her pen against her notepad. "That means we have a clear timeline. Whoever did this knew about the padlock. He came prepared to cut it off so he could move the body into the shed. I find it hard to believe that happened in daylight."

"Whoa." Leon held up a hand. He liked and respected Laurie, but sometimes that no-nonsense approach of hers was like a bulldozer rolling over a nutshell. "Let's back up a little, Detective. Are you saying that during the night, while Flora and I were in the house with the twins, someone was on the property moving a body into the shed *and* setting fire to the house?"

His thoughts strayed to that incredible kiss. When Flora was in his arms, they had been standing right by the kitchen widow. The roller blind had been up. Moments before, Leon had looked out into the night and seen nothing. But what had been going on behind the cover of darkness?

"Looks that way." Laurie flipped to a clean page in her notebook. "I need to ask you some questions. If that's okay?"

Flora nodded. "Whatever it takes."

"When was the last time you saw Jennifer?"

"It was on the first day the Ryerson Center opened. I had met her once before that. We had a staff induction day a week before the official opening. Several of the employees were new in town. Jennifer and I chatted about the difficulties facing single women starting out in a new place. It was the only real interaction I had with her."

Laurie scribbled a few notes. "And she worked at the Ryerson Center for one day?"

"Technically, she only stayed for the morning," Flora said. "She took her lunch break and didn't come back. One of my colleagues, Dr. Rajiv Laxman, called her to find out if she was okay. She told him then that she was leaving. Something about a family emergency." Her eyes widened. "It wasn't her Raj spoke to, was it?"

"It seems unlikely," Laurie confirmed. "I'll need to speak to Dr. Laxman to find out more about that conversation."

Flora sucked in a breath. "My *shed*. I kept the boys away from it, but still—"

Leon knew exactly what she was picturing. Two little figures playing with a ball. Laughing and tumbling as they kicked it toward the shed. The ancient door creaking open…

He gripped her hand. "We will find the person who is doing this." The look he gave Laurie was almost fierce. "Right?"

"Of course." Laurie nodded her agreement. "But, the discovery of Jennifer's body, coupled with the new information from Bulldog Warren and the social media smear campaign, takes this investigation in a whole new direction. Although we can't close down the Alan Grayson angle completely, it's looking more and more likely that Flora is the target."

"Damn it, Laurie." Leon ran a hand through his hair. "Just blurt it out, why don't you?"

She gave him her unblinking cop stare. "That's what I do. I tell it like it is, then I catch the bad guys."

"Wait." Flora cut across their conversation. "What

are you talking about? Who is Bulldog Warren? What new information?"

"Sorry." Leon turned back to her, annoyed that he'd let himself be distracted and that the worry and confusion in her eyes had deepened as a result. He would do anything he could to take that expression away. Giving his own feelings an outlet by snipping at Laurie wasn't helping. "I had a visit today from one of Alan's former patients. It was the same old story. Misdiagnosis. Expensive, unnecessary treatment over many years. Only, in this case, the patient, a man called Bulldog Warren, had taken his case to a malpractice lawyer. Alan had already received a letter informing him of Bulldog's intention to claim."

Flora took a moment to process the implications of what he was saying. "All this time we thought Joy and Lilith could have been murdered because they had information that would lead to a malpractice charge against Alan Grayson. But that now seems unlikely because he was already facing such a charge."

"Exactly," Laurie said. "Killing them would have been a waste of his time."

"So, why were they killed?" Flora asked. She looked from Laurie to Leon and back again. "Was it because of *me*?"

"The three women who were killed all have a link to you. And it's clear that someone is targeting you in other ways." Laurie's voice was gentle. "But we can't rule anything out. It now seems increasingly likely that the murderer and whoever is harassing you *is* the same person. And, since Alan Grayson has gone missing, and even though there are some questions about his involvement, he is presumed innocent, and he could also be a victim. We have to look at this from every angle."

Flora looked lost. "I don't understand. I didn't know anyone in town when this started happening. And I'd barely spoken to Jennifer when she went missing."

"Which means we can't ignore the possibility that the person doing this has no connection to Stillwater. The timing of these events and your arrival here could be a coincidence." Laurie pursed her lips. "Although that's not a word I generally use. Bearing in mind that we could be looking for someone who has a grudge that has nothing to do with Stillwater, I've issued a statewide alert for Luella French. I already have an alert out for Alan Grayson. Even though it looks less likely that he is our murder suspect, the malpractice evidence against him is mounting."

"Maybe Alan became unhinged by these events." Leon disliked speculating in this way about a man he had, until recently, considered his friend. "If he wasn't thinking clearly, perhaps he thought he could weather the storm of Bulldog's lawsuit if he got rid of Joy and Lilith?"

"Anything is possible," Laurie agreed. "But we don't know how many other cases of malpractice we will uncover during the course of this investigation. There could be dozens. Alan would have had to become very disturbed very fast to decide he was going to kill them all."

"And that doesn't explain why Jennifer was murdered and her body hidden in my shed." Flora rubbed her hands along her upper arms as she spoke as though trying to warm herself. Since the day was sunny and bright the gesture was an indication of her emotional state rather than the temperature. Leon drew her closer and she turned her head to smile at him.

At the same time, something bumped his leg. Hard. He looked down and a small, brown-and-white goat gave him a side-long glance before trotting away. It was a measure of how his day was going that he devoted only a passing thought to the encounter.

"You mentioned a social media smear campaign," Flora said.

Leon wished he could spare her the pain of this but bringing it to her attention would be preferable to having her stumble across it accidentally. And he had no doubt that the person who had started those malicious online rumors would find a way of letting Flora know about them. It was better for her to find out this way.

"Laurie is already shutting it down—"

"I want to see it, please." Flora's face and voice were determined.

Reluctantly, Leon drew his cell phone out of his pocket. "You don't have to do this."

"Yes, I do." She waited while he found the page Tegan had shown him earlier. Although her eyes widened as she scrolled through it, she didn't speak. When she handed the cell phone back to him, she turned to Laurie. "Can you find out who created it?"

"I'll try, but it's unlikely," Laurie said. "The account will have required an email address, but my guess is that will have been set up for the sole purpose of creating this page. An attempt to trace the internet provider—or IP—address of the computer on which the social media account, or email address, was created is likely to draw a blank. We'll make the attempt, but mobile technology makes it easier for people planning this sort of attack to cover their tracks."

Flora shook her head. "This is getting even more confusing. Jennifer's murder and the information from Bulldog Warren make it seem like I'm being targeted and that, because it started so soon after my arrival here, it can't be linked to anyone in Stillwater. But that—" she pointed to the cell phone in Leon's hand "—that *is* about Stillwater."

Laurie sat up straighter. "You're right. My God. That campaign against you is totally targeted to a Stillwater audience."

"What the hell is going on?" Leon asked. "Flora arrives in Stillwater and…what? Someone decides he, or she, doesn't like the way she looks, the tone of her voice, the color of her lipstick? So they kill her receptionist and two of her patients, vandalize her car, and set fire to her house, whilst also running a social media smear campaign to drive her out of town?"

"And then try to drive me off the road as I was on my way here." Flora pointed to her car. There was a large dent in the left wing and the bumper was hanging off.

"What?" Leon's already elevated stress levels hit critical and kept on going.

"Did you get the registration details?" Laurie was already flipping to a clean page in her notepad.

"No. I was too busy trying to stay alive." Flora exhaled. "Sorry. But I didn't even think of it. I was on a quiet stretch of the Elmville road, just before the turnoff for Eternal Springs. A silver SUV with blacked-out windows drew level with my car. When there was no one else around, he swung into me. I'm sure he was trying to drive me into the drainage ditch at the side of the road. I managed to accelerate past him and make the turn." She gave a shaky laugh. "It wasn't a popular move with the truck whose path I crossed."

"Damn it, Flora." Leon had a mental image of her Honda Civic swinging across the path of an oncoming truck. "You could have been killed."

Her eyes were bluer than ever as she gazed at him. "I could have been killed if I'd stayed on that road and taken my chances with that SUV. This way, I had a fighting chance of getting to Eve's place." She turned to Laurie. "But Leon is right. It looks like someone took one look at me and decided they wanted me out of Stillwater so bad it was worth killing for. It feels like there's no reason behind this."

"There will be a reason," Laurie said. "It probably won't be as simple as the ones Leon outlined. It's unlikely to have anything to do with how you look or speak. But when we find that reason, we'll know who the killer is."

Leon reminded himself that he was looking at a woman who had a hugely successful track record when it came to catching murderers. Laurie herself had been the target of one of Wyoming's most prolific serial killers, but she had captured the Red Rose Killer. He had to have faith that she would do the same again. In the meantime, he wasn't taking any chances with Flora's safety.

"I can take care of you and the boys when you are under my roof, but what about the rest of the time?" He fixed Laurie with a determined stare. "She needs a bodyguard."

Flora shook her head. "My patients require privacy. And I don't want this to hit the Ryerson Center any harder than it already has. A doctor turning up for work with her own security guard in tow? That's not going to help our reputation."

"At least it's the weekend tomorrow. That gives us some breathing space. Let me talk to Cameron. He may have some ideas about how we can organize this. In the meantime, I'll take some pictures of your car and get forensics to check in case the other vehicle left traces of paint on your wing." Laurie got to her feet. "Will you be at the animal sanctuary awareness day?"

"I don't think…" Flora's expression was cautious.

"I'd advise you to come along. Be cautious but try to keep things normal."

When she'd gone, Flora huffed out a breath. "Keep things normal? How am I supposed to do that?"

Leon was pleased to see a slightly militant sparkle had replaced the defeated look in her eye. "I don't know. But let's start with something easy like removing your jacket from that goat's mouth."

Because Leon had arrived at Eve's place in Laurie's car, he traveled back to town with Flora. Despite the damage, her vehicle started just fine, and the journey was uneventful. Laurie had contacted the local DMV but there was no record of the SUV with blacked-out windows that had tried to drive Flora off the road.

When they reached Stillwater, Leon suggested he should call the fire station. "If Andy Mellor gives the go ahead, we could see if any of your clothes and the boys' stuff is worth saving." She felt his gaze probing her profile. "That's if you feel okay about going back to your place?"

Flora knew what he meant. Her little house was different now. Someone had not only started a fire while her boys slept upstairs, but that person had also dumped Jennifer Webster's body there. Those things hardly contributed to the homey feel she'd tried so hard to create.

"I have to go back. If I don't, he wins." She spared a second glance Leon's way. "But you'll be with me, right?"

"Always."

Always? In any other circumstance, that word might be considered a declaration. When Leon didn't follow it up with any more information, Flora figured she was letting her overwrought imagination skip too far ahead. It was possible he meant that word in relation to their friendship. In which case, shouldn't she be feeling glad instead of slightly disappointed? After all, she was convinced it was too soon for anything more. Right?

Except when she looked at Leon's carved profile and strong muscles, or gazed into his green eyes, she wasn't sure keeping her distance was such a good idea. It felt a lot like she was standing at the edge of an emotional precipice. And she didn't know whether she was more afraid of what would happen if she jumped or turned back.

Was this all part of the danger she was in? Was she seeking solace in Leon's arms because, on some subconscious level, she saw him as the protector she needed? Since Danny's death, she had been both Mom and Dad to her boys, striving every day to make sure they were never disadvantaged because they only had one parent. Deep down, she knew she'd done a good job. It hadn't always been easy. Juggling the demands of work and home had been hard, but she'd tackled both with determination. Things had changed since their arrival in Stillwater. She had been under intense pressure. Fear was a constant unseen presence breathing down her neck.

Was the attraction she felt toward Leon stronger because of that? Could it be simply a primitive response, a basic need to find security for herself and her boys? She smiled inwardly. If that was the case, she had to question her own judgment. Yes, Leon was physically strong. He had already assured her that his army training had provided him with the skills he needed to protect her. Most important of all, she knew he *wanted* to look after her and the boys.

But…seriously? If all she needed right now was a big, strong man, she could have made life easier for herself. Leon was *not* the straightforward choice. Yet, the more she got to know him, the more she *wanted* to know him. And that wanting had nothing to do with his strength and his looks. It was about the way he made her feel. Yes, he made her feel safe. But, when she was with him, she felt warm and cherished. There was also a whole world of new emotions involved.

She didn't want to get into comparisons. That would be unfair to Danny, and she couldn't see any reason to go there. Even so, there was an inevitability about thoughts of "then and now." At seventeen, she had tumbled confidently into love. Her heart had been light and free, and she had been sure the sweet sunshine that bound her to Danny and filled her with warmth would last forever.

The girl she'd been then had not experienced what she felt now. This wasn't warmth. It was raw heat, searing every part of her and depriving her of the ability to breathe properly when Leon was around. Stripping away her defenses, it was growing stronger with every passing minute. When she looked at Leon, Flora saw her own yearning reflected back at her. She didn't know how long they would be able to sustain this level of need without it consuming them. All her internal debating counted for nothing in the face of such primal need. But if they let go of the tight rein they both were keeping on their emotions? What then?

Leon ended his call and interrupted her soul searching. "Andy said they've completed the investigations at your house. There's an officer finishing up there, so he'll let us in."

They drove along Lake Drive in silence and Flora pulled into her own pathway, thoughts still in turmoil. As she switched off the engine, Leon shifted in his seat to face her and her questions were answered. Where this man was concerned, she would trade sensible for wanton. If he'd let her...

"I was watching your face as you were driving." *You were? Oh, my days.* She hoped he hadn't been able to see too much of what she was thinking. "I know it's hard, but Laurie is right. Let's try and keep it normal."

Her lips curved upward. Did he know he'd taken her idea of normality and shaken it up like an overeager kid with a snow globe?

"Stillwater normal takes some getting used to," she said.

As they left the car and approached the house, Flora

could clearly see the fire damage on the front facade. It was less than she'd expected. Although smoke had blackened the boards all the way to the second-floor windows, the fire had only taken hold in the porch. Rick Morris, the firefighter who had helped cut Stevie free from the playground equipment, was waiting for them inside the house.

"It looks a mess, but it is safe." He pointed to some rough timber beams that had been used to shore up the porch ceiling. "The structural work won't take long. Replacing the furnishings and decorations will be the big job."

Flora stepped inside the family room and her stomach clenched in time with her indrawn breath. It wasn't just the lingering smell of smoke that made her feel that way. She'd only started getting the house straight. Some of the furnishings were from her apartment in Denver, others had come with the place when she'd bought it. It hadn't been perfect, but she'd done her best to make it a cozy home for the twins.

Now, everything was covered in a layer of soot. It looked like a scene from a movie in which an artsy director had decided the best effect would be a single gloomy color. A slither of light sneaking through the closed drapes somehow made everything look worse.

"The whole house?" she asked Joe, struggling to keep the quiver out of her voice.

"It's not as bad upstairs." His expression was sympathetic. "You may be able to salvage some stuff from the closets."

With feet that suddenly felt like lead weights had been attached to them, she mounted the stairs. Leon followed close behind. Joe was right. The smoke damage wasn't as bad in the bedrooms.

"By the time we've washed these clothes and got rid of the smell, they'll be fine." Leon pulled open drawers in the twins' bedroom and ran his hand through the garments. His brisk approach saved Flora from sinking to the floor and never getting back up.

"There are suitcases under the bed in my room."

With Leon's help, it took only minutes to pack the most important items, including some toys that could be scrubbed clean. Since Flora had no desire to linger, they hurried back downstairs. She grabbed her bag from the closet. Although it was grimy, at least she had her cell phone, her wallet, and her notebooks back. As they reached the front door, fire chief Andy Mellor was on his way in. He nodded to them, his expression grim.

"This is bad business."

Privately, Flora thought the damage to her home and the concealment of a body on her property should be described using stronger language, but she kept that opinion to herself.

"Who found the body?" Leon asked.

"I did." Although Andy's voice remained calm, Flora caught the flash of anger in his eyes. "I was checking the shed to see if the items used to start the fire might have been stored out there. Looked to me like she'd been wrapped in a tarp to move her. Then whoever placed her there had pulled the covering back, so the body was on display to the first person who entered the shed."

"Was that meant to be me?" Flora asked as she and Leon returned to the car. "Or is the killer trying to make it look like I murdered Jennifer?"

He looked back at the house. "We could waste a lot of time trying to get inside this maniac's head. Even if we succeeded, I don't think we'd like what we found. Let's focus on the good things and go pick up the boys."

She smiled. "You're right."

The grin he flashed her way was filled with a new-found confidence. While Leon was defending her and the boys from the bad guy lurking in the shadows, he was also fighting his own demons. And it was doing him a whole lot of good.

"I usually am."

She bit back a laugh. "Have you been taking flirting lessons from Tiny again?"

He sighed as he got into the car. "Is that your way of telling me I'm charm-impaired?"

"On the contrary. I have a feeling you could be a master flirter in disguise." Flora started the engine and backed out of the drive.

"Really?" He shifted in his seat, turning fully to face her. "Care to elaborate?"

"Oh, I don't know. It just occurred to me that maybe the very best flirts might pretend to be bad at it in order to lull their victims into a false sense of security." If only this was all they had to occupy their minds. This light-hearted banter with the hidden will-they-won't-they subtext the only unknown.

"Victim?" Leon sounded like he didn't know whether to be amused or outraged. "That makes me sound even more like Tiny."

"Well, yes." She shot him a side-long glance. "Although I'm hoping that you'll draw the line at jumping out of the bushes and knocking me over next time you want to kiss me."

There. She'd said it. *Next time.* She'd let him know she wanted him to kiss her again. *Over to you, Leon.*

He didn't respond, but another swift glance in his direction showed her he was facing forward. The corner of his mouth tilted upward very slightly, and her heart soared. They drove the rest of the way to the daycare center in silence.

Once they were through the security checks and inside, Flora took one look at the twins and was reassured. They clearly hadn't spent the day pining for her. On the contrary, they were daycare poster boys. Their borrowed clothes sported an interesting array of stains including paint, mud, yogurt, and glitter. As they ran across the room, she noticed Frankie had painted one of his sneakers green.

"Dr. Leon! Dr. Leon!" Flora watched in amusement as Stevie and Frankie hurled themselves on Leon, twining around him like monkeys climbing a tree. She liked the way he handled their exuberance. Catching hold of them, he wrapped a strong arm around each as he lifted them off their feet. Laughing, he tried to make sense of their excited chatter.

"I'm not sure when I became the invisible mom," Flora commented to Daisy.

"He'll make a good dad." Daisy's gaze was on the exchange between Leon and the boys.

Flora frowned. That was way too many steps into the future. It wasn't something she'd even considered herself—not seriously—and it certainly wasn't something she wanted to discuss with Daisy. Luckily, she was spared the necessity of replying when Leon hauled his squirming burden toward them.

"Let's go home. I'm fairly sure my instructions just included something about pasta."

Flora's eyes met his. *Home.* Did he know what he'd said? It almost didn't matter that she didn't have a roof of her own right now. It didn't even matter that this all felt too fast. As they made their way out to the car, *this* felt like home and family. Leon and her boys. And, after everything that had happened over the last few days, Flora was going to grab that safe, warm emotion and clutch it to her with both hands.

Chapter 11

"How do you do that on your own every night?" Leon looked around the bathroom in amazement as he spoke.

There was about an inch of water left in the tub with the twins. The rest was on the floor. Or on him and Flora. Even his eyelashes were wet. The twins had displayed a determination that was breathtaking. They took splashing to tsunami levels, hurling water at each other to the accompaniment of ear-splitting squeals. Somehow, Flora had managed to wash them despite the seismic activity.

"It was easier when they were smaller." Deftly, she scooped Stevie up, wrapped him in a towel, and handed him to Leon. "I used to sit them in a plastic laundry basket and put that in the tub. The day they learned how to get out of the basket was memorable for all the wrong reasons." She repeated the towel maneuver with Frankie but kept hold of him. "I must admit, having another pair of adult hands around is like heaven."

Her gaze caught on his and held for an extra second or two. It had been this way all through dinner. Everything seemed to have taken on a double meaning. Eyes, lips, and hands were all overemphasized. If they accidentally brushed against each other, the air around them was so highly charged it was as if Leon could see electrical particles shimmering in the atmosphere.

At the same time, he was enjoying the change Flora and the twins brought to his quiet home. It took some getting used to. It was also set to the backdrop of some manic animal antics.

A long-suffering Bungee had come home and been greeted with fawning adoration by Tiny. None of Bungee's usual tactics had worked. His "no touching" vibe never had any effect on Tiny, but this time the dog's exuberance had gone into overdrive. He had missed his friend and he was determined to show him how much. The fact that the friendship was one-sided seemed lost on him.

Even with the relative peace that followed, the evening had been taken up with preparing dinner, then ensuring the twins ate it without a food fight. Once the ensuing mess had been cleaned up—a task of industrial proportions—and the twins had played outside for half an hour, the task of persuading them into the bath had begun.

Persuading? I meant "strong arming."

Flora did this *every* night? It was like taming a lion in a hurricane. Crazy, mind-spinning, exhausting… Leon had already forgotten his former, peaceful existence. This was real life, and he was loving every minute.

Was this what his life with Karen would have been like? He had no way of knowing if this joyful domestic chaos would have been part of his future. He felt a tug of release, secure in the knowledge that, mayhem or not, they'd have been happy.

Once the twins were dried and dressed in matching pajamas that had been salvaged from Flora's house, they were finally exhibiting signs of tiredness. Sitting at the kitchen table, they drank warm milk and ate rice cakes with peanut butter in unaccustomed silence. When Flora announced it was time for bed, Leon was expecting a fight. Instead, the two boys shuffled sleepily from their chairs.

"Want Tiny." Frankie wrapped his arms around the dog's neck.

"Want Dr. Leon." Stevie latched on to Leon's leg.

"Tiny and Dr. Leon can both come and say goodnight," Flora said. "But they will not be sleeping in your room." She gave Leon an over-the-shoulder glance as they went up the stairs. "I thought I should make that clear now, before anyone tries to claim you as a teddy bear substitute."

There it was again. That slight crackle in the air. Although…*teddy bear?* Where Flora was concerned, his thoughts were far from safe and cuddly.

Both boys were almost asleep by the time they were tucked into the twin beds in the smallest room. It was the one Leon had occupied as a child, and he ducked his head slightly to avoid the low beams, smiling as he watched Flora's face. She was radiant with love when she kissed her children good-night, reminding him of the way his own mom had once looked at him. It felt good to have that family warmth restored to his home.

Flora switched off the overhead light, leaving a night-light casting a soft glow over the room. After a last look at the angelic faces on the pillows, they made their way quietly downstairs to the kitchen.

"Coffee?" Leon asked.

"No." As if it was the most natural thing in the world, something she did every day, Flora stepped up close and wrapped her arms around his waist.

He gazed down at her for a moment, his mouth a fraction of an inch from hers. Her breath touched his lips, and Leon smiled. "I guess we're not very good at this 'keeping our distance' thing."

"I don't want to be good at it." She pressed closer, and he moved his hands up to grip her shoulders. "I want this. *You.*"

The initial brush of her lips against his was an instant hit of heaven. The time he had spent picturing this moment had ramped up his anticipation into the stratosphere. But nothing in his imagination matched the perfection of holding Flora in his arms. Starting slow, the kiss warmed up fast.

They melted into each other, the suppressed passion of the last hours and days rising as his lips pressed harder against hers and their tongues tangled eagerly. The feel, the taste, the scent of Flora…everything about her set him alight. Deep inside him, the heat intensified and spread like a forest fire, sending sparks shooting through his whole body. Had he really believed he could fight this?

Their movements were slightly clumsy. Both of them were out of practice, and they were almost strangers. Alongside the intensity, there was a desire to gauge each other's likes and needs, to know when to speed up or slow down, and how far was too far. For Leon, the answer to that last one was simple. Never too far. He couldn't get enough of her.

When they finally broke apart, he stared down at her. With her parted lips, flushed cheeks, and half-closed eyes, she took his breath away. He wanted to cling to this moment. Breathless, reckless, aching… All of those things were proof he was alive. More than that, they were about Flora. She was the one who had revived him.

Even so, the doubts crept in. "I'm still not sure either of us is ready—"

Flora shook her head. "For what? A walk down the aisle? Promises of forever? I agree." She sucked in a breath. "But I don't want to sleep alone tonight, Leon."

He gave a soft laugh. "I don't imagine we'd do much sleeping."

"There's only one way to find out." Flora's tilted chin and sparkling eyes were a challenge. One he wasn't going to refuse.

He moved his hands down from her shoulders to her upper arms. "There's just one problem."

Her brow furrowed. "What's that?"

"I've been celibate for the last four years. I've had no need of protection, and I'm clean out."

"And I came off birth control." She started to laugh. "So here we are. Two doctors who can't get laid tonight because we have no access to protection."

"We could improvise." Leon moved his hands down to her hips.

"What did you have in mind, Dr. Sinclair?" Her eyes were teasing.

"Rather than stand around here talking, Dr. Monroe, why don't I give you a demonstration?" With one swift movement, he scooped her up into his arms. Flora gave a little gasp, then wound her arms around his neck.

As Tiny bounded eagerly forward to follow them out of the kitchen, Leon shook his head. "Stay." The dog slithered to a reluctant halt and, heaving a canine sigh, slunk back to his bed.

"My God," Leon said. "The world just took a turn for the better. Tiny did as he was told."

"Ahem." Flora leaned back to get a look at his face. "The world took a turn for the better for *that* reason?"

He swung around, heading for the stairs. "I told you I was out of practice. Is talking about the dog not a valid seduction technique?"

Shaking with laughter, she buried her face in the curve of his neck. "You may be out of practice, but you're not doing so bad."

Leon set Flora on her feet and closed the bedroom door, the smile in his eyes warming every part of her.

The room was cozy, furnished in a traditional style with burnished wood and patterned rugs and throws. When Leon closed the drapes and switched on a bed-side lamp, golden light illuminated the scene. He lost no time in coming back to stand before her.

"Sure this is what you want?"

"So much." It was true. There was no more room for doubt. It was there in his eyes as well as in her words.

Slowly, she undid the buttons of the white work blouse she hadn't found time to change out of. Holding his gaze with her own, she took her time. One by one. When the last button was undone, the garment fell open, revealing the swell of her breasts above her cream-colored lace bra. With a shrug of her shoulders, she let the blouse slip to the floor.

She hadn't planned to put on a show, but the flare in Leon's eyes as he watched her ignited an answering response deep and low in her core. She *wanted* to be on display before him, wanted to be responsible for the hungry look on his face.

Reaching behind her, she undid the clasp of her bra. Catching the lacy cups as they fell forward, she paused a moment before dropping her hands and tugging the straps free of her shoulders. Even though the room was warm, her nipples tightened instantly. Was it anticipation? Or the appreciation in Leon's gaze as he drew in a ragged breath? Possibly it was a combination of both.

Flora turned half-away from him to ease down the zipper at the side of her skirt. When she stepped out of it, she was wearing only a pair of high-cut lace panties and her black heels. This time Leon's sharp intake of breath was accompanied by a muttered half-curse. He took a step closer at the same time that Flora bent forward to slip off her underwear. Excitement thrilled through her as he leaned over and placed a kiss on her right shoulder.

"Oh." She let go of a long sigh, leaning her head back against his chest as he lifted his hands to her hair.

Fumbling slightly, he found the pins that held her chignon in place and removed them. Flora shivered as he swiped her curls aside and his lips whispered over the back of her neck. There was something incredibly decadent about being naked while Leon was fully dressed.

"You're beautiful." The smile in his voice, the husky warmth, the total lack of hesitation all added to her desire.

"Mmm," Flora murmured dreamily as he ran his fingers through her hair. It was as if his touch released the tension of the day, and she savored the moment. Slowly, he turned her to face him.

With his hands on her hips he drew her in close and placed his lips on hers. The kiss was long, deep, and unhurried. When they parted, Leon looked as shaken as Flora felt.

She couldn't begin to describe the emotions he aroused in her. She had never felt more alive than in this moment with his eyes on her body. Appreciating her. Wanting her. *Needing* her. This was their time, their place. Everything that had gone before meant they were able to value it more.

She reached out a hand for his belt buckle. "Your turn."

Leon disposed of his clothing faster than Flora had. Shrugging out of pants, shirt, socks, and shoes at the same time as she kicked off her black heels. When they faced each other again, her eyes were drawn to the impressive bulge in his boxer briefs. How had she lived so long without this wonderful throbbing, clenching ache? As Leon moved toward her, the answer was simple. It wasn't about wanting a man. She hadn't felt this way until now for a reason. This was about *him*.

He pulled her close again, the determined expression on his face making her knees buckle ever so slightly. Placing a hand on her right buttock, he gave it a firm squeeze before letting his fingers gently caress her flesh and tease the divide between each cheek. Flora stood completely still, enjoying the intimacy of his caress.

"I love your ass." He breathed the words into her hair. "From the first moment I saw you, I dreamed of touching you this way."

The words were too much, and she squirmed against him, her imagination going wild. When she looked up, Leon was staring at her as if he was afraid he'd wake up at any second and find this was all a dream.

She kissed along his collarbone. "I'm real."

Taking his hand, she led him to the bed. They lay on their sides, facing each other, and Leon ran a hand along the curve of her waist, stopping at her hip. "I feel as nervous as a kid doing this for the first time."

"It is the first time." Flora reached up and cupped his cheek. "For us."

He slid one hard thigh between hers and she delighted in the contrast between their bodies. His strong, hers soft and yielding. As he tipped her onto her back, she gripped his shoulders, feeling his muscles bunch beneath her fingers. Slowly he made his way down her trembling body, kissing various parts of her as he went. The pulse at her throat, the small hollow between her neck and collarbone, then teasing the upper curve of each breast.

Flora gasped as his lips closed over a hardened nipple. His tongue teased the sensitive tip, swiping back and forth until she cried out and twisted as longing boiled through her. Emotion surged to the surface and her throat tightened. The tears that stung her eyelids were a result of the sheer force of her feelings and she blinked them away, not wanting to miss a single, perfect moment.

He moved lower, until he was holding her thighs apart with his shoulders. As he ran his fingertips lightly over her outer lips, Flora arched her back and opened wider. His movements were soft, slow, almost playful as he stroked and teased her sensitive flesh. At the first flick of his tongue, she whimpered.

Leon kissed, licked, and sucked, holding her hips down with his hands as Flora writhed against him. That first touch had brought her to the edge. Now, she was almost sobbing, her whole body shaking, hurtling toward the precipice. Her climax hit hard, flinging her into shuddering, gasping delight.

Leon continued with long, slow swipes of his tongue, even as her body jerked and spasmed. Her head was filled with color and light, normality returning gradually.

"Oh. That was…" She drew in a lungful of air.

He moved back to lie next to her. "Incredible? Amazing? I thought so."

"But you haven't—" She blushed. "At least not yet."

He smiled. "I was hoping you might be planning to do some improvising of your own."

Flora hooked her fingers into the waistband of his boxer briefs. "In that case, these will have to go."

* * *

Leon reclined against the headboard and succumbed to the bliss of Flora's lips moving down his body. He allowed his last few conscious thoughts to linger on how this felt. There was no guilt or pain. Only a sense of release and rightness.

He knew now that his feelings weren't supposed to be locked away. His body wasn't meant to be shut off from its natural urges. And this? Being with Flora? This felt like it was meant to be.

As Flora wrapped her lips around his straining erection, his concentration zeroed in on her, on her warm, wonderful mouth and her soft, fluttering fingers. In that moment, nothing else mattered.

Flora's fiery mane was a tousled curtain, hiding her from sight as she slowly bobbed her head up and down. Leon gently pulled her hair back, giving him a clear view of the delightful erotic image.

Flora swirled her tongue around his sensitive head before running it up and down the underside of his shaft. The result was a pleasure so extreme it was close to torture. The sucking and flicking heated his blood to boiling point. As Flora perfected her rhythm, and that wicked tongue continued to dance a series of caresses over his throbbing flesh, one hand reached lower to gently cup and stroke.

Watching her through half-open lids, Leon groaned. "Yes. Just like that."

In response, she purred with pleasure, the sound triggering a vibration that made him moan. He gripped her hair tighter with one hand, the other twisting the sheet almost into a knot. She looked up and he was lost in the vivid blue of her eyes.

The familiar tingle started deep and low. His groans became urgent and Flora responded by shifting position. Deprived momentarily of the delicious warmth of her mouth, Leon ground out a protest. "Don't stop."

He needn't have worried. Using her hands in time with her mouth, she applied the perfect pressure. Leon's toes curled as she moved faster, licking and sucking, while pumping with her fist. He was breathing hard, his back arching as he neared his climax.

The tip of Flora's tongue lapping against the most sensitive part of his body was causing his hips to buck up and down, and he managed to give a warning. "I'm getting close."

She stared right into his eyes and sucked harder. Leon gasped as his whole body tensed and his release hit. Flora kept her lips firmly planted around him as he cried out her name. Slamming his hand down on the mattress, he bucked and writhed as the world exploded around him.

Spent, he slumped back on the mattress. Flora crawled up the bed and curled into his side. From somewhere, he found the strength to pull the bedclothes over them.

"Tomorrow, we are getting those condoms."

She chuckled, her soft breath tickling his ear. "I agree, but the improvisation was fun."

"Fun?" He tightened his arms around her. "It was wonderful."

The words were inadequate. He couldn't begin to tell her what it meant to have her in his bed, their limbs entwined, her head on his chest. He didn't know how to convey the peace their passion had brought him.

"This—" Flora lifted her head to look at him. He caught a glimpse of tears in her eyes and understood their source. She wasn't crying because she was sad. She was crying because, like him, she was letting go. "It feels good, doesn't it?"

"It feels perfect."

Reassured, she nestled back into his arms. "Tell me what to expect at the animal sanctuary tomorrow."

"Well, it's a sanctuary and there will likely be some animals..." Flora dug an elbow into his ribs, and he laughed. "Okay. I predict it will be busy."

"Why?" Flora stroked a hand lazily up and down his arm.

"Because people are still intrigued by Steffi and her story. Although she keeps out of the limelight these days, it doesn't mean the attention has completely died down. There may even be some press there."

"You're talking to a newbie in town, remember?" He could hear the confusion in Flora's voice.

"Of course. I forgot. You remember the Anya Moretti story?" Leon asked.

"The famous actress who went on the run when she was wanted for murder? Didn't it turn out she was wrongly accused, and she married the guy who helped her clear her name?" Flora leaned up on one elbow. "Are you saying that Steffi Delaney is Anya Moretti?"

"That's right. She gave up the celebrity lifestyle when she married Bryce, but, like I said, there is still a residual interest in her story."

"Oh." The glowing look faded from Flora's eyes and

she chewed on her lower lip for a moment. It was easy to follow her thoughts.

"You can't let that social media page stop you from going out and encountering new people," Leon said.

"My rational self tells me that, but there is a little voice inside me that wonders how many people at the animal sanctuary tomorrow will have seen that social media page. My picture was splashed all over it, so I'll be easily recognized." She looked pale and vulnerable with her hair tumbling about her shoulders. "I'm new in town. For many Stillwater residents, those lies will be the only thing they know about me."

"Hey." He drew her back down into his arms, holding her tight against him. "I'll be at your side. Cameron and Laurie will be there, and I'll introduce you to Bryce and Steffi. There's also Cameron's other brother, Vincente, and his wife, Beth. If anything, it's a good chance for you to get to know more people. Trust me. It will be fine."

Gradually, he felt her start to relax. "I do trust you."

"Good. Because I have just had another innovative idea."

Her chuckle vibrated through his chest. "You have? Tell me more."

He lifted her hair and whispered in her ear.

Flora gasped. "Dr. Sinclair, you are a wicked man."

"I hope to be. If you'll let me, Dr. Monroe."

She squirmed with pleasure as his hand moved down her body. "I'm all yours."

They were the sweetest words he'd heard in a long time.

Chapter 12

The following day dawned bright and clear and, although Leon could tell Flora still had some reservations, they planned to set out for the animal sanctuary just after lunch.

Their departure was delayed slightly when Tiny tried to eat Bungee's dinner. The ensuing disagreement resulted in both cat and dog bowls being upturned. Water was spilled, and food scattered across the kitchen floor.

"While we're at the sanctuary, maybe we should ask Steffi if she accepts donations?" Leon asked as he and Flora cleaned up the mess.

"You think we should take her some dog and cat food?" Flora was on her knees, wiping up water, but she paused to look at him as she spoke.

"No, I think we should give her Tiny and Bungee."

She looked so beautiful as she started to laugh that his heart almost flipped over. "You don't mean that."

"I could be persuaded." He softened the threat by leaning forward to kiss the tip of her nose.

The twins were sitting at the table with paper and crayons, drawing pictures of the animals they hoped to see at the sanctuary. When Leon finished sweeping the floor, he wandered over to look at their artistic endeavors.

"Is that a dinosaur?"

"It's a lion." Frankie's tone expressed his opinion of Leon's intelligence. It wasn't high.

"Ah, it was the color that confused me. I don't think we'll see many lions today, especially not green ones." Leon studied Stevie's drawing and decided against trying to decide what it depicted. "What's in your picture, Stevie?"

"Rabbit." Stevie's tongue protruded from the corner of his mouth as he concentrated.

"We *will* see lots of them," Leon said.

"Want a rabbit like in Stevie's picture." Frankie bounced up and down in his chair.

Leon looked at the squiggles on Stevie's page. "They won't look quite like that."

"Want a rabbit. Want a rabbit." Stevie looked up from his picture and joined in with his brother's chant.

"Great." Leon glanced over his shoulder at Flora. "That's all we need. Bungee can chase the rabbit and Tiny can chase both of them. Why don't we just get a whole Noah's Ark?"

She came to stand beside him, leaning her head

briefly against his upper arm. "Oh, Leon. Have we completely destroyed your peace?"

"Yes." He checked to make sure the boys weren't looking, quickly pulled her into his arms and kissed her. "And I love it."

When he released her, she regarded him with a slightly bemused expression. "We are not getting a rabbit."

The words were greeted with outraged wails. Leon made an attempt to alleviate the twins' disappointment. "There will be ponies—"

"Want a pony!"

"I didn't mean that." He rolled his eyes at Flora. "I was going to suggest they could go for a ride."

"They'll forget about it when we get there," she assured him.

"In that case, I think we should get going before they trick us into agreeing to get them a python or something."

Flora was still laughing as they loaded the twins into the car and set off. Leon was glad. He preferred this light-hearted mood to the troubled expression he saw in her eyes every now and then when she thought he wasn't looking. He just hoped Laurie had made some progress with her investigation.

Bryce and Steffi Delaney lived with their six-month-old daughter, Katerina. Their home was a large, rambling ranch house close to Funnel Hill, a peculiar inverted hill formation that could be seen for miles around. The animal sanctuary covered acres of land and included stables, kennels, farmland, and other buildings.

"The primary aim of the center is to find new homes

for abandoned or abused domestic and farm animals. If we can't re-home them, they stay here." Steffi was greeting visitors as they arrived. Even though she was his friend and he'd known her for some time, Leon still found it hard to accept that this woman had once been famous for the designer outfits in which she'd graced the world's red carpets. Now, Steffi was dressed in faded jeans, a sweater in an indeterminable color, and boots that were splattered with unmentionable sludge. "We also take in wild animals if they are injured or suffering."

Steffi saw Leon standing at the back of the group of new arrivals and waved. Handing the introductory-talk job to one of her assistants, she came over. After hugging Leon, she gave his companions the smile that had once brought Hollywood to its knees. Its impact was only slightly reduced by the muddy smear across her left cheek.

Squatting to their level, Steffi greeted the twins. "Hi, guys. Have you come to see our animals?"

Leon had already learned that Frankie usually took his cue from his bolder twin, so he was surprised to see him step forward before Stevie.

"Want to see rabbits." Frankie took Steffi's hand. "And ponies."

"And dinosaurs." Stevie decided he needed to go bigger and better.

Steffi didn't flinch. "We may be fresh out of dinosaurs. But we can do rabbits and ponies. And pigs, goats, sheep, and horses." She looked up at Flora with a smile. "I can see you have your hands full."

Leon quickly did introductions. Although the place

was bustling, the atmosphere was carefree. Steffi led them toward the farm animals, and he could see Flora starting to relax. As they walked, they were joined by Bryce, who was pushing his sleeping daughter in a stroller.

"This is Flora Monroe, and her boys, Stevie and Frankie."

Bryce gave him a quick side-long glance. Barely noticeable to anyone else, Leon knew what it meant. It was an acknowledgment of how far the two men had come since the early days of their discharge from the army. Back then, PTSD had affected them in different ways, and they had supported each other, forging a bond that no one else could understand. That glance was Bryce's way of saying *"Look at us now."*

Partners, kids, stability, contentment. That was what Bryce was seeing. Although Leon's relationship with Flora wasn't at the same stage as his friend's, he knew Bryce, more than anyone, would recognize when he was happy. And no one, especially Leon himself, could have anticipated this. That he would meet a woman who had seen her own share of heartache, and that they would begin each other's healing process. No matter what the future held for them, what they had here and now was special.

The twins were enchanted with the various animals. As they strolled around the farm area, they were joined by Bryce's half brother, Vincente, his wife, Beth, and their daughter, Lia.

"I'm glad you left the guard dog at home today," Bryce said. It seemed to be some sort of joke between the brothers.

Vincente rolled his eyes. "We have a collie called Melon. He has the herding instincts of a sheepdog without the skill. You can imagine what happens when he gets in amongst all these animals."

Leon laughed. "I'm just glad to learn we're not the only ones who have a dysfunctional pet." He realized he was talking naturally about him and Flora as "us." *How's that whole "not ready" thing working out for you?*

He wondered if Flora had noticed. If she had, her smile gave nothing away. "Tiny certainly puts the 'fun' in 'dysfunctional.'"

They greeted other people, including Daisy and some of the other staff from the daycare center. Leon noticed Tegan was with them and figured she had already made her mind up about taking the new job. He couldn't blame her.

His knees buckled abruptly, and he looked down to discover the source. The little brown-and-white goat he'd seen at Eve Sloane's place gave him an oblique stare before turning to head-butt Vincente.

"Hi." Eve had the goat on a collar and leash like a dog. "I did call and check it was okay to bring Scape. I thought it might do him good to meet other goats."

As she spoke, Scape deftly slipped his head out of his collar and skipped away from her. Eve made a dive to catch him and went sprawling on the ground. Several people, including Steffi, joined in the chase. The ensuing scene resembled something from a slapstick movie.

Scape cavorted around the farm pens, helping himself to food, climbing on equipment, and greeting the other animals with evident delight. The whole time, he stayed just out of reach of the hands that were trying to grab him. It was an impromptu performance, one that provoked much laughter and was set to the backdrop of Stevie's and Frankie's squeals.

"Want a Scape!"

When the mischievous creature was finally cornered by Bryce and Vincente close to the pig enclosure, Leon turned to see what Flora thought of the show. To his surprise, she was standing slightly to one side. Two women had approached her, and she had turned away to listen to what they were saying. From the look on her face, it wasn't good.

He moved quickly to her side, catching the tail end of the women's comments.

"…not wanted here."

"…suggest you just pack up and get out of our town."

Leon knew the women by sight. They were both Alan Grayson's patients and he searched the recesses of his memory to put names to their faces. Aline Stibbe and Dolores Moon. The Stillwater rumor machine wasn't all bad. Often, if word got out that someone was struggling, or there was a problem, the scandal spreaders were the first to mobilize and offer their help. Not these two. They represented all that was bad about the town gossips.

Leon remembered when he had been down on his luck. Aline and Dolores had delighted in telling malicious tales about him. They had never let a little thing like the truth stand in the way of a good story.

"What's going on here?" Leon asked.

Dolores had the grace to look sheepish, but Aline

folded her arms across her chest. "We're just saying to her face what other people are thinking."

Out of the corner of his eye, Leon noticed Beth taking the twins by the hand and leading them away. He would thank her later for her thoughtfulness. Deliberately, he placed an arm around Flora's shoulders.

"And how do you know what other people are thinking, Aline?" He was pleased with the way he kept his voice calm. It was a long way from what he was feeling.

Her smile was triumphant. "The 'Doctor Death' page says it all."

"That page is the subject of a police investigation. I'd be very careful how you engage with that. And if you have any information about it, Chief Delaney will be very keen to talk to you."

"I sure will." Leon hadn't realized that Laurie had approached them, but she drew closer now. "Particularly as I'm investigating that page, and the messages in it, as harassment. I'd like you ladies to stop by my office on Monday and discuss that further."

"Oh, no." Aline shook her head vehemently. "That's okay, Chief Delaney. It was a misunderstanding."

"The only misunderstanding here is if you thought I was issuing an invitation." Laurie looked from one to the other. "I *will* see you both Monday. Let's say ten a.m., shall we?"

Leon waited until the two women had sidled away before he checked on Flora. Although she was pale, she gave him a weak smile. "I guess I was expecting it."

"You should have called me over as soon as they approached you," he said.

"They did it quite skillfully, almost like they had

something friendly to say. By the time they turned nasty, I didn't want to draw attention to what was going on in case the boys noticed." She leaned her head against his shoulder. "I'm okay. Really. What about Eve? Did she survive the goat-scapade?"

"She's gone. She wasn't injured, but she didn't want to risk a repeat performance," Steffi said as she joined them. "All goats are crazy but that one takes it to a new level." She turned to Flora. "Eve said she'll see you Monday. And Beth has taken Lia and your boys to ride on the ponies."

"What do you want to do?" Leon asked. "You've had a shock. Do you want to get a hot drink?"

"No." Flora's voice was firm. "We brought the boys here to enjoy a day out. That's what I want to do."

"I'm glad to hear that," Steffi said. "Because you may need to start with some explanations. They seem to think they will be taking all these animals home."

A few hours later, Flora and Leon accepted Steffi's invitation to join the Delaney family for dinner. They gathered in the large, cozy farmhouse kitchen, where Bryce served up delicious chili while Steffi organized drinks.

Flora watched the twins playing with Vincente and Beth's daughter, Lia. Although she was almost a year younger than Stevie and Frankie, there was no question about who was in charge. The little girl gave the boys her orders and they obeyed without question.

"I need to take her home with me," Flora said to Leon.

"Just copy her style," Leon suggested. "If they don't

do what you want, stamp your foot and threaten to throw your toys at them."

In this company, she felt some of her troubles ebbing away. It was as if the house, and its occupants, offered a place of safety. The care Bryce and Steffi gave to the animals in the sanctuary spilled over into their approach to guests. Flora felt comfortable with these people. This was the atmosphere she had hoped to find when she made the move to Stillwater.

Laurie joined them. "I won't discuss the investigation if you don't want me to."

Leon looked at Flora. "It's your choice."

"I guess we need to hear what's happening." Flora was resigned. This wasn't going away until the killer was caught.

Laurie's ever-present notebook was in her hand and she flipped through it. "We found Jennifer Webster's car. It was hidden in the trees near Wilderness Lake. Forensics are still working on it, but from the amount of blood we found, I'm confident she was killed in the vehicle."

"Do you have any idea what happened?" Leon asked.

"I'm speculating here," Laurie said. "But, based on what I know, for some reason, Jennifer allowed someone else to get into her car while she was on her lunch break. That person persuaded, or possibly forced, her to drive to a quiet location. At that point, he stabbed and killed Jennifer. The murderer then moved the body to the trunk and drove the car to the hiding place."

Leon glanced at the twins and Lia to make sure they were still occupied with their game. "Was the body in the trunk until the murderer moved it to Flora's shed?"

"I think that's the most likely scenario." Laurie nodded. "If that wasn't the case, the killer had to move the body a few times. From the trunk, to another hiding place, then to the shed. It's possible, but it adds another move that wasn't necessary."

"You're talking as though this is logical." Flora spoke in an undertone. "Yet none of it makes sense. Jennifer didn't know anyone in town. Who would she have picked up in her car during her lunch break?"

"That's what we need to find out," Laurie said. "I spoke to Dr. Laxman, but he couldn't give me any more information about the call he made to Jennifer's cell phone. It lasted only a few minutes, and he had no reason to believe it wasn't her he was speaking to. Jennifer either arranged to meet someone, which, given what you've said, seems unlikely, or her killer tricked her into letting him into her car."

"To do that, he must have come across as trustworthy." Flora thought of her own situation. "We talked about not knowing our way around, how hard it was to get to know new people. Jennifer wasn't an outgoing person. I can't see her picking up just anyone." She glanced from Laurie to Leon. "She *had* met Alan Grayson before. He came to the center for a meeting with the trustees when they discussed the possibility of a merger."

"Why would Alan kill a young woman he'd only just met?" Leon asked. "I can stretch my imagination far enough to accept that desperation might have led him to kill Joy and Lilith, but this?"

"Whoever killed her would have been covered in blood," Laurie said. "Jennifer was in the driver's seat and the killer was in the passenger's seat. The killer then drove the car to its hiding place. Even if he carried a change of clothes with him, it would have been impossible to get rid of all the blood."

Flora rubbed her hands up and down her arms. She felt a sudden chill that had nothing to do with the warm room. "You said it was likely that all three women were killed because of their links to me. Jennifer's murder certainly doesn't feel random. It seems too convenient that she arrived in town and was killed almost immediately."

Laurie frowned. "That's a good point."

"I didn't know I was making a point," Flora said. "I was just thinking aloud."

Laurie's notetaking was in full flow when Cameron wandered over and presented his wife with a glass of sparkling water. "I know it's no use to tell you to stop working, but you can at least avoid dehydration."

Although Laurie rolled her eyes, the glance they exchanged was filled with affection and understanding. It tugged at a point in the center of Flora's chest, but, where it would have once caused pain and reminded her of what she'd lost, it now triggered a different emotion. One that felt like hope. She caught Leon's eye and the smile that flickered between them felt as warm as a hug.

"Did Laurie tell you what we discussed?" Cameron asked.

"We've been too busy talking about the investigation," Laurie said.

"One of the biggest issues for all of us is your safety, but we don't want to spook your patients," Cameron said to Flora. "It seems to me we could solve that problem with my original proposal… The one that Alan Grayson turned down."

Leon frowned. "You mean the merger between the Ryerson Center and the Main Street Clinic?"

"Yes. It wouldn't be formal, of course, because you don't have that authority. But while Alan remains missing, you could operate your clinic out of the Ryerson Center's premises." Cameron's calm tones made the proposal sound straightforward.

Flora could see Leon thinking the idea through. Although she'd dismissed his suggestion that she needed a bodyguard, she couldn't deny that having him close would make all the difference to her well-being. She didn't want someone else. *He* made her feel safe. Even so, Cameron's suggestion was a big step, particularly as Leon wasn't a senior partner at the Main Street Clinic.

After a moment or two, he gave a decisive nod. "That could work."

"What about your patients?" Flora asked.

"They can still see me. They will just need to come to a different building," Leon said. "And, since I suspect my receptionist is about to quit, the timing is good."

"We can get a message out to your Monday appointments and divert future calls to the Ryerson Center." Cameron was already in organizational mode. "A vague story will suffice. I find 'operational issues' covers most things."

"My husband the businessman." Laurie fluttered her eyelashes at him, before switching back to her brisk manner. "I'll leave you to work out the logistics. Call me if you need anything."

When they were alone, Flora turned to face Leon.

"Are you sure about this? I've already turned your home life upside down. Now, your working arrangements are being disrupted because of me."

"Will I have a desk that doesn't have one wobbly leg?" She nodded. "And a swivel chair that actually swivels?" Another nod. "Do you have a coffee machine that produces coffee instead of weak, brown sludge? And air-conditioning that works?" She was laughing now as she continued to nod. "Then try and stop me being there with you on Monday morning."

A few minutes later, his attention was claimed by Vincente and Flora turned to find Bryce at her side. "I guess this wasn't the introduction you were hoping for when you moved to a new town."

Flora smiled. "You could say that."

He looked across at where Leon was deep in conversation with his brother. "You know, if I had a problem, I can't think of anyone better to turn to than Leon Sinclair."

She raised her brows. "He might be surprised to hear you say that. He told me he was a mess when he first came back to Stillwater, and that you helped him pick up the pieces."

"He's been through a lot. People will tell you he's an alcoholic. I've heard Leon himself say it enough times." He pulled his gaze away from Leon and looked at Flora. "I'm no expert, but I'm not sure it's true. Although the last thing I want to do is give anyone false hope, I think he was using drinking as a crutch."

"Isn't that the nature of alcoholism?" Flora asked.

"Of course, but in Leon's case, I believe it was a temporary symptom of PTSD. I can't promise that he will never slide back into addiction. All I can tell you is what I observe as his friend. I sometimes accompany him to his weekly Alcoholics Anonymous meetings. I'm also his sponsor. He can call me anytime, if he needs to. Since he left rehab, not only has he not touched a drink, he hasn't *wanted* to. He turned himself around." He smiled. "That took courage and stamina."

She returned the smile. "You do a good job of talking him up."

"Don't tell him." He looked slightly alarmed. "We're guys. We're supposed to trade insults and off-key jokes."

An hour later, the twins were drooping with tiredness as Flora and Leon loaded them into their car seats.

"Come and see us again soon." Steffi hugged them both. "The circumstances are different, but we know how this feels. You'll get through it and come out stronger."

As they neared Stillwater, Leon pointed to the lights of a gas station. "Pull in here."

"I don't need gas," Flora said.

"I know, but it has a twenty-four-hour convenience store attached."

She turned off the highway and pulled into the parking lot. "Do we need groceries that can't wait until morning?"

He cast a glance over his shoulder at the twins. They both appeared to be sleeping soundly. Even so, he leaned closer and spoke quietly. "No, we need condoms."

Instantly, there was movement behind them. Flora clapped a hand over her eyes, anticipating what was coming.

"Condoms?" Stevie murmured sleepily.

His twin was more alert. "Want one."

Leon prepared to exit the vehicle. "Maybe you should distract them by bringing up the subject of rabbits again?"

He was gone, leaving Flora to deal with the fallout before she could think of a suitable response.

Chapter 13

"I don't understand how they can have been falling asleep when we left Bryce and Steffi's place only to be bouncing off the walls once we got back here." Leon collapsed onto the sofa, stretching his long legs in front of him. He felt like he'd just wrestled an alligator instead of getting three-year-old twins into bed.

"Once they get that second wind, it's a nightmare." Flora flopped down next to him. "The only consolation is that they should sleep late in the morning."

"Good. Because I'm exhausted."

"Are you?" She turned to face him. "That's a shame."

He smiled, sliding an arm around her shoulders and drawing her closer. "Is it?"

"Hmm." Her eyes sparkled as she looked up at him. "You know, given your recent shopping expedition."

"I might be coaxed into staying awake."

She got to her feet in one swift movement, holding out her hand. "Let me try out my powers of persuasion."

As he followed her up the stairs, Leon reflected on how easy this was. Exhilarating and arousing, but comfortable at the same time. As though they had been together for longer. *Meant to be.* The phrase stayed with him as they stepped into the bedroom.

They took their time removing their clothing, with lingering kisses accompanying each item. When they were naked, Leon lifted Flora onto the bed and lay next to her. He cradled her close, imprinting her skin on his. It was a sensation like no other. An intimacy that went beyond anything physical. A fulfillment that meant more than just sex.

He'd stopped questioning how they'd reached this point so fast. His life had been in darkness and Flora was the power surge that had switched the lights back on. She had restored him, giving him back his enjoyment of life. His desire for her was part of that…an exquisite, magical craving that was demanding his immediate attention.

Flora broke free of his hold, disrupting his thoughts as she kissed his upper body. Leon lay still, enjoying the feel of her lips on his chest, ribs, arms, and neck. He trailed his hands over the smooth skin of her back as the mood shifted from laid-back to urgent.

"Leon?" She paused between kisses.

"Yes?"

"Are you still feeling tired?" She rested her chin on his chest.

"I may have regained some of my energy."

"Are you feeling strong enough to reach for a condom?" Her smile was teasing.

"I seem to be pinned down by a beautiful woman…"

Flora gave him a playful shove. "Is that your way of telling me I have to do all the work?"

Leon tucked his hands behind his head. "If that's the way you want it, you won't hear me complaining."

She reached across him, her hair tickling his chest as she groped on the locker beside the bed. With a condom in her hand, she leaned over him. "I think I can still remember how to do this."

Tearing open the foil packet, she rolled the latex down his hot, hard length. Leon sucked in a breath, as he met her gaze, all signs of teasing gone now.

Straddling him and gripping his hips with her knees, Flora reached between them and grasped him with one hand.

"It's been a long time," he said, as she guided him to her.

"For me, too." Her voice was husky.

"I'm warning you in case—"

"Doesn't matter." She leaned forward to kiss him. "We have more condoms."

Leon debated trying again to explain that this might not last long. Instead, he lifted his hips, pushing up as Flora lowered herself. When she drew in a sharp breath, he paused. "Is this okay?"

She gripped her lower lip between her teeth. "It's wonderful. It's just…you know…"

Even though she was wet and ready, her muscles were tight around him. Those heavenly sensations, once so familiar, took some getting used to after all this time.

"Yeah. I know." He drew her down into a kiss. "We can go slow."

Gradually, through their combined efforts, she stretched until she was able to sink all the way onto him.

"There are no words for how good this feels," Leon murmured.

Flora's response was a soft moan. For a minute or two, they remained still, exchanging long, slow kisses, adjusting to a storm of emotion that threatened to overwhelm them. Leon knew that, if he started to move, it would be out of control. Instead, he wanted to let Flora set the pace. Slowly, she straightened. Raising her hips, she lifted up and pushed back down.

Leon groaned and strained upward to meet her. "So close already."

"Me, too," she gasped.

Her movements sped up. At the same time, Leon raised on his elbows until he could cover one of her nipples with his lips. His tongue circled the hardened tip and he felt Flora's thigh muscles begin to quiver.

It was like their rhythm was in time with the beat of his heart. Darts of pleasure danced up his spine and spread along his nerve endings. His connection to Flora went beyond the onslaught of passion that was tearing him apart. She had saved him, brought him back to life, and she was in his soul. Those things took their bond to another level.

The physical sensations were incredible, but it was the emotions that drove him toward a climax so intense it was savage. As the pressure inside him reached boiling point, he felt Flora begin to spasm around him.

Gripping her hips, he held her tight and surged

deeper. They rocked together as the explosions overtook them. Leon was overwhelmed by closeness, warmth, and euphoria. As he coasted down, his uppermost feeling was one of security. With Flora, he could let go of everything except this. Her. Them. Here and now.

After a moment, she started to move away, but Leon tightened his arms around her. "Not yet."

She nuzzled into his neck. "I don't want to squash you."

"You won't. I like it." The truth was he was reluctant to break the connection.

Eventually, Flora raised her head. "Seriously, I'm losing the feeling in my legs."

He laughed, tipping her carefully to one side. Sliding from the bed, he went to the bathroom to take care of the condom. When he returned, he wrapped his arms around Flora.

"Now…sleep."

She snuggled close. "Okay. If you insist."

The following morning, Leon suggested they should take advantage of the fine weather and head out onto the Stillwater Trail. The lower part of the trail was popular with tourists, while higher up was for serious hikers and hunters. Starting out in town at the edge of the Ryerson River, it wound inland and upward until it reached the highest point in the county, the treacherous climb known as the Devil's Peak.

Although the path started out deceptively flat, as it approached the first expanse of water known as Tenderness Lake, it grew steeper. By the time the trail reached mountain-encircled Wilderness Lake, the gradient was punishing.

"What do you think?" he asked Flora. "Will Stevie and Frankie be able to manage to hike as far as Tenderness Lake?"

"They are quite good at walking, but they often tire on the way back," Flora said. "I have a pull-along wagon at my place. I bought it last year, but the twins were getting a little heavy for me to manage on my own. Between us, we should be able to handle them easily."

When they arrived at her house, and he saw the look of apprehension cross her face, Leon felt his anger levels rise. Who was doing this? Was Flora being deliberately targeted? It looked that way, but was it still possible the murders would turn out to be unrelated to the harassment? Laurie was certain the killings and harassment weren't random, so what was the reason behind them?

"Is there something else that links them?" He spoke his thoughts out loud.

"Like the Stillwater Dozen?" Flora asked.

He shifted in his seat, turning to face her. "You mean the baking club?"

"Joy and Lilith founded it, remember? It was how they became friends," she reminded him. "It's another connection between the two women, although I'm not sure how Jennifer would fit into that picture."

"I'm sure Laurie has looked into it, but it might be worth reminding her." He viewed the front of the house. "Do you want me to go in there?"

She gave him a grateful glance. "Yes, please. I know I have to do it again sometime, just as I have to get the repairs organized. But..."

He placed a hand on her knee. "You don't have to explain it to me."

It was true. She didn't have to tell him how she was feeling. The ease with which they had slipped into understanding each other felt natural and unhurried. He guessed that, at some point, they would need to take stock. Everything had happened so fast, and the circumstances were far from normal. Right now, it felt okay to just enjoy being together. There was no pressure to force a discussion about where this was going.

Flora explained that he would find the folding wagon under one of the beds in the boys' room. As he entered the house using her keys, sadness gripped him. All the hard work Flora had put into building her little home had been destroyed by a malicious act.

Why?

As he mounted the stairs, his eyes were drawn to the kitchen window. It still bothered him to think that, as he had drawn Flora into his arms that night, someone could have been outside, dragging Jennifer's body into the shed.

If they had been able to see out into the darkness, they might have glimpsed what was going on. It was a foolish notion, though. The optics worked the other way around. The person on the *outside* would have been able to see *in*. Whoever was out there in the darkness would have had a clear view into the kitchen. With the window blind up, an unseen watcher could have observed their kiss…

For some reason, the image troubled him more than the idea of looking out and seeing the killer moving the body or the arsonist prepping the fire. He shook the thought aside. He couldn't let this get to him. From the start, he'd decided his role was to protect Flora and the twins, and for that he needed to keep a clear head.

Once he'd located the wagon, he went back outside. As he approached the car, he heard singing and clapping. Flora was keeping the boys entertained, and the sweet simplicity of the moment made his breath catch in his throat. He was finally able to look at family life and not think about what he'd lost. Flora and the twins had welcomed him into their little world, and he'd stepped into it gladly. For an instant, he wondered how it would feel if he had to step back out again.

"Dr. Leon!" The boys' cries greeted him through the open window, interrupting his thoughts and spurring his feet onward.

He stowed the wagon in the trunk next to Tiny's crate and returned to the car. "Ready to go hiking, guys?"

"I'm not sure what they think today will involve," Flora said. "They've been out for walks with me many times, but now Dr. Leon is involved, there has been speculation about dragons and popcorn."

"I'm hoping a big dog and a Frisbee will prove just as popular."

They left the car at one of the rest stops and headed out on the trail. Although the path climbed steadily, the incline was moderate enough for Stevie and Frankie to chase Tiny without tiring. The day was warm, with clear skies above the higher peaks, and there were a few other people out enjoying the scenery. Partly shaded by tall pines, the trail was cooled to a pleasant temperature and their walk was accompanied by the sounds of trickling water, bird song, and the scampering of animals through the undergrowth.

As they climbed higher, the first view of Tenderness Lake appeared through the trees, sunlight glinting on its waters. Above them, the dizzying summit of the Devil's Peak soared into the blue.

When they reached the water's edge, Flora unpacked their picnic lunch and they sat on flat rocks to eat. When the twins had finished their food, she took off their sneakers and socks and rolled up their pants so they could play in the shallows.

"I'm just glad I brought them a change of clothes." She smiled as they threw stones into the lake and tried to catch Tiny as he charged past. "This is the life I wanted for them when I decided to move out here."

Leon leaned back, letting the sun warm his face. "What made you choose Stillwater?"

"My parents had friends who lived close to Yellowstone. We visited a few times when I was a kid and I always remembered how beautiful it was. I'd started thinking about making the move to a small town and, when I saw the position advertised at the Ryerson Center, the pictures of Stillwater I looked at stirred up those childhood recollections."

"Why did you feel the need to leave Denver?" Leon watched her face as she talked, the light and shade of her expressions captivating him.

"It was partly the memories of what happened to Danny. I was the widow of the cop who got shot, and I wanted to shake off that identity. Don't get me wrong, people were kind, and Danny's police colleagues looked out for me, but I didn't want to be that person forever. And, I guess I didn't want the boys living in that shadow." Her mouth turned down slightly. "With Danny gone, I didn't have any ties to keep me there."

They sat in silence for a few minutes, watching the boys play. Leon could feel Flora's gaze on his profile. She had been honest about her past and the impact of Danny's death. It was only natural that she would have questions for him. Was he finally ready to dig deep inside himself and face the answers?

"Karen was p-pregnant when she died." There. He'd said it. Almost without a stutter. The world hadn't stopped turning. The sadness hadn't gone away, either. But it no longer felt like broken glass filling his heart. He hadn't noticed the point when it changed and became a hollow ache.

Flora reached for his hand and held it to her cheek. "I'm so sorry."

His throat tightened painfully, and he nodded, unable to trust his voice. He didn't know whether to be glad or sorry when a wail and a splash had them both jumping to their feet and running to haul Frankie out of the water.

Fortunately, the little boy was unharmed and seemed more upset at being told the game was over than about his fall.

"Time to break out the dry clothes." Flora met Leon's gaze over her son's head, and the understanding in her eyes was as sweet as a hug.

That first sentence about Karen had been a leap into the unknown. He'd had no idea how he would react. Now it was over, the relief was enormous. The guilt, the responsibility for his wife's death, they were still there, coiled tight inside him. But he'd made an effort to open up about his feelings. He was starting to rejoin the human race.

Flora had been right. The twins' stamina flagged on the way back down the trail and they were happy to sit quietly in the little wagon while Leon pulled them along. When they were about halfway to the car, they passed a determined group heading in the opposite direction. They carried backpacks that were clearly heavy and were moving fast up the hill. One of them was Daisy Cain, and she waved a hand as she pounded along.

"That looks like hard work," Flora said.

Leon watched the group as they turned a corner. "I run this trail myself, but it gets steep from here, and, unlike them, I don't carry weights."

"I'm not surprised Daisy needs to be fit. Looking after two children is hard enough. She does it with twenty, or more, all day, every day." Flora placed her hands on the small of her back and stretched. "Maybe I should ask her for some workout tips."

"I think you should start easy," Leon said. "How about a slow walk back to the car, followed by pizza for dinner?"

She grinned. "Dr. Leon, that sounds like my kind of workout."

The next few days fell into a pattern of near normality. For Flora, having Leon working alongside her didn't feel awkward or unusual. They slipped into an easy routine. Dropping the twins at daycare together, they then traveled to the Ryerson Center, went about their separate working days in the same building, and met up again at the end to collect the boys.

Flora had a horrible sense of playing by the killer's rules, waiting for his next move. Leon's presence close by reassured her, though. She'd passed the point of questioning whether he was the right person to make her feel safe. He did, and that was what counted. The fact that he made her feel a whole lot of other things? Right now, she was going with the flow, feeling her way around all these new emotions. Her heart and her head both had a lot to deal with.

Although she didn't want to get inside the mind of the person who was doing these awful things, she couldn't help wondering about the motive behind the murderer's actions.

"It's like he wants to frighten me *and* make me look bad," she said to Laurie when the police chief called at Leon's house with an update on the investigation.

They sat on the porch, watching the twins play on the lawn with their toy cars. Leon had gone into the kitchen to make coffee, and the peaceful domestic scene jarred with the subject of their conversation. No one should have to talk about murder on a summer evening. Flora grimaced. No one should have to talk about murder entering their lives, *ever*.

Leon came out of the house carrying the coffee, which he set on the table. He took a seat next to Flora.

"The break-in at my house, the vandalism to the twins' planters and my car, the fire, the attempt to run me off the road—" Flora ticked them off on her fingertips. "They could be intended to scare me off."

"But you said he wants to make you look bad as well," Laurie said.

"This is going to sound weird." Flora had turned the idea over in her mind several times, becoming convinced it made sense. Crazy sense, if there was such a thing. "Joy and Lilith were my patients and they were killed soon after they'd seen me. The 'Doctor Death' page came right out and said it was *because* they'd seen me. And Jennifer's body was moved to my shed."

"You think he's killing them, so he can taint you?" Laurie asked. "Blame you for the murders, or at least use them to blacken your name?"

"I've been thinking about it a lot," Flora said. "And I wonder if that could be his motive."

"It's been on my mind as well," Leon admitted. "But I suspect there could be another target. One we haven't considered." Both women turned inquiring looks his way. "It occurred to me that this could be about the Ryerson Center."

His words were followed by silence. Flora swallowed hard. "You mean because of Jennifer?"

"Partly. We couldn't see where her death fitted with the others. Maybe this explains it," Leon said. "But what really got me thinking was the 'Doctor Death' page. Specifically, the way it twisted the newspaper article about the opening of the Ryerson Center. That reporter really focused on you, Flora. He made you the face of the new center."

She spread her hands in a helpless gesture. "That wasn't the way I wanted it. I even contacted the editor of the Stillwater *Sentinel* to protest about the tone of the piece. I was not responsible for the way the article criticized local doctors."

He smiled reminiscently. "I know that now, but it stung at the time. And Alan was furious."

"You think this brings us back to Alan as a suspect?" Laurie asked. "That he was enraged by the article and targeted Flora and the Ryerson Center because of that?"

"I'm not sure I would go that far. But Alan didn't keep his feelings to himself. He was angry, and he talked about how he felt. He also told anyone who would listen that the Ryerson Center would kill off the Main Street Clinic," Leon said. "What I am saying is, that, even before she arrived in town, Flora was on the radar of anyone who had a grudge against the Ryerson Center. That newspaper article put her in the firing line."

"So he wants to drive me out of town and discredit the center? By killing our receptionist and patients?" Flora shivered. Could Leon be right? It was the closest thing they had to an explanation for what had been happening. "All because that article was critical of local doctors?"

Laurie was flipping open her notebook. "Who, apart from Alan Grayson, was going to lose out when the Ryerson Center opened?"

Leon held up a hand. "That would be me."

"You were with Flora when Joy's body was found and when Lilith was killed. You were also together when Jennifer was moved to Flora's shed. That means we can discount you as a suspect," Laurie said.

"Thank you." Leon gave her a wry smile.

Laurie appeared not to notice the trace of sarcasm. "Is there anyone else?"

"There would have been Tegan Jackson, the receptionist at the Main Street Clinic, but she's just taken another job," Leon said. "Although she has always been loyal to Alan, I can't see her carrying that over to the point where she would kill to protect his business."

"You'd be surprised what people will do when they feel cornered." Laurie scribbled Tegan's name in her pad. "This opens up a new angle. As well as talking to Tegan, I'll need to speak to your colleagues at the center again, Flora. I interviewed them about Jennifer's death, of course, but they may have noticed other things without being aware of what was going on. Possibly, some of them have been targeted at a lower level."

Flora gripped her coffee cup, inhaling the aromatic scent. "I think I'd rather the killer was Luella French. At least we'd know who and why even if we didn't know where she was hiding out."

"I may have some information on that," Laurie said. "Six months after she threatened you, Luella was arrested on prostitution charges in Montana. I don't have any information about her after that, but I have a call lined up tomorrow with the arresting officer in the Billings Police Department. I'm hoping he can give me some details that will help me track her down."

"What about the baking club Joy and Lilith founded?" Flora asked. "Is it possible there's some connection there?"

"The Stillwater Dozen? I've spoken to most of the members, but my inquiries didn't lead anywhere," Laurie said. "You know, Flora, the Dozen would be a great way to get involved in the community. I even go along to meetings myself sometimes. They're holding a bake-off next week at the memorial hall to raise money for the new school sports field."

As she finished speaking, her cell phone buzzed. She took the call, listening intently for a few minutes. When she finished, her expression was grim. "Rajiv Laxman has been attacked."

Flora felt her world tilt off balance. "Is he…"

"Don't worry. He sustained only minor injuries. I'll have more details when I've spoken to him." Laurie got to her feet. "It looks like Leon's theory could be correct. Maybe the Ryerson Center is the real target."

Flora wrapped her arms around herself as she began to tremble. "That doesn't make me feel any better."

Chapter 14

In the midst of the madness, Eve Sloane had been a ray of sunshine. Within hours of starting work at the Ryerson Center, she had the reception desk and appointments system running like a charm. Despite the shock of Jennifer's death and the ensuing police investigation, Eve's pleasant personality and organizational skills had enabled the other staff to focus on their work.

The next morning, she arrived at the same time as Leon and Flora, looking slightly mussed up. "Let me guess." Leon held the door open, so she and Flora could enter the building ahead of him. "Scape?"

He already knew it was a safe bet.

"Isn't it always?" Eve sighed as she brushed a few leaves from her hair. "He ran off just as I was about to leave this morning. Luckily, I managed to get him back after a short chase through the trees."

Although Eve rolled her eyes when she shared hilarious stories about her troublesome pet, it was obvious she was as fiercely attached to him as Leon was to Tiny.

"I'm not a goat expert, but couldn't you leave him to find his own way home?" Leon asked.

"Goats are supposed to have a strong homing instinct, but, for some reason, Scape doesn't have that ability." Eve shrugged off her jacket as she spoke and took up her position behind the reception desk. "I'm always worried he'll get lost."

They had arrived early at the center in response to a request from Laurie. The police chief had asked Eve to contact all Ryerson Center employees and get them to attend a meeting. With impeccable timing, she walked through the doors with her husband at her side.

Cameron's expression was concerned as he approached Flora. "How are you?"

Her smile was tight. "I've been better."

He nodded. "Your safety, and that of the other staff, has to be the priority."

They went through to the conference room, where most of the other employees were gathered. Since the seats around the large, central table, were already occupied, Leon, Flora, and Eve stood at one side. Laurie and Cameron took up a central position where they could be seen by everyone.

Before they started to speak, the main doors opened, and Flora gasped. "Raj! What are you doing here?"

"The same as you." He only managed half a smile

because of the bruises and swelling to the right side of his face. "I work here, remember?"

Flora crossed the room to his side. "Will it hurt if I hug you?"

"I'll risk it." He held out his arms and they exchanged a quick embrace. Leon caught a glimpse of emotion on Raj's face and guessed he was hiding just how much the attack had affected him.

The nurse gave up her seat for Raj, and he eased carefully into it. Leon studied the other man's face. There was a deep cut across his right cheekbone with vivid bruising around it. That side of his face was so swollen that his eye was completely closed.

"Is everyone here?" Laurie asked Eve.

Eve consulted a checklist. "Everyone except Dr. Vivien McAuley. I tried calling her, but she didn't answer so I left a voicemail message."

Laurie glanced at Cameron. "I think we should start and bring Dr. McAuley up to speed later." He nodded, and she turned to address the assembled group. "This meeting is not intended to alarm you, but I feel it is only fair to inform you that I am linking the attack on Dr. Laxman to the murders of Jennifer Webster, Joy Valeski, and Lilith Bronson."

There was a murmur of surprise and consternation around the table. Laurie waited for a moment or two to allow the impact of her words to sink in. "There is a possibility we are dealing with a killer who has a grudge against the Ryerson Center."

"Does that mean we are all in danger?" The question came from Julie Ricks, the physiotherapist.

"I can't rule out that possibility." Even though Laurie never shied away from the harsh messages, her calm manner made them less frightening. "But I called this meeting to talk about how we can protect you."

"I'm here on behalf of the trustees," Cameron said. "We'll do whatever it takes to ensure your safety."

"Maybe if we knew how Raj was targeted it would help others avoid the same situation," Leon said.

"Dr. Laxman, do you feel able to share your experience?" Laurie asked.

"Sure, if it helps," Raj said. "I was working late, catching up on paperwork. When I came out of the building, I went straight to my car. As I unlocked the driver's door, I heard a noise and turned my head. Chief Dclancy thinks that could have saved my life."

Laurie nodded. "It seems likely the attacker intended to hit Dr. Laxman over the back of the head."

"When I turned, he got me on the side of my face instead," Raj said. "Even though I was stunned, I didn't go down. I knew if I did I was lost. He hit my shoulders and body with a baseball bat, but I fought back. As soon as I did, he ran off."

"Did you get a look at him?" Leon asked.

"No. He had a dark mask or balaclava over his face," Raj said.

"You could have been killed, Raj." Julie Ricks looked slightly queasy.

Leon glanced at the faces around the table. Even without Julie's comment, it was obvious that everyone was aware of the seriousness of the situation.

"Even though you didn't see his face, did you form any other impressions about him?" Leon knew the police would have already asked Raj these questions, but he was keen to get as much information about the assailant as he could.

"It all happened so fast." Raj frowned in an effort to remember. "He was about my height, so average for a man. I didn't get the sense that he was heavy-set or muscular. Other than that, I didn't notice anything. There was nothing distinguishing about him, but I was kind of distracted by that whole fighting for my life situation."

"What if he wasn't waiting specifically for Raj?" Julie asked. "What if he was just hiding in the shadows, waiting for the next person to leave the building?"

It was a good question, and every eye turned toward Laurie for the answer. "I can't rule anything out," she said. "Which is why you all have to be careful. Don't work late on your own. When you leave the building, do it in pairs or groups. Consider vehicle sharing until we have this person in custody."

"But when will that be?" Julie's voice rose on a note of hysteria. "I mean, surely the center should close until he's caught?"

Cameron looked around the room. "That has to be your decision. My concern is that, if we close the Ryerson Center, we risk leaving the people of Stillwater, and the surrounding area, without vital medical services."

"What do you propose?" Leon asked.

"Since the police are all involved in the investigation, the trustees have agreed to employ a private security firm until this is over," Cameron said. "But, if anyone feels they can't continue working here while the attacker remains at-large, we will allow you to take a paid leave of absence. Your employment at the Ryerson Center will be protected until the investigation is concluded and we'll be working to ensure that local people have access to a full range of medical services."

Silence fell over the room, but no one moved. Even Julie, who had appeared nervous, remained in her seat.

"My job is to care for people." Flora's voice was quiet but determined. "I don't know what this person's motive is, but he's not going to stop me."

There were nods and murmurs of agreement.

"I don't want to alarm anyone." Eve looked at the clock on the wall as she spoke. "But it's past the time Dr. McAuley would usually be here, and her first appointment is in ten minutes."

"Can you contact her?" Flora asked. Although she was turned away from him, Leon could hear the concern in her voice.

"I've tried, but my calls are still going direct to voicemail."

The morning dragged by. In between seeing her patients, Flora checked in with Eve to see if there was any news about Vivien. The answer was the same each time. "Chief Delaney said she'd call when she has any information."

"She hasn't called, so what does that mean?" Flora asked Leon, when they grabbed a half-hour lunch break in her office.

"Maybe that she doesn't have any information?"

"Has she found Vivien? *Not* found her? Is Vivien okay? Not okay?" Flora pressed a hand to her forehead. "I don't know whether hearing nothing is good, or bad."

He took her hands in his, drawing her to him. As always, his nearness acted like a balm, soothing her and reducing her anxiety. "Let's accept it as a positive sign. There's nothing else we can do right now."

She leaned against him. "I just have a picture of him running off after attacking Raj, still looking for a victim—"

"Hey." Leon lightly gripped her chin, tilting her face up to his. "Don't torture yourself with this. It's interesting that this person has never attacked you directly. He's burned your house, gone after people around you, but not attacked *you*?"

She nodded. "If I wasn't so tired, I might find that interesting. Even scary."

The afternoon passed in a blur. Several emergency cases cropped up and needed to be seen as well as the scheduled appointments. By the time Flora was able to draw breath, it was 5:00 p.m.

"Chief Delaney is in the conference room. Dr. Sinclair and Dr. Laxman are already there," Eve said, when Flora finally emerged from her office.

Flora headed for the meeting room with a sinking heart. She knew before she got there that this wasn't going to be good. If Vivien had been found alive and well, Laurie could have called to give them that information. The fact that the police chief had taken time out of a busy murder investigation to show up in person was not a hopeful sign.

"We're tracking Dr. McAuley's phone. There is no sign of her at her home, and her vehicle is missing." Laurie came straight to the point before Flora even sat down.

"That means the murderer could have gotten to her

the same way he did to Jennifer," Flora said. "She could have been killed in her own car."

"Before we jump to that conclusion, let me ask you what you know about Vivien McAuley." Laurie looked at Flora, then Raj. "I'm assuming you met her for the first time when you all started working here at the Ryerson Center, is that correct?"

Flora looked at Raj and saw her own confusion reflected on his face. "Yes."

"Did she share any information about her background?"

"She told me she was from Minnesota," Raj said. "And she went to medical school in Nebraska."

"I'm not sure I ever heard her talk about her family." Flora made an effort to remember. "She's a very private person."

"Why is this relevant, Laurie?" Leon asked.

"When we found out that Dr. McAuley was missing, I naturally instigated a search for her. I also did a background check. Five years ago, Vivien McAuley and her husband, David, were involved in a car crash in Colorado Springs. They were taken to the nearest hospital, where David died of devastating head injuries. Vivien, who wasn't seriously injured, refused to believe that he could not have been saved. Distraught with grief, she threatened to sue the doctors who treated him. Not content with that, she vowed to ruin the non-profit organization of which the hospital was a part."

"Let me guess," Leon said. "That hospital was part of the Mountain States Health Group?"

"Yes." Laurie flipped through her notes. "After Vivien's

lawsuit was unsuccessful she took an ER job in Cheyenne. From there, she came here to the Ryerson Center."

"Wouldn't this have shown up on her pre-employment background checks?" Flora asked.

"Vivien hasn't broken any laws," Laurie said. "I doubt she'd have been given the job here if the trustees knew she'd sued the company, but there isn't a question about that on the application form. I'm guessing there will be in the future."

"Are you saying that Vivien, having failed to get her revenge by conventional means, deliberately targeted the patients and staff of the Ryerson Center?" Leon asked.

"No." Flora spoke before Laurie could reply. "I've only worked with Vivien for a short time, but I can't believe she's a killer."

"I agree," Raj said. "She is a kind, compassionate person and a dedicated doctor."

"Could Vivien have been the person who attacked you?" As Leon spoke, Flora focused on his calm voice, using it to keep her grounded. *Vivien?* How could this be happening?

Raj fell silent for a moment. "I honestly never considered that it might have been a woman."

"But it could have been?" Laurie said.

"Vivien is as tall as me, so I guess so." Raj sounded like the words were dragged from him reluctantly. "But, if she is the killer, why would she run now?"

"Maybe she was afraid she went too far when she attacked you?" Laurie said. "Possibly she believed that, since the attempt on your life went wrong and you fought back, you would be able to identify her."

"So now, as well as searching for Alan Grayson and Luella French, you are also looking for Vivien McAuley?" Flora battled to keep the incredulity out of her voice.

"I know it must seem we are adding to the list of questions instead of finding answers." Laurie's voice was sympathetic. "It's often like this in a big case. Before we get a breakthrough, it can feel like there are so many threads we will never untangle them all. Right now, finding Dr. McAuley has become the number one priority. She's either a suspect, or she is in danger."

When Laurie had gone, Flora leaned back in her chair. Her insides were like ice water, her thoughts slow, as though what she had just heard had made them clumsy.

"I know you've both had a shock and you don't want to hear this about a colleague you like and respect." Leon leaned forward, his hands clasped lightly on the table in front of him. "But Vivien had vowed to cause harm to the Mountain States Health Group. Why would she come and work for one of its medical centers unless she intended to carry out that promise?"

"Even if her intention was to do some damage, I just can't see her as a killer," Flora said.

Raj nodded. "My imagination won't stretch far enough to picture her attacking me."

Leon got to his feet. "One thing is for sure. We won't solve anything by sitting here worrying about it. It's been a long day. Let's go home."

It was only as Flora accompanied him from the room that she realized that, when he said the word "home," she thought naturally now of his house. Her already low mood dropped several degrees further. Could she really have lowered her guard so far without noticing?

Flora had known when she accepted Leon's offer of protection that she was vulnerable. Even so, she had believed she was strong enough to give in to the attraction between them and deal with the consequences later. Now she was starting to doubt her ability to do that.

She knew Leon cared for her. He didn't need to say the words out loud. But he had been upfront about his inability to offer her anything long term. She had believed a temporary relationship was enough for her, and this was a bad time to find out that wasn't the case. Her heart had been through so much, and the fear of losing another man she loved was like a knife tearing through old scars. Could she recover from that? Was she willing to risk it—for herself or her boys?

She glanced at Leon's profile as they walked to the car. Somewhere along the line, her feelings had changed. She wanted more. Maybe he did, too. If she was willing to take the next step, would he be prepared to take it with her?

As several days passed with no incidents and no news of Vivien, Leon wondered if Flora was beginning to reluctantly question her own judgment about her colleague. She went about her daily routine with all her usual determination but was quiet and introspective. When she thought no one was looking, he would catch a downcast look on her face that was at odds with her usual sunny approach.

Physically, she was as warm and responsive as always, but he sensed an air of detachment about her that troubled him. It was as if a new barrier had arisen between them and he had no idea where it had come from.

He hadn't spoken about Karen again since his first attempt to open up to Flora about his past. He wasn't sure why. In that instant, he had felt ready to tell her everything. In many ways, he still did. But events had overtaken them. Was now the right time for him to pour out his heart? More importantly, was Flora in any frame of mind to hear the truth about his past?

Even though things had quietened down, the investigation was still ongoing. His head was telling him now was not a good time to make any decisions about the future. At the same time, his heart was giving him other messages.

Being with Flora and the boys had opened up a whole new world to him, one he had never dared dream he would see. Within a short space of time, they had become his family. At first, he had been afraid he was using them to replace what he had lost when Karen and the baby died. But he was able to take a step back and view the situation objectively. Flora, Stevie, and Frankie were important to him in their own right, not as substitutes for anyone else.

They were a little team who had slipped into his life and taken over his heart. Almost without noticing how it had happened, he found himself missing the boys when they weren't around. He would automatically plan child-friendly activities and look forward to the chaos they brought to his once peaceful life.

He had grown accustomed to stepping over discarded toys. All his belongings were now placed above toddler height. He understood that Stevie and Frankie would wipe their hands, mouths, and noses on his clothing. Refereeing unreasonable squabbles had become part of his everyday life. He'd even learned it was wise to spell out any words that might trigger an outburst of "want." Every time he heard the twins call him "Dr. Leon," his heart soared. Their laughter was one of the sweetest sounds he'd ever heard. When he tried to picture his life without them, he found it impossible.

Even so, Flora was at the center of everything. She had thrown Leon off his dull path and forced him to look at his life differently. And he liked this new view. More than anything, he liked having her at the center of it.

Since there were also three-year-old twins in his new vista, any periods of introspection were short lived. Bedtime was always interesting and, on this particular night, Stevie and Frankie were more determined than ever to prolong the inevitable.

Having requested toast for supper, Stevie promptly gave his to Tiny, then started to cry. "Tiny ate my supper."

Leon turned away to prepare more toast, only to be interrupted by the sound of more crying from Frankie. "Stevie ate my supper."

"This could be a long night," Flora said, as she and Leon each carried a twin toward the bedroom.

Two bedtime stories later, the boys were still wide awake.

"Want a song." Frankie wriggled around in his bed like a pajama-clad worm.

"Okay." Flora tucked the bedclothes around him again. "But you have to lie still and listen."

"Want Dr. Leon to sing a song."

"Uh." Leon sent a helpless glance in Flora's direction. "Singing is not one of Dr. Leon's strengths."

She smiled. "They won't care. It's like a story—they just want to listen to your voice."

Leon sat on Stevie's bed, dredging his memory for the words of a song his mother used to sing to him at bedtime. Feeling slightly self-conscious under the gaze of his audience of three, he began to sing. After a few lines, Stevie reached up and placed a hand over his mouth.

"Sing better, Dr. Leon."

"That's the best I can do." Leon's voice was muffled by the small fingers covering his lips. He met Flora's eyes and found hers were brimming with laughter.

"Mommy do it." Stevie turned his head to look at Flora.

She came to sit beside Leon and he rested his chin on her shoulder as she crooned a lullaby in a soft voice. Stevie's eyelids began to droop, and a glance across the room showed that Frankie was sprawled across his bed, already asleep.

It was a moment of perfect peace. They were caught up in the center of a horrific murder inquiry, but, for Leon, the rest of the world had drifted away. There was just this. Serenity, comfort, and warmth. Everything he needed was right there within his grasp. In that room. If he had the courage to take it.

Flora's voice grew quieter, then ceased. She drew Leon's arm around her waist and they sat in silence for a few more minutes, checking that the twins were really asleep. Finally, she gave a long, slow sigh. "I think we're safe."

Once they'd sneaked from the room, Leon paused outside the door. "Three-year-old music critics. My self-esteem is in tatters."

Flora rose on the tips of her toes to press a kiss onto his lips. "Don't worry, I still—" He didn't know what she'd been about to say. After a heartbeat's hesitation, she recovered quickly. "Like your singing."

"You do?" He gripped her hips, drawing her closer. "Wow. No one's ever said *that* to me before."

Her eyes twinkled with mischief. "When I said 'like,' I don't want you to get the wrong idea. I don't think you're quite ready to perform publicly."

He placed a hand over his heart. "You just crushed my hopes of a music career."

She chuckled, the sound reverberating through both their bodies. At the same time, Leon's cell phone buzzed. He rolled his eyes and reached into his pocket.

"It's a message from Laurie. She's on her way over. She's gotten more information about Alan Grayson's departure from Stillwater, and it seems likely that the investigation will take a new course."

Chapter 15

"Alan Grayson walked into a police station in Nevada this morning." Laurie started talking as soon as Leon opened the door. "He'd seen an online news article about the murders here in Stillwater and read that there was a police alert out for him. He's been staying with relatives near Las Vegas ever since he left town. Apparently, he takes this sort of trip regularly. The good doctor has a gambling problem…"

Laurie followed Leon and Flora through to the family room. They took a seat on the sofa and she sat on a chair that was catty-corner to them.

"I'm traveling to Nevada tomorrow to interview him," Laurie said. "Alan was in Stillwater when Jennifer Webster and Joy Valeski were killed. If, however, he can prove where he was when Lilith Bronson was murdered, it makes him look less likely as a suspect for the first deaths."

Leon couldn't help a feeling of relief. He had never been able to picture his former boss as a murderer.

"What about the allegations of malpractice against him?" Flora asked.

"A medical malpractice suit is usually a civil case. It's generally only in extreme situations, resulting in intentional harm such as gross negligence manslaughter, that criminal prosecutions are brought. In this case, matters are complicated by the fact that two of Alan's accusers are dead. Bradley 'Bulldog' Warren is pursuing a civil claim. If, as I suspect, his story prompts other patients to come forward, Alan could be facing a long and costly legal battle. But, at present, it's not a police matter."

"So we are back to two suspects for the murders?" Leon said. "Luella French and Vivien McAuley?"

"No." Laurie retrieved her ever-faithful notebook from the depths of her tote. "That was my other piece of news. Remember I told you Luella French was picked up on a prostitution charge six months after she threatened you, Flora?"

"Yes." Leon hated the wary note he could hear in Flora's voice. He wanted to take it away and make sure it never came back.

"She was given a six-month sentence but served only two before she was released on parole. Three weeks later, she died of a drug overdose." Laurie looked up from her notes. "You never had anything to fear from Luella. She was a sad individual who couldn't take care of herself. She certainly didn't have the time, strength, or energy to carry out her threats against you."

Flora slumped forward, elbows on her knees, as she covered her face with her hands. Leon slid an arm around her shoulders, drawing her against his side. He had to lean close to hear the words she was whispering. "All this time…"

Although she was pale, she regained her composure fast and straightened. "I'm sorry. I've spent a long time looking over my shoulder. It's a strange feeling to find out there was never anyone there." The corners of her mouth turned down. "Until recently."

"At least the focus of the investigation is narrowing," Laurie said. "Joe Nolan will take over while I'm in Nevada. Get in touch with him if there's anything you need. And do me a favor. Make sure you enable the emergency function on your cell phones."

"Already done," Leon assured her.

When Laurie had gone, Leon drew Flora into his arms. She rested her head on his shoulder and stayed that way for several minutes. When she looked up, she managed a shaky smile.

"I didn't know how much Luella's threats had affected me until I heard Laurie say she was dead."

"Being threatened at the trial of the man who killed your husband must have been hard," Leon said.

"It was a horrible time. All of it. Danny's death, the investigation, the trial…" Flora's hands twisted in her lap and she stared down at them as though they held the clues to what had gone on back then. "But the worst part was not being able to help the feelings."

"You mean the grief?" Leon could identify with that.

The nothingness that took a hold of the soul and burdened the body. The heaviness where once there had been a heart. The ever-present, bitter taste of loss.

"That, of course." She raised her eyes to his, and he saw a momentary hesitation in their depths. Then she plunged onward. "But there was more to it. I felt—" she sucked in a breath "—*cheated*."

Leon could see how much it was hurting her to talk this way. He took her hands in his. "You can tell me."

"I'd been robbed of all the things we should have had." A frown pulled her brows together as she tried to explain. "And, for a while, I was angry that Danny had left me. Left *us*. That he'd put his job first. That he'd gone into that derelict warehouse. That he'd faced a drug dealer knowing I was at home carrying our child. Because he never got to know there were two of them."

Those words told Leon a lot. They filled in the blanks about Flora. About her fierce independence and determination to protect her little family. About the fearful look he glimpsed in her eyes sometimes when she looked his way, particularly when they should have been at their happiest. Danny hadn't wanted to leave her. She knew that. But deep down inside, in the part of her that was hurt and damaged by his loss, she felt he had abandoned her when she needed him most. And she was scared that it could happen all over again.

Leon could understand her fears. They had tumbled into something neither of them understood. Agreeing they weren't ready for forever was all very well, but they both knew this had come to mean more than they'd ever intended at the start.

He didn't know how much he could do to reassure

her, but maybe he could continue the conversation he'd started when they were out by the lake. Perhaps he should share a deeper insight into who he was and why his life had veered so far off course? He owed it to them both to try.

Some of his soul-searching must have showed on his face, because Flora reached up a hand and cupped his cheek. "It works both ways. You can tell me."

Would he tell her? Flora watched the emotions play across Leon's face like sunlight on a pond. She already knew part of the story. That his wife, who he had clearly loved with all his heart, had died in a car crash. And he had told her himself that Karen had been pregnant at the time.

They were the facts. What about the rest?

Finally, he spoke. "I was responsible for Karen's death."

Flora gripped his hands. "Why do you think that?"

He was silent for so long that she thought he couldn't continue. When he did, his voice was low and raw. "When we met, we were both students. We never had any money. I was in medical school when we got married and Karen worked as a librarian. There was never any spare cash. One day, she saw some pictures of a luxury hotel in a magazine, and she joked about how she wanted to go there one day. It became her thing, you know? Every time something bad happened, she'd say 'ah, but one day, we'll go to *our* hotel.'"

A sigh shuddered through him and Flora threaded her fingers tighter between his. She tried to picture how he had been back then in the early days with Karen.

Stunningly handsome, of course, fun-loving and laughing, sure that the future they wanted would be theirs.

"Then, when we found out she was pregnant, the joke changed. She laughed about how there would be no luxury hotels for us. Not with a young family." He managed a slight smile. "So I decided to surprise her."

Leon bowed his head, and his chest rose and fell hard as he struggled to keep control.

"You don't have to tell it all right now," Flora said.

"If I stop, I may not start again." He rubbed a hand over his face. "And I want you to hear all of it."

She leaned closer and pressed her lips to his temple. "Just do it in your own time."

"It was New Year's and I was home from Afghanistan. All Karen knew was that we had a reservation somewhere special. When we set off, it was snowing lightly, but the weather worsened as we got closer to the hotel. There were two routes we could have taken. The mountain road was the fastest, but the conditions weren't good. The route through the valley would have slowed us down and we risked missing our dinner reservation. In the restaurant she'd always dreamed of visiting." He swallowed hard, the sound clicking in his throat. "I took the mountain road."

He started to shake, his whole body shuddering as though he was suffering some terrible fever. Wrapping her arms around him, Flora held him tight until the trembling subsided.

"You're almost done," she said, and he nodded.

"We were traveling uphill, and the truck was coming down. The driver lost control and slid across into our lane. It wasn't his fault." He blinked hard, and a tear spilled down his cheek. "There was only one person to blame."

Flora gripped his chin, turning his face to hers. "Leon, it was an accident. A terrible, heartbreaking accident. No one was to blame."

"I had a choice. Karen and our baby died because I chose wrong." His jaw muscles were so tight they barely moved as he spoke. "I failed them."

She could see the gulf of pain in his eyes, and already knew how deep his feelings of guilt went. Undoing that message wasn't going to be easy. But this man had stepped up and offered Flora and her boys his protection, despite the huge burden he was carrying. In her eyes, that made him worth fighting for.

"This is probably not the best time for a philosophical discussion, but I don't know how much of our destiny we control. Perhaps it's very little," she said. "When I told you how I felt about Danny's death, about how angry I was? Even though I still feel that way sometimes, I also wonder, what if he hadn't died?"

Leon frowned. "What do you mean?"

"If Danny hadn't given his life to catch that dealer, how many people would have died as a result of him still being on the streets, still selling drugs?"

"You think your husband was *meant* to die that night?" Leon asked.

"I find it makes it easier if I can believe that." She kept her voice level and gentle. "Have you ever considered that the outcome might have been the same, even if you *had* taken the road through the valley that night?"

He stared at her for a moment or two, his expression impossible to read. Then, with a sound midway between a groan and a sob, he caught her up into his arms and held her as though he would never let her go.

The next morning, Flora scurried around the kitchen drinking coffee and searching for a missing shoe, while Leon tried to organize the twins. They were running late, having sacrificed organization for an extra half hour in bed.

"Do you want to go to the bake-off at the memorial hall this evening?" Leon removed bits of cereal from Stevie's hair as he spoke.

Flora was on her hands and knees under the table, but she paused and looked over her shoulder at him. He could tell what she was thinking. Did she want to attend a gathering of Stillwater residents, most of whom would have seen the "Doctor Death" page?

He continued before she could refuse. "I had a message from Bryce. He and Vincente are going head-to-head in a baking challenge. Wyoming meets Italy. Apple pie versus chocolate torta. It should be fun."

"Why not?" Flora reversed out from under the table. "I've heard so much about the Stillwater Dozen, maybe it's time to see it in action for myself."

Leon reached down and helped her to her feet, planting a quick kiss on her lips as he did. They hadn't slept much the previous night, their passion fueled with a new intensity.

He couldn't say he was miraculously cured of his guilt and self-loathing over Karen's death. But he had been able to articulate what he felt, and Flora had listened to him with sympathy and understanding. Talking

to her had made him feel…*lighter.* Some of the weight
had been lifted from his shoulders.

"Dr. Leon kissed Mommy." Frankie snickered behind
his hand while Stevie smacked his lips together noisily.

Flora's shoe was finally found—in Tiny's bed. Dashing out, they arrived at the daycare center, where Tegan
Jackson was waiting at the door. The twins greeted her
with pleasure.

"That's a relief," Flora said. "They seem to have gotten over that reluctant phase."

Stevie took Tegan's hand. "Dr. Leon kissed Mommy,"
he announced loudly.

"Oh, my days." Flora rolled her eyes. "He's going to
tell everyone, isn't he?"

"At least they've forgotten about the condoms," Leon
murmured.

The rest of the day felt refreshingly normal. Leon
barely saw Flora, whose workload had increased because of Vivien's absence. His own schedule was full,
but when he did have some down time, he found his
mind straying to Laurie's interview with Alan. It still
shocked him that a man he had always considered honorable could fall so far.

If Laurie was correct, and Alan was in the grip of a
gambling addiction, he needed help. Dependence took
many forms and had different outcomes. His patients
didn't deserve the treatment they had received, but, in
many ways, Alan was a victim himself. Leon, who had
an understanding of what it meant to deal with an addiction, didn't envy Alan the fight ahead.

His last appointment of the day was with Daisy Cain.
Daisy had been one of Alan's patients, but a quick check

of her medical record showed that, apart from a routine annual physical, she rarely visited the Main Street Clinic. With her balanced diet, dedication to exercise, and tall, toned physique, she was the healthiest specimen Leon had seen in a long time.

"Calf pain." Daisy removed her sneaker and sock and rolled up her pants before extending one long, well-muscled leg. "I think it could be my Achilles tendon."

"Normally I would ask questions about stretches, footwear, and correct mileage increase." Leon took her right ankle in one hand as he examined her lower leg. "But I know you'll have all of those things covered."

"I forgot you're a runner yourself, Doctor."

"I'm not in your league." Leon flexed her foot. She didn't flinch, which was strange. If she was experiencing pain in her Achilles tendon, he'd have expected that movement to trigger a reaction. "Can you stand and walk across the room, please?"

Daisy did as he asked. She showed no sign of a limp, or pain, as she crossed Leon's office and returned to take the seat opposite him. "Do you like this place?"

The question took him by surprise. "It's a very modern facility." It was a lame response, but the best he could do on the spur of the moment.

"It's not the same, though, is it?" Daisy leaned forward. "I mean, it's not like the Main Street Clinic?"

"It's certainly different." Leon wasn't quite sure where this was going. Somehow, his doctor-patient consultation had been hijacked and he was being interviewed. "You don't have flat feet—"

"Your patients must miss that homey atmosphere." She shook her head. "And Dr. Grayson... So many people are asking about him. Do you know when everything will be back to normal?"

Aha. He could see what was going on here. Daisy was leading the charge for the Stillwater scandal-lovers, trying to get information about what was happening with Alan. Leon wondered if there was actually anything wrong with her leg.

"Take a break from the hill running. That will put extra stress on your tendons." He spoke briskly, ignoring her question. "Take anti-inflammatories for pain, and use the rest, ice, compression, and elevation strategy."

Daisy was gazing at him with an expression that was almost hungry, presumably hoping for some snippets of information. When she didn't move, Leon got to his feet. "If that's all?"

"Oh." She blinked. "Yes. Thank you, Doctor."

Leon watched her as she left. No sign of a limp. Shaking his head, he typed up his notes. He hadn't figured Daisy for one of the die-hard gossips. Maybe she genuinely was missing Alan and wanted to know when he'd be back. It was something Leon would have to think about. Currently, his own career was tied in with what happened at the Main Street Clinic, and it was unlikely the place would stay open given the problems Alan was facing.

A knock on his door roused him from the contemplation of an uncertain future. When Flora entered, his whole body responded to the smile in her eyes, warmth replacing the tension in his limbs. He held out his hand, and she stepped up close.

"I am so ready for a quiet night at home." Leon pulled her down onto his lap.

"I thought you wanted to go to this bake-off thing?"

He groaned. "Bryce had better not be kidding me when he says he makes the best apple pie in Stillwater."

It was a beautiful evening as they drove along Lakeview Drive toward Stillwater City Hall. As the sun dipped behind the mountains, the heat of the afternoon gave way to a pleasant coolness.

After picking up the boys, they had gone home to change into casual clothes. Flora wore a cotton skirt that ended just above her knee, with a light-weight sweater on top. As they left the car and crossed the parking lot, she took a moment to admire the fit of Leon's jeans and T-shirt. With all these people around, it was probably a good idea to restrain the impulse to keep touching him.

Flora was relieved to note that there were other children going into the building. She'd been slightly wary about taking her exuberant duo to an event of this type, but the groups of people making their way into the building included some who looked the same age as, or even younger than, the twins.

Although she had been inside the city hall building, Flora hadn't been to any events in the Clarence Delaney Memorial Hall.

"Is it named after someone in Bryce's family?" she asked Leon as they followed hand painted signs advertising the bake-off.

"Clarence Delaney was Cameron, Bryce, and Vincente's great-grandfather," he said. "Apparently, he was well known for his charitable work. Although, the way

Bryce tells it, he was also known for his womanizing and hell-raising."

They entered a huge room at the rear of the main building. The decor was elegant with a mosaic tiled floor, plaster columns, and chandeliers that harked back to another era.

"Everything happens here," Leon said. "Barn dances, rock concerts, bake sales, and children's Christmas parties. When part of the roof collapsed a few years ago, there was talk of closing the place down. There was an online petition asking if a modern town really needed a turn-of-the-century relic. The answer was a resounding yes. Most of the townsfolk thought that losing the memorial hall would be like ripping the heart out of Stillwater."

All around the sides of the room, stalls had been set up. As well as the cakes, pies, bread, and other delicacies produced by the members of the Stillwater Dozen, there were craft booths and traditional games. The air was a heady mix of delicious scents: cupcakes competing with the funfair aromas of Flora's childhood. The noise level made her wince. On a stage at the far end of the room, the contestants were setting up in preparation for the bake-off competition.

The twins instantly pulled on Flora's hands like puppies straining on a leash. With no real idea of what was going on, they wanted to see everything.

"Ducks!" Stevie tried to drag her one way.

"'alloons!" Frankie exerted equal force in the opposite direction.

"Before you break your poor mommy in half, let's

agree to do hook-a-duck first, then the balloon-pop."
Leon took hold of Frankie's hand.

They toured the booths, laughing at the twins' excitement. Although Flora remained alert for signs of people watching her with distrust, she didn't see anything troubling. Aline Stibbe and Dolores Moon were selling homemade cookies, but neither of them looked her way.

Beth was at the wheel-spin booth with Lia, who greeted the twins by trying to steal their cotton candy. A few minutes later, Steffi arrived, carrying a sleeping Katerina in a baby sling.

"Aren't you two on opposing sides?" Leon asked her and Beth. "Should I get in the middle and keep you apart?"

"I think we'll be fine as long as we don't reveal any baking secrets," Beth said.

"I'll be glad when this is over." Steffi looked at the stage, where Bryce and Vincente were gathered with the other contestants. "If I have to try one more apple pie prototype, I won't be responsible for the consequences."

"I don't think it's occurred to either Bryce or Vincente that someone else could win," Cameron said, as he joined them.

A bell signaled the start of the competition and they moved toward the stage. There were twelve contestants, who were competing in pairs. The three judges would taste the food baked by each pair and decide on a winner. The six winners would go forward to the next round and compete against a new partner. The judges would then decide on the final three, who would be awarded bronze, silver, and gold medals.

"I thought you'd be judging," Leon said.

"I recused myself on the grounds that I will be needed as a referee when my brothers come to blows."

The first round was over quickly, with both Bryce and Vincente making it through to the next stage of the competition. The other contestants didn't seem to mind that the focus was on the banter between the Delaney brothers, or the fact that the entire audience was clearly divided between the two of them. By the time the judges had decided on the final three, Bryce and Vincente had each roused their supporters to fever pitch.

Flora had Frankie in her arms, and Leon was holding Stevie. Although the twins didn't understand what was going on, they were caught up in the atmosphere and were shouting first for Bryce, then for Vincente. As the head judge diplomatically announced a tie between the Delaney brothers, Flora felt a hand on her shoulder. Turning, she saw Detective Joe Nolan standing just behind her.

"Can I speak with you?" His expression told her he wasn't bringing good news.

Beth noticed what was happening and stepped forward to help. "They are serving cookies and juice for the kids over in the refreshment booth. Why don't I take your boys with Lia?"

Flora waited until Beth, Steffi, and the children had gone before she turned to face Joe. "What is it?"

"Not here." He led her and Leon outside the hall and into a corridor. After a quick glance to check they were alone, he spoke quietly. "We've found Vivien McAuley's body."

Chapter 16

"I don't have much information for you, except that the circumstances were similar to Jennifer Webster's murder." Joe Nolan's voice was apologetic. "Dr. McAuley's vehicle was hidden in dense woodland off the Elmville road. Her body was in the trunk. When I spoke to Chief Delaney, she asked me to make sure you were informed immediately."

"I knew Vivien wasn't capable of murder." Flora's voice was quiet, her face unnaturally white. She lifted a shaking hand toward her lips. "Raj… He was attacked. Someone needs to tell him."

"I'll go from here to inform Dr. Laxman," Joe said.

Leon placed an arm around Flora's shoulders. He knew she was struggling with grief for her colleague, but there was a deeper message that troubled him. "This means you have no suspects."

"We'll continue to investigate every lead." Joe's standard response told Leon everything he needed to know. The police had nothing.

He wasn't blaming them for that. It was just a fact. They were no closer to finding the killer than they had been when he and Flora walked into Joy Valeski's kitchen and found her lying in a pool of her own blood. The leads they had followed so far—Luella French, Alan Grayson, and Vivien McAuley—had all proved false. The real killer was still out there, and he, or she, wasn't going to stop.

"Be careful." Joe was clearly thinking the same thing.

"We will." Leon's voice was grim as he gripped Flora's hand.

When Joe had gone, Leon took hold of Flora's shoulders. He didn't need to ask if she was okay. One look was enough to tell him she wasn't. She pressed her face to his chest, unable to halt the storm of tears that gripped her. Murmuring words of comfort, he held her until she was wrung out and hung limp in his arms.

After a minute Flora straightened. "Do I look horrible?" Her eyes were red, her face was blotchy, and the words were accompanied by a sniff.

"You look beautiful."

"If you really believe that, you should get an eye test." She gave a watery chuckle. "I need to go to the restroom and splash some water on my face before I go back into the hall."

"I'll wait here." He watched her walk away, astounded by the strength that she continued to demonstrate throughout this nightmare. Despite the horrors that were thrown her way, she met every challenge head-on. No wonder those twins of hers were little fighters. They had courage stamped into their DNA.

When Flora returned, her appearance had improved. Only close scrutiny would detect signs of recent tears.

"Let's get the boys and go home," Leon said, and she nodded gratefully.

They had to push their way through the crowd to get to the refreshment booth. Although Beth and Steffi had managed to get a kids table for Lia and the twins, the adults were forced to stand nearby. Bryce and Vincente had joined them and were showing off their medals.

"Is everything okay?" Cameron asked.

"No." Leon quickly filled him in on the details of their conversation with Joe Nolan.

"Two members of staff are dead, and one has been attacked. With the threats to you as well, maybe we do have to think about taking more serious measures," Cameron said to Flora. "I'll call in at the Ryerson Center tomorrow."

Even though the hall was noisy, their attention was claimed by Lia, who started crying loudly. "I want pie."

Beth knelt at the table to comfort her. "You have cookies and juice."

"I want pie." Lia pointed to Frankie's plate. Unlike Lia and Stevie, Frankie had a neat slice of pie on his plastic plate next to his half-eaten cookie.

Beth looked up at her companions with a frown. "Where did Frankie get this pie from?"

Leon moved fast. Snatching up a napkin from a

nearby table, he grabbed the piece of pie from Frankie's plate and wrapped it up.

"Did you eat any pie?" he asked Frankie.

"N-no." The little boy looked up at Flora for reassurance.

"It's okay, sweetie." She came to kneel beside the table, placing an arm around each twin. "Did you see who gave you the pie?" They both shook their heads, and Flora looked up at the group of adults. "Did anyone see anything?"

"Sorry." Vincente spoke for all of them. "There are so many people around."

Leon was examining the piece of pie, his blood running cold as he realized what he was looking at. "The cherry filling is crammed with small pieces of broken glass."

Flora shivered as she looked around at the throng of people. "He's *here*."

"*He* could be anyone." Leon clenched a fist against his thigh.

Thankfully, they had thwarted a deliberate cowardly attempt to harm an innocent child. Someone must have been watching and waiting to seize a chance to leave that tainted pie on Frankie's plate. It was carefully planned. Who could be capable of such evil?

If he could find the answer to that question, he would know it all.

They drove home in near silence, even the twins picking up on the somber mood. It was only as they pulled up at the front of the house that Frankie spoke.

"Don't like pie." His voice was subdued, unlike his usual robust self.

As Flora choked back a sob, Leon placed a hand on her knee. After a moment or two, she nodded, signaling that she was okay.

"Some pie can be nice," he said, maintaining a calm tone as he answered Frankie. "How about we try making some together at the weekend? What kind would you like to make?"

"'anana," Frankie said.

"Choclit." Stevie put forward his own favorite flavor.

"Banana and chocolate pie, it is." Leon smiled at Flora, pleased to see some of the panic leaving her. "I may need to take a few tips from Bryce."

"How about 'never cook with three-year-olds'? That would be my tip." Flora managed a faint smile before she climbed out of the car.

When they got inside the house, there was no time for conversation. Tiny's greetings were always insanely over-the-top, but, on this occasion, he clearly sensed that something more was needed and stepped up a gear. The lunging, whining, and spinning reached new, and dangerous, levels.

Leon and Flora had to scoop the twins up to protect them from the flailing paws, tail, and tongue. Once Leon opened the door and ushered Tiny outside, peace was restored. He was pleased to see that the twins were laughing.

"I'm glad someone finds living with an out-of-control greeter entertaining." He reached out a hand to Flora. "It's been quite a day."

"When do we have any other kind?" She returned

the pressure of his fingers. "I'll get these two into bed while you call Detective Nolan."

Joe Nolan's shock was obvious as he listened to the details of the incident. "Could the little guy have died if he'd eaten that pie, Doctor?"

Leon closed his eyes briefly, not wanting to picture that scene. "It's a real possibility. The best case is that Frankie would have badly cut his mouth and spat the glass out. If he'd swallowed it… Yeah, it could have done him some major damage."

"You think whoever gave it to him knew that?" Joe asked.

"I think he didn't care." Leon fought down the rising tide of anger and helplessness. "I think he wanted to scare Flora so much it didn't matter what happened to her little boy."

He ended his call after discussing plans for keeping the twins safe and started fixing coffee. Flora reappeared sooner than he'd expected. "They were both asleep as soon as they were tucked up in bed."

Leon carried the coffee through to the family room. Flora curled into a corner of the sofa, and he sat next to her. Although he didn't want to talk about the killer, didn't want to bring that evil into this comfortable setting, there was something he needed to say. "It's a long shot, but it's worth getting that piece of pie analyzed."

"I already thought of that. I'll take it into the Ryerson Center lab tomorrow." Flora leaned her head back on the cushions. "I can't do this, Leon."

He frowned. "I don't understand."

"He's won. I can't stay in Stillwater."

Leon took a moment to process what she was saying. He could understand her reasons for wanting to leave. The twins were her whole world. Any danger to them was worse than a threat on Flora's own life. But this felt all wrong. Not just because it was giving in to what the killer wanted, but because this was their home.

The though hit him with perfect clarity. This was where Flora belonged. In Stillwater. In this house. With *him*. Because he loved her. She and the twins were his family. Now he needed to get past his fear of commitment, so he could find a way to tell her.

"Can we talk about this?" The realization had hit him hard and fast, and he needed to buy some time to process it.

"My boys have been threatened. I don't think there's anything else to be said." She looked exhausted, as though every last bit of fight had been drained out of her.

"I need—" The nerves kicked in and he stumbled over the words. "I need you here with me."

"Why?" Flora's gaze probed his face, willing him to open up to her.

Do it. He tried to make himself say the words. "So I can protect you and the boys."

She leaned forward to touch his cheek, her smile sad. "Wrong answer."

When Flora got to her feet and left the room, Leon stayed where he was, listening to her footsteps as she walked along the hall to the bedroom. The click of the door closing was like a knife in his heart.

Wrong answer. He'd blown his chance to tell her he loved her. He knew why, of course. Because, as soon as the words rose to his lips, he saw a snowy road and an out-of-control truck. He heard Karen's scream followed by a deathly silence. He had lost one woman he loved and their child, and he was scared to take the chance a second time.

Go to her. Tell her.

He attempted to get his limbs to move, but every second that passed made it harder. In the end, he opened the door to let Tiny back into the house and the two of them slept on the sofa.

Even though she willed her body to relax, Flora knew she wouldn't sleep. Her emotions were in tatters. The faceless killer with a grudge against the Ryerson Center had found her weakness. Every time she thought about it, she wanted to grab up the twins and run. Her instinct was to escape, to hide, to put as much distance as she could between them and the place where this nightmare was happening.

Panic was strangling her ability to think rationally. She had to stay strong, but her reactions were those of a terrified child. Shaking. Tearful. Desperately in need of reassurance.

From Leon.

As the constricted feelings intensified, and she was choked by the very air around her, he was the person she wanted to reach for. She had come to rely on his strength and dependability. The questions she had once had about his steadiness were long gone. His kindness, his patience…his love. She needed them wrapped around her.

Because he did love her. She knew it as surely as she knew she loved him. At first, she had been too scared to acknowledge the truth and take a chance on love a second time around. Now, she was too scared of losing him *not* to take a chance. As long as Leon was at her side, Flora knew she would be okay.

When he had told her that he felt responsible for Karen's death, she had finally understood why his fear of commitment was so much greater than her own. While Flora's reservations were based on a fear of abandonment and the needs of her boys, Leon's anxiety went deeper. He had convinced himself he wasn't worthy of love. Believing that he had let Karen down, he was terrified it would happen again.

Flora didn't know if he'd reached the point of admitting to himself that he loved her. Now and then, she thought she'd glimpsed that recognition in his eyes, or seen it in the familiarity between them. She knew it was there in the honesty of their bodies when she lay naked in his arms. Knowing he was worth waiting for, she had been prepared to take things slowly.

That was before fate, in the form of a killer with a slice of pie, had intervened. Because now she had to get the twins away from this nightmare. And she had to do it fast. With her emotions in freefall, she had hoped that, when she told Leon she was leaving, he had been about to tell her how he felt. Instead, he had come out with his standard line about protecting her and the twins. It was his shield. The excuse he used to guard his heart. They both knew it. Could they get past it?

Flora needed to get the boys as far from Stillwater as she could, possibly forever. If Leon wasn't ready to do long-term, how could she ask him to uproot himself from the town he loved? The answer was simple. She couldn't.

She had no way to predict the future. If they were meant to be together, it was possible this was a bump on their road map. Maybe the killer would be caught quickly, and she could come back again. There were a lot of unknowns in that sentence. It was hard to pin her happiness on the outcome of a police investigation.

When Leon didn't come to bed, she wasn't sure how to react. Should she go to him and tell him how she felt? Force him to confront the truth? What if he wasn't ready, and he denied his feelings? Then she would lose the tiny sliver of hope she still had. No matter how much she craved his arms around her right now, she had to give him the space he needed.

Somehow, she managed to catch a couple hours of restless sleep. When she woke feeling like she'd been hit by a truck, she staggered to the shower. Emerging only slightly refreshed, she dried her hair, dressed, and went to wake the twins. The sounds of laughter coming from the kitchen told her Leon was one step ahead of her.

Pausing in the doorway, Flora took in the scene before anyone noticed her. Empty cereal bowls on the table indicated that breakfast was already over. Leon was kneeling on the floor sorting a pile of laundry, ready to place it into the machine. He was enlisting Stevie and Frankie's help, but the twins were deliberately muddling up the colors.

"Blue," Stevie said, placing a green T-shirt on the pile.

"Arghh!" Leon grabbed him and tickled him, provoking squeals of laughter from both boys.

"Red!" Frankie jumped up and down as he placed a pair of blue jeans on top of a stack of white clothes.

Leon dived for him, but Frankie skipped away and took refuge behind Tiny. A pursuit ensued that involved one doctor, two three-year-olds, and a dog. It wasn't entirely clear who was chasing whom. Bungee, who had been curled up in his cat bed, gave the participants a look of disgust as he stalked from the room. The end result was a four-way rough-and-tumble.

"Come on, guys." Leon sounded slightly breathless as, with a twin under each arm, he returned to the pile of clothing. He set them on their feet. "Before we finish the laundry, remember what we talked about?"

"There are safe people, and not-safe people." The twins chanted the words together like a line from a nursery rhyme.

"And what do you do if you think someone isn't safe?" Leon asked.

"Find a safe grown-up. Stay with them."

Leon high-fived them both. "Now, let's get this laundry started before mommy arrives."

"Too late." Flora managed to get past the lump in her throat and get her voice to sound halfway to normal. Emotionally, she was being torn in two. How could she walk away from *this*? How could she stay?

"Hey." Leon came toward her, and she wished she could do something about the look in his eyes. The one that said he wasn't sure how to act around her anymore. "We didn't want to disturb you."

She caught hold of the front of his shirt. "I don't know what to do…"

"Not now." Even though his eyes held a measure of

nervousness in their green depths, his smile still had
the power to punch into her chest and flip her heart
over. "We can talk later." He nodded toward the clock
on the wall. "Because you have exactly five minutes to
grab some coffee, while I persuade the twins that this
laundry is a serious task."

Reluctantly, she released him and headed toward the
freshly made coffee. "After what happened yesterday,
I don't feel good about letting Stevie and Frankie go
to daycare."

"I spoke to Joe Nolan about keeping them safe when
I called him yesterday." Leon looked over his shoulder
as he loaded the machine with laundry. "I just didn't
have a chance to discuss it with you."

She regarded him steadily over the top of her coffee cup. "Go on."

"He's going to stop by the daycare center before it
opens this morning and explain the situation to the staff.
The security in Daisy's place is first class, anyway. No
one gets in without passing through a thorough check
at the reception desk. But Joe will also have an officer
stop by each hour during the day to ensure everything
is okay, plus he'll place an alert on the cell phone num-
bers of all the daycare assistants."

Flora picked up her jacket from the back of a chair.
"I'm still not sure."

"What's the alternative?" Leon's reasonable tones
calmed some of her anxiety. "Are you planning on taking them into your patient consultations? And it's important to keep life as normal as possible for the twins."

"You're right, of course." She looked at the two little

figures, who were sprawled on the floor with Tiny. "It's just…you know—"

"I do know. Believe me, it's hard for me as well," Leon said.

Reason and instinct were fighting a battle inside Flora, her protective impulses refusing to be silenced. Like a tiger watching over her cubs, she was prepared to face any threat, and fight any danger. She could only do that if she kept the twins at her side.

But Leon was right about security in the daycare center. It was one of the first things she'd checked out when she'd arrived in Stillwater and looked for a suitable place for the twins. There was probably a marginally better chance of breaking into the First Stillwater Bank vaults than there was of getting into Daisy's Daycare unannounced.

She gulped down the last of her coffee. "Two conditions."

"Name them."

"We take turns to call Daisy for regular updates throughout the day." He nodded. "And, if the anxiety gets too much, I'll leave work early and collect the boys."

"As long as I can impose a condition of my own," Leon said. Flora raised her brows in surprise. "It's the same as yours." He looked at the twins with a slight smile. "If the nerves get to *me*, I may be the one who needs to leave early to make sure they're okay."

Chapter 17

"I can't believe that we are having this conversation." Flora looked stunned. "After the hopes we had for the Ryerson Center, how can we possibly be sitting here discussing its closure?" Only half an hour had passed since the last check-in with the daycare center but it felt like a lifetime.

Cameron's expression was somber. "The last thing I want to do is shut these doors, but I've said all along that safety must come first. We now have two members of staff and two patients who are dead, as well as the attack on Rajiv. In addition, you have been the subject of repeated harassment. That has now spilled over and your son has also been targeted. I have to question whether we can stay open."

"Reputation is everything, especially in the early

days of establishing a new business." Leon couldn't believe how far he'd come. Was he actually advocating *for* the Ryerson Center? He'd been opposed to this place from the start. Alan Grayson had been right in his prediction that this new facility would be the end of the Main Street Clinic. Although the reasons were not those Alan had been shouting about, the end result was the same. But so much had changed since the days when Alan had been voicing his hostility to anyone who would listen. "That isn't different for a medical practice. Even if your intention is to close temporarily, I doubt you'll sustain enough public confidence to reopen again."

"You are echoing the opinion of the Mountain States Health Group," Cameron said. "Having invested heavily in this center, management is reluctant to see it close."

"Maybe you should wait for Laurie's return before you make a decision?" Leon said. "This is tied into the police investigation, and she may have more information."

He looked at Flora and Raj, who both nodded their agreement. When Flora didn't mention her plan to leave Stillwater, Leon wondered if she might be having second thoughts. Her comment earlier about not knowing what to do implied that was the case, but he hardly dared let himself hope. All he wanted to do was get to a point where he could put things right between them. He could only trust it wasn't too late.

"What about the pie that was given to Frankie? Is it being analyzed?" Cameron asked.

"The police agreed to allow the laboratory here to do the tests," Flora said. "I spoke to James Barrett, the senior technician, and he will expedite the results. He may even have something by the end of the day."

"That's good news," Raj said. He was clearly struggling to come to terms with Vivien's death. His eyes were swollen and bloodshot, and his normally neat black hair stood up at awkward angles.

"Not necessarily," Flora sighed. "James said the information he can get from a sample of food is likely to be limited."

They had already delivered the news of Vivien's murder to the rest of the staff. Early morning meetings were becoming commonplace at the Ryerson Center, and they never spelled good news. Although word had filtered out that the police had found a body, and most people had already made the connection, the mood throughout the center was one of shock and sadness. Leon could also see a healthy dose of fear on most faces. The sense of "who next?" was almost tangible.

The rest of the day passed in a timeless bubble. Leon and Flora had devised a schedule for calling the daycare center, working around their appointments. Leon found himself looking at the clock to check if it was time to call, only to find the hands hadn't moved. Then, when he thought minutes had passed, he'd realize it had actually been an hour. Each time he spoke to Daisy, she assured him that the twins were fine.

"You spoke to Daisy?" Flora said, when he managed to grab a few minutes to speak to her. "I've only managed to get Tegan. Daisy has been too busy to take my calls."

Leon frowned. "That's not good. Daisy must know how important this is."

"Tegan has kept me up-to-date with how the boys are doing. That's all I want. Besides…" Flora gave him a side-long glance. "It doesn't surprise me that Daisy would rather speak to you."

Leon frowned. "Why?"

"Oh, it's occurred to me once or twice from things she's said that she may have taken a liking to you."

The words stirred something inside him. A discomfort he didn't understand. It would certainly explain that strange conversation the other day when Daisy had come to see him with that almost certainly fake tendon problem. The look on her face when she'd talked about things returning to normal had troubled him. Maybe Flora's explanation was the reason why.

Unsure how to respond, Leon managed an embarrassed smile. "Must be my magnetic personality."

Flora brushed her fingertips lightly over the back of his hand, and the contact thrilled through him. "Among other things."

After his last appointment, Leon went with Flora to the laboratory to meet with James Barrett, the lab tech. He beckoned them over to his desk and pointed to his laptop screen.

"I'm typing up my report now. I don't know how much use it will be when it comes to helping the police catch the killer." James gave a helpless shrug. "The pie filling wasn't made with fresh cherries. Most over-the-counter pie fillings come in a can, but this was from a jar. Whoever baked this pie smashed a glass jar and mixed the pieces into the filling after it was baked. I could tell that from the differences between the cooked filling in the pie and traces of raw cherry on the glass. The pie crust is also ready-made."

"This suggests the killer isn't a proficient baker," Flora said. "Maybe not a member of the Stillwater Dozen?"

"Unless he, or she, is attempting to throw the police off the scent? Or, when plotting the crime, perhaps the finer details of the recipe weren't important?" Leon tried to picture the sort of person who would cold-bloodedly bake that pie and place broken glass in it, planning all the time to offer it to a child. "I guess the police may be able to check on sales of cherry pie filling and pie crust."

Flora's despondent expression told him she thought as little of that idea as he did. After thanking James, they headed out to the parking lot. Once they were in the car, Leon drew a breath.

"Flora, I need to talk to you..." He swore softly under his breath as his cell phone buzzed. "Why? Why now?"

She smiled. "Answer it. It could be Laurie."

He drew his cell from his pocket, his heart dropping when he saw the caller display. *Daisy's Daycare.* With fingers that felt clumsy, he swiped to answer.

"Dr. Sinclair?" Although her voice was oddly muffled, he could tell it was Tegan. His blood turned to ice as he realized she was crying. "Please hurry. I've already called the police..."

As Leon sped toward the daycare center, Flora alternated between feeling completely numb and totally terrified. Her stomach clenched in a hard, cold knot of nausea, and she fought off the light-headedness, willing herself not to faint. Something was terribly wrong.

Her precious babies were in danger, and every instinct in her was crying out to go to them.

She pressed her knuckles to her temples, feeling as though she might go crazy before they even got to Main Street and found out what was going on.

"Hang in there." Although Leon's voice was shaky, his hand on her knee restored some of her sanity. "Just a few more minutes."

She focused on his touch, staring at his fingers, telling herself to stay calm. It could be nothing. A minor accident. A bumped head. Stevie had gotten his arm stuck again. Who was she kidding? *Tegan had called the police...*

As soon as Leon drew to a halt in front of the day-care center, Flora was scrambling for the door handle, tumbling from the car and almost falling over. The few seconds it took her to run into the building were the longest of her life. Once she and Leon passed through the security system at the reception desk and were admitted to the main play area, her worst fears were confirmed. There was no sign of the sweet, familiar faces of the twins.

"Tegan is in the kitchen with Detective Nolan." One of the assistants, her face pale, directed them to a room at the rear of the building.

As they stepped inside, Tegan, who was seated on a chair with her back to the door, turned her head, and Flora gasped. Tegan's left eye was swollen closed, and a lump the size of a golf ball bulged above her cheekbone. Blood dripped from her nose down the front of her shirt, and her bottom lip was split. Joe Nolan held a cold compress to the back of her neck.

Although there were obvious questions about how she got in that state, Flora had other things on her mind. "Stevie? Frankie?"

Her eyes searched the small room, even though it was obvious that the boys weren't there.

Tegan choked back a sob. "Daisy took them."

Flora's head began to spin, and her knees gave way. Leon caught her as she lurched forward.

"What do you mean she 'took them'?" Leon's voice sounded far away, dulled by the roaring of blood in Flora's ears. She hooked an arm around his waist and held on tight, refusing to give way to the dizziness. Her boys needed her to stay strong.

"I'm so sorry." Tegan was obviously having trouble speaking because of her injuries. "I tried to stop her."

"Why don't you tell us exactly what happened?" Joe said.

Tegan gulped in air and sat up straighter. "No one really comes into the kitchen at this time of the day, but I had a headache and I needed some water to take painkillers. When I opened the door, I saw Daisy going toward the exit with Stevie and Frankie. We were all on high alert to take care of the twins, so I knew straight away something was wrong. I asked her what was going on and she…she attacked me."

Flora thought of the assault on Raj. He had been subjected to the same fury as Tegan. When he was asked if his assailant could have been a woman, Raj had been undecided. Daisy was as tall as Raj, with a powerful, muscular build. Was she his attacker?

She has my boys…

"I tried to fight her. I couldn't even call for help, or

tell the boys to run, because she was punching me in the face, coming at me like a boxer in a fight. Then she shoved me back and I hit my head on the corner of the cabinet. I fell and maybe blacked out for a few seconds. When I managed to get to my feet, there was a car pulling away from the staff parking lot."

"*A* car?" Joe said. "Not Daisy's usual vehicle?"

"No," Tegan said. "It was an SUV with blacked-out windows."

"That sounds like the vehicle that tried to run me off the road." Flora plunged further into the sensation that she was wading through her own nightmare.

"I'm going to need details of that vehicle and Daisy's cell phone number," Joe said. Once Tegan had given him the information, he moved fast, making calls to his colleagues in the Stillwater Police Department and the West County Sheriff's Office.

"What's going on?" Flora's voice sounded alien to her own ears. Raw with pain and confusion. "Why would Daisy take my boys?"

Her mind was spinning with possibilities. Could Daisy be trying to save the twins from a threat? But, if that was the case, why would she attack Tegan? Unless... Did Daisy think *Tegan* was a danger to Stevie and Frankie? Surely not.

"I don't know." Leon's face was grim. "But I intend to find out."

She couldn't ask the other question out loud. The one that hovered on the tip of her tongue. The one that had to remain unsaid. If the words were spoken, they would become a possibility. But they remained on repeat inside her mind. Over and over. Taunting her with their awfulness.

What if you never get that chance? What if Daisy harmed the boys before they could get to her?

Joe ended his calls and turned back to them. "I've got an Amber Alert on Daisy, the twins, and her vehicle. I'm also trying to trace her cell phone, and I've sent a couple officers over to check out her home address."

"There must be something more we can do." A new wave of panic crashed over Flora. Every minute they spent here took Stevie and Frankie farther away from her.

"The chief has just returned from Nevada. She's coordinating with Sheriff Harvey to get a helicopter search underway," Joe said. "The terrain around here is easier to view from the air."

Flora gave a little moan and Leon drew her tighter against his side. As he did, his cell phone buzzed, and he groaned. "Again?"

When he withdrew his cell from his pocket, his expression changed so suddenly it was as if he'd been slapped. Looking stunned, he held the phone up so Flora could see the display.

"It's Daisy."

"I've sent a message to the chief to see if she can get a fix on Daisy's location," Joe said. "Put this call on Speakerphone. We have no idea what she's going to say, so just stay calm and listen. Let's find out what she wants."

Leon had no idea why Daisy would contact him instead of Flora, but he figured he was about to find out.

With a heart that was hammering out of control, he answered the call.

Daisy spoke before he could say anything. "Is *she* with you?"

He guessed that she meant Flora, but he decided to act dumb. "Who?"

Daisy's laugh jarred like fingernails scraping down a chalkboard. "Don't play games, Doctor. Not now I've finally gotten your attention."

"If you mean Dr. Monroe, yes, she's right here. She wants to know if her boys are okay." Flora's fingernails dug painfully into his side.

"Them? Oh, they're fine." Daisy's dismissive tone sounded unnatural.

"What's this about?" Leon fought to keep his tone calm.

"You really don't know." She laughed again, a different sound this time, soft and disbelieving. "All the things I've done to get you to notice me, and you still haven't figured it out?"

Leon was a doctor. He knew his heart hadn't really just thudded to a standstill. It was an illusion. So was the sensation that his mouth was so dry he couldn't speak. But the horror of what he was hearing was like a series of electric shocks tingling through him.

Could it be true? Flora had said Daisy had a crush on him. Was it that simple? Could this whole thing have been about Leon all along?

"You're going to have to explain it to me, Daisy."

"I was waiting for you. I thought you weren't ready for a new relationship." There was a bitter edge to her voice that chilled him. "Then *she* came along. Dr. Monroe. How ironic was that? While I was doing everything I could to save the Main Street Clinic, you were falling for the very person who was going to destroy it."

Joe gestured to Leon to try to get Daisy to expand on what she was saying. Wishing he didn't have to do this to Flora, didn't have to add to the look of distress in her eyes, he plunged on. "What were you doing to save the Main Street Clinic?"

"I'm sure you've figured it out by now. Dr. Grayson said the Ryerson Center would be the end of his practice. Then that article in the Stillwater *Sentinel* confirmed it." She gave a snicker. "By the way, that reporter? He didn't leave town."

Leon swallowed hard. "What happened to him?"

"You're an educated guy. Figure it out. Back to my story. I thought that, if you lost your job, you might leave town. I couldn't risk that, so I had to do something about it." The matter-of-fact way Daisy spoke chilled Leon even further. It was as if she was talking about a minor decision like what to have for dinner. "The *Sentinel* reporter made it clear. Dr. Monroe was the person who was trying to ruin everything. If I wanted to bring down the Ryerson Center, I knew she was the one I had to get rid of."

Leon closed his eyes briefly. It didn't give him any satisfaction to know he had been right. The Ryerson Center had been the target, but, in Daisy's eyes, Flora had been entwined with it. When he opened his eyes, he noticed Laurie slipping silently into the room.

"I could have killed her, of course." Daisy continued in the same conversational tone.

The statement triggered a thought and Leon gestured

for something with which to write. Laurie handed him her notebook, and he quickly scribbled a few words. *Has she killed before?* If that was the case, he didn't know how Daisy could have gained a childcare qualification or passed the required background checks. But, in his opinion, most people didn't discuss murder in such a casual manner.

"What I really needed was to taint her so completely that no one in Stillwater would ever step foot inside the Ryerson Center," Daisy went on. "*Dr. Death.* It has a ring to it, don't you think? Jennifer Webster, Joy Valeski, Lilith Bronson, and Vivien McAuley would probably agree. Rajiv Laxman should have been on that list. I don't like admitting failure, but he got away from me. Once he started fighting back, I couldn't stick around in case he figured out who I was."

"If you wanted to make it look like Flora killed them, why were you also trying to scare her?" Leon asked.

"Because watching her squirm was *fun*." There was so much venom in the words that Leon could see his own shock reflected on the faces of the other people in the room. "You wouldn't deny me a little amusement would you, Leon?" Leon's skin crawled at the flirtatious tone. Luckily, Daisy didn't seem to require an answer to her question. "Of course, once I saw how close you and she were getting, I had to get serious. That kiss in her kitchen? With the window blind open and the light on? Anyone could have seen you. It just happened to be me when I was busy getting the padlock off her shed."

Leon thought back to that night, and how he'd speculated later about what had been going on beyond the darkened glass. It had bothered him more than it should.

With hindsight it was easy to put his feelings of disquiet down to a subconscious sense that someone had been outside looking in. It was unimportant. If Daisy hadn't seen the kiss, she'd have picked up on the attraction between him and Flora some other way. He shouldn't feel guilty because a killer didn't like what she'd seen. He shouldn't, but he did.

The police had their confession. It was time to direct the conversation to the most important question. They needed to find out what it would take to get the twins back. "What do you want, Daisy?"

"That's easy." She paused, and Leon held his breath. "I want *you*."

Chapter 18

"We've got her location," Laurie said, as Daisy abruptly ended the call. "She's out on the Elmville road, near the Eternal Springs plunge pool. Her vehicle appears to be stationary."

Flora knew the area Laurie had described. It was close to Hawk Farm, where Eve Sloane lived, and she had taken the twins to see the point where the waterfall cascaded into a deep pool when they had first arrived in Stillwater. The terrain was rugged and hostile. The thought of her boys out there in the clutches of a ruthless killer, as darkness was falling, made her feel sick.

"What are we waiting for?" she asked.

"Flora, you have to leave this to the police." Laurie's voice was firm.

"If you think I'm going to wait here while that

woman—" Her voice wobbled, and she took a moment to get it under control. "Not happening."

"I understand what you're saying, but we now know Daisy's actions have been fueled by her obsession with Leon and her hatred of you. Both of you need to stay away from her." Laurie was walking out of the room as she spoke. Joe Nolan followed close behind.

As the door shut behind them, Flora turned to Leon in anguish. "I don't want a confrontation with Daisy, but I can't stay here. Not while my boys are out there."

"That's okay. Nor can I." He grabbed her hand and broke into a run.

"Bring them back safe," Tegan called after them.

Flora felt like her blood was setting her veins on fire. Trying to hold it together was turning the weight in her chest into a huge, heavy boulder. Every breath scorched her lungs. If it wasn't for Leon's comforting presence, she'd have crumpled into a helpless heap by now. It was probably a good thing that all law enforcement in the area was otherwise engaged as he gunned the engine and pushed the car to its limit. The scenery, lit by the last rays of sunlight, flashed past the passenger window.

"The boys don't like the dark," she murmured.

She turned her head in time to see Leon's jaw tighten. "The police should be close by now."

The longer Stevie and Frankie were out of her sight, the more extreme her imaginings became. She punished herself with thoughts of "if only." If only she hadn't taken them to daycare that morning. If only she'd left early and collected them after lunch. If she'd never brought them to Stillwater…

Leon flicked a glance in her direction. "Stop torturing yourself." His attempt to sound soothing didn't work. She could hear the pain thrumming through his words.

"I will if you will."

He sighed. "That obvious, huh?"

"I know how much you care about them." Her voice hitched like flesh snagging on barbed wire.

A few minutes later, the highway ahead was busy, and Flora pressed a hand to her lips. Two West County Sheriff's Office patrol vehicles blocked the road, and a whumping sound overhead indicated that a helicopter was nearby. Beyond the roadblock, she could see more police vehicles and people moving around.

Leon glanced at Flora's tight-fitting skirt and heels. "We are not going to get past Sheriff Harvey or his deputies. How do you feel about a walk through the trees?"

"Whatever it takes."

Switching off his headlights, Leon pulled off the highway and into the shelter of a clump of trees. When they left the car, the roar of the waterfall sounded close, and they plunged straight into thick undergrowth.

"We need to approach the police position from behind." Leon crouched low, drawing Flora down with him. "If they see us, we won't get close."

Although they didn't have far to go, it wasn't easy to make their way through the dense scrub that covered the ground. By the time they drew level with the police vehicles, Flora's arms ached from catching hold of the branches as Leon pulled them aside for her. Scratches crisscrossed her palms, and fronds tangled in her hair.

She and Leon were on a slight elevation, looking down on a clearing above the assembled group of police officers. Through a gap in the trees, they could see that the police were surrounding a vehicle that had pulled off the highway.

"Is that the one that tried to run you off the road?" Leon whispered.

"Could be. It's the right size and shape." All she really cared about was that Stevie and Frankie might be behind those blacked-out windows.

Laurie was standing nearby conversing with a tall, dark-haired man. From his uniform, Flora guessed she was looking at Sheriff Glen Harvey. She took a second to approve of him. He looked like someone she would trust to take care of her boys.

"Why are they just standing around?" she muttered. "Why don't they do something?"

"They can't." Leon's softly spoken words struck terror into Flora's heart.

Of course the police couldn't do anything. They were in a hostage situation. Daisy was shut inside that vehicle with Stevie and Frankie. One move from the police and she would…

The thought was choked off as she was grabbed from behind and hauled roughly away from Leon. Her attacker clamped one hand around her neck in a tight choke hold and the other over her mouth.

Although there was enough light for her to see, she didn't need the look of horror on Leon's face to tell her what was happening. The grip on her throat loosened, but in its place the sharp, cold edge of a blade pierced her skin. Warm blood trickled down her neck.

"One step closer and I'll slice so deep your medical training will be worthless." Daisy's voice froze Leon in his tracks.

"How did you get out of the car and past the police?" He glanced over his shoulder as he spoke. Flora could almost read his mind. Laurie and Glen Harvey were about forty feet away. He could call out to them, but, if he did, Daisy would slit Flora's throat before the law enforcement officers could even turn their heads.

"I wasn't in the car when they got here," Daisy sneered. "I'm not stupid. You think I didn't know they'd be tracing that call? Of course I did. It was what I needed. How else was I going to get you where I wanted you?"

And there it was. Daisy had been clear all along about what she wanted. *Leon.* Everything she did was with one single-minded focus. The harassment, the murders, kidnapping Stevie and Frankie, now this. Leaving her car where the police could find her had all been part of the plan. She had known Leon and Flora wouldn't be able to stay away from the twins.

Where are *the twins?*

With a knife to her throat and a hand clamped over her mouth, Flora couldn't even ask the question. She and Leon had walked into Daisy's trap...and, if things went her way, only one of them would be walking out again.

When they first heard from Daisy, Leon had enabled the emergency function on his smart phone. If he could trigger it, a pre-recorded audio message warning that he was in immediate danger, and giving his precise location, would be sent automatically to four contacts. Two of those contacts were Laurie Delaney and Joe Nolan. All he needed to do was press the power button on his phone three times in a row. The only problem with that strategy was that his cell phone was in the left front pocket of his pants.

He tried to keep his eyes on Flora's face instead of focusing on the way that lethal-looking blade was piercing the soft flesh of her neck. If he could distract Daisy, and keep her talking, maybe he could reach a hand into his pocket.

"What do you want me to do?"

"I want your undivided attention," Daisy said.

"You have it." With a knife to Flora's throat, he wasn't about to get distracted.

"I thought you were still grieving for your wife. If I'd known you were ready to move on, that you wanted a family, I'd have told you how I felt. You'd have known I loved you, and there'd have been no need for any of this." Daisy sounded almost reasonable. "So you see, none of it is actually my fault."

If Leon hadn't already known she was unhinged, those words would have been enough to convince him. "I can see why you would feel that way." As he spoke, he inched his hand toward his pocket.

"You have to understand how it feels. It's been so long since I was able to think of anything except you. I had to find a way to convince you to be with me. If you just let me into your life, we can have it all. Yes, we'll have to leave Stillwater, but we'll be together, and you'll thank me for my determination. One day, we'll brag to our friends about how I took the initiative and won you over."

Oh, they were in so much trouble. Daisy really thought this was leading to a happily-ever-after? That she could persuade him to love her? Or maybe she thought she could force him...

"Let Flora go, and we can keep talking." His fingertips brushed his cell phone.

Daisy gave a soft laugh, and Flora's whole body jerked as the knife pressed deeper. "Not happening. I'm the jealous type."

"Wait—" Leon's finger found the power button on his cell phone and relief almost brought him to his knees. "You haven't heard what I have to say."

"Go on." In the dim light, he could see both wariness and curiosity on Daisy's face.

He knew he would get only one chance at this. Hitting the power button on his phone was the easy part. One. Two. Three. *Done.* He wanted to heave a sigh of relief, but he didn't have time. Because now he had to keep Daisy talking. And speaking had never been his strong point.

"I wasn't just grieving for Karen." He kept his eyes on Flora's face. Daisy could pretend this speech was about her. He wanted Flora to know the truth. This was for her, and every word was coming straight from his heart. "It was beyond grief. I was punishing myself. I believed I didn't deserve to go on living when she had died. But I wasn't living. I wasn't even existing. Every breath felt like a wasted effort."

Every time he almost stumbled over the words, the love he saw in Flora's eyes kept him going. Even through her fear, she was guiding him on, reassuring him that she knew he was talking to her. Only her.

"Then, you came into my life, and everything changed. I'm not going to pretend it was easy. I was scared, afraid to let go of the control I had over my feelings. I was in a safe zone, and I told myself I didn't want to step out of it."

Both women were gazing at him, and he wondered how much he was fooling Daisy. Could she be so deluded as to seriously think he was pouring his heart out to her? Leon didn't care. He had finally found the courage to speak.

More importantly, he could see what Daisy couldn't. He could see the figures closing in on her from behind.

"It was when I thought I'd lost you that I knew how wrong I'd been. If you love someone else as much as I love you, you have to start caring for yourself as well. That meant I had to forgive myself. Every moment I spent dreading that the past would repeat itself became a waste of our future." Tears were streaming down Flora's face as she listened to him. "I didn't believe I was worthy of a second chance at love, but now I know everyone deserves to be happy. If you'll take my hand now, I swear to you I'll never let it go again."

His final sentence was more than a declaration. It was also a signal to action. As he finished speaking, Flora held out her hand. Leon grabbed it and pulled her toward him at the same time that Glen and Joe seized Daisy from behind. Wailing with fury, Daisy tried to swipe with the knife, but Glen already had her wrist in a firm grip. She screamed in his face as he calmly removed her weapon. Seconds later, Glen had her hands cuffed behind her back as he informed her of her rights.

Flora was trembling all over as Leon held her tight against him. "Let me take a look at your neck."

She shook her head. "Not now. The twins…"

* * *

As Flora raced toward Daisy's car, Laurie stepped in front of her, blocking her path. "I'm sorry. My officers need to check the vehicle over before you approach it."

"My boys are in there—" Flora made a movement to push past her, but Leon caught hold of her wrist.

"Laurie's right. Daisy could have done anything to that car." She strained against him for a moment before collapsing into his arms with a little sob. "It won't take long." He stared at Laurie over Flora's head. "Will it?"

The police chief returned his gaze, her face solemn. "I hope not."

Two cops wearing protective clothing commenced a detailed search of the area around the SUV, checking the grass before moving on to the car itself. One of them lay on his back and used a flashlight and mirror to examine the underside of the vehicle. His colleague checked the exhaust, fenders, tires, and wheel arches.

"If the boys are looking out of the window, and they can see me, they won't understand why I'm not going to them," Flora said. There was no noise coming from the vehicle, and that troubled her. She'd have expected the boys to be crying or shouting for her. The silence was a worrying sign.

What have you done to them, Daisy? Her nerves ratcheted up another level, alarm screaming through her bloodstream.

While the two officers continued checking the vehicle for hidden traps, the others were following orders from Laurie and Glen. The two patrol cars that had been blocking the highway moved, re-opening the road to traffic. One of the sheriff's deputies pulled his vehicle up close to the scene, and Glen escorted Daisy toward it.

The cop slid out from under the SUV. "Getting ready to open it up."

"No sign of any booby traps on the passenger side." His colleague slowly opened the door, and Flora held her breath.

"The vehicle is empty, Chief Delaney."

Flora's world swam out of focus. As she sank to her knees, Glenn and Daisy drew level with her.

"Where are my boys?" She would plead with a cold-blooded killer if she had to.

Daisy turned her head, looking up toward the distant sound of roaring water. "Eternal Springs."

A soft smile touched her lips, and Flora realized with horror that she was enjoying this final moment of triumph.

Leon squatted on the grass beside her as Flora covered her face with her hands. She was only dimly aware of the sheriff calling one of his deputies over. "Get the prisoner into the vehicle and take her to the cells. I need to stay here and liaise with Chief Delaney on the search for the missing kids."

"Search?" Flora turned to look at Leon. "Daisy said…"

"She said Eternal Springs. That could mean anything. It doesn't have to mean they went into the waterfall. It could be that she left them close by. Or she could be lying." He took her hands and pulled her to her feet. "The police will use the helicopter, dogs, get local trackers involved, anything it takes."

"Why don't they make her tell them what she did?" Flora asked.

She looked across to where one of the deputies was holding Daisy's arm as he guided her to his patrol car and put her in the back seat. As she watched, Daisy swung her legs around. With incredible strength and agility, she kicked the deputy in the chest with both feet. He fell back, hitting the ground. As he did, Daisy sprang from the vehicle at a run.

Both Laurie and Glen drew their weapons, but neither of them got a chance to fire, or even issue a warning. With a burst of speed, Daisy ran onto the highway. Right into the path of an auto-transport carrier.

Leon wrapped his arms around Flora, and she turned her face into his chest gratefully, blotting out the horror of what she'd just witnessed. It was an effective, but messy way to commit suicide. All around her, she could hear the chaos of shouted instructions, but her brain refused to get beyond one simple, selfish message. After a collision with a huge, fast-moving vehicle, Daisy must surely be dead. She could no longer torture them...but she also wouldn't be able to tell them where the twins were.

It took a few seconds for Flora to register that her cell phone was ringing. She shook her head in disbelief. "I can't talk to anyone."

"It's probably Bryce or Vincente wondering why they got an emergency message from me," Leon said.

Flora fumbled her cell out of her jacket pocket, frowning at the display. "No, it's Eve Sloane." The whole town must know by now that her twins were missing. Why would anyone call her in the middle of a crisis? Even so, Eve had never struck Flora as the sort of person to intrude or seek gossip.

She swiped to answer the call. "Not now, Eve—"

"Flora? Oh, thank goodness you answered. I have your boys with me."

"The twins witnessed Daisy attacking Tegan, they were taken away from the daycare center, then they were lost in the dark." Leon could see Flora almost gnawing through her lower lip as he pulled up in front of Eve's house. "They must be so scared."

Eve had told them she would leave the front door open. Once Flora left the car, she dashed into the house ahead of Leon, sliding to a halt in the kitchen doorway. Stevie and Frankie were seated at Eve's small table.

"Hi, Mommy." Frankie waved a hand in greeting. "We have cookies and milk."

"So you do." Leon could hear the tears in Flora's voice. She stepped up close and, placing an arm around each of them, drew both boys into an embrace.

"'nuff hugging now, Mommy," Stevie said, after submitting for about half-a-minute.

"Is it just me?" Leon viewed the two boys as they returned to their cookies. "I don't think they look too traumatized."

Flora managed a shaky laugh. "You could be right." She turned to Eve, who was watching the reunion with a smile. "The police are on their way, and they will ask all sorts of questions, of course... But how did you find them?"

"I didn't find them. Scape did," Eve said. She smiled at the look of amazement on Flora's face. "He escaped again. I caught sight of him heading through the trees toward the waterfall. Because it was dark, I took a flashlight and went after him. I thought I was going crazy when I got close to Eternal Springs and I heard the sound of children's laughter. The next thing I knew, I shone my flashlight through the trees ahead, and your boys were coming toward me with Scape between them."

"Scape is safe people," Stevie said. The words tugged hard on Leon's heartstrings as he remembered the conversation he'd had with the twins just that morning.

Eve spread her hands in a helpless gesture. "They kept telling me that."

"I've been trying to teach them that, if they are in danger, they should find someone safe," Leon explained. "And they did. They found Scape, who brought them to you."

"And we can never thank you enough," Flora said, as she hugged Eve.

"Daisy is not safe people." Frankie frowned as he brushed milk from his top lip.

"Oh, sweetie…" Flora pulled out a chair and sat next to him, taking his hand.

"She's bad." Stevie nodded.

"How did you know she was bad?" Leon asked.

"'cos she made Stevie's arm stuck." Frankie calmly helped himself to another cookie as he spoke.

Flora gasped. "Are you saying it was *Daisy* who trapped your arm under the play equipment?"

"Yes." Stevie rubbed his arm before turning to smile at Leon. "Dr. Leon got me out."

"So it wasn't daycare you didn't like," Flora said. "It was Daisy."

"That explains why they were happy to go in when Tegan was there to greet them." Leon shook his head. If only they'd asked. But would the twins have been able to explain their fears?

"I don't believe this. The police have been floundering around clueless for weeks and, all the time, my babies knew who was to blame." Flora placed her head in her hands.

"Wait until we tell Laurie she could have handed this investigation over to a couple of three-year-olds and a goat," Leon said.

With perfect timing, Laurie called out from the hall. Seconds later, she and Glen Harvey entered the small kitchen, making it immediately appear over-crowded.

"Hey." Laurie smiled at the twins. "Everyone is very glad to know you guys are safe."

Stevie looked Glen up and down before quickly moving the cookie plate closer to him and his brother.

"We're not going to keep you long," Laurie said to Leon and Flora. "I'm going to take some details from Ms. Sloane. Then, tomorrow, we'll get an officer who is trained in dealing with young children to come to your home and speak to your boys." She lowered her voice. "The suspect didn't survive the collision, but we still need to make sure we have all the facts."

Eve repeated what she'd told Leon and Flora about how she found the twins while Laurie made notes. Flora also recounted what the boys had told them about Daisy's role in trapping Stevie's arm.

"One thing I wanted to ask about was if Daisy knew Jennifer Webster?" Laurie asked.

"Yes," Flora said. "The Ryerson Center had an introduction day for the staff a week before it opened. Jennifer and I both attended. In fact, we were chatting in the foyer when Daisy came to the center to drop off some paperwork for me about the daycare center." She raised a hand to her throat. "I actually introduced them."

"That answers the question about why Jennifer would have given Daisy a lift. I figure Daisy faked a problem with her car, or some other difficulty. I guess we'll never know for sure," Laurie said. "We're done here for now. I'm sure you want to get your boys home."

Once Laurie and Glen had gone, Eve walked outside with them.

"Thank you again," Flora said. "Although those words don't come close to what I really feel."

"There's the other hero." Leon nodded across at Scape, who was standing on top of a pile of logs. When he saw them, the goat jumped down and pranced over.

Stevie and Frankie greeted Scape with pleasure. The animal responded with bleats and headbutts that had them chuckling.

"We owe you our thanks as well." Flora rubbed the top of Scape's head. He gave her one of his oblique glances and nibbled the hem of her skirt.

By the time they got home, the twins were asleep. "Cookies and milk for dinner and no bath?" Flora said. "It's incredible the way standards slide following an abduction."

When the twins were tucked up in bed, Leon placed an arm around Flora's shoulders and they stood for a long time, staring down at the boys as they slept. Leon was awash with the most intense relief he had ever known. The fear he had felt when the twins were missing had almost destroyed him. He had lost one child in his life. He couldn't bear the thought of more pain. Only the need to be there for Flora had moved him forward and kept him going. Now, he was grateful for the depth of his feelings. He was living and loving again, instead of coping in a way that numbed him and shut him away from reality.

Flora took his hand and led him from the room. When they were outside the door, she raised his palm to her cheek and held it there. "What you said...back then—"

"I meant every word. I love you, Flora. You and the boys are my life now."

She nodded, tears glistening on the ends of her lashes. "My boys have never had a dad, and I'd convinced myself they didn't need one. That was because I was scared. Not just for them, but for myself. I felt love had let me down when Danny died, and I was afraid to give my trust again. When I fell so hard and fast for you, I had no confidence in my instincts. It took time for me to accept that I couldn't fight it. You are the best dad my boys could ask for...but it's so much more than that. You're perfect for me." Her smile was radiant through her tears. "Asking me to take your hand, and hold it forever... I love you, Leon, and those are the sweetest words I've ever heard."

He drew her close. After everything they'd been through, just holding her like this was a precious gift he had believed they might never have.

Flora leaned back and looked up at him. "Take me to bed. I want to fall asleep in your arms without worrying about what tomorrow will bring."

Chapter 19

The next two days were a form of therapy. Leon and Flora didn't really talk about what had happened. Instead, they concentrated on loving each other and caring for the twins.

Although Flora watched the boys like a hawk for signs that their ordeal had adversely affected them, it didn't seem to be the case. They were as lively as ever, tumbling with Tiny, playing together one minute and squabbling the next, funny, curious, demanding, and delightful.

The daycare center was temporarily closed, but Beth and Steffi had called to offer their help. The boys enjoyed dividing their time equally between the animal sanctuary and Beth and Vincente's lakeside home. Flora had called Tegan to find out how she was and learned that there was a plan underway among the daycare staff to reopen the center.

"We don't want all the good things about the place to go to waste," Tegan had explained.

"I don't know if I want them to go back there," Flora said to Leon when the call was over.

"We can decide that when it happens," he said. "And we can see how the boys themselves feel about it."

Having eaten dinner, they were spending the evening in their favorite place on the porch, watching the twins play on the grass. The knowledge that they no longer had to look over their shoulders was a form of therapy in itself. As a doctor, she knew that true healing would only take place when they explored and shared their emotions. That might be with each other. Possibly the twins would need professional help, as might she and Leon. They could take their time to find out.

"How did your conversation with Alan go?" she asked.

Leon's mouth turned down. "Much as you'd expect. He didn't try to hide anything, and he's full of remorse. I can't see him returning to Stillwater, which means, of course, that the Main Street Clinic will definitely close."

Flora knew how hard it had been for him to make the call to his former boss, but she admired him for doing it. In his meeting with Laurie, Alan Grayson had admitted to multiple cases of medical malpractice. He faced an uncertain future littered with lawsuits and a lengthy battle with his gambling addiction. Although he couldn't condone his actions, Leon wasn't prepared to turn his back on the man who gave him a chance when most people had written him off.

The silence was interrupted by the sounds of an approaching car engine. Leon shielded his eyes against the evening sun. "Cameron and Laurie."

"I guess we had to hear more about the investigation sooner or later." Flora sighed as she got to her feet.

Although an officer had been out to the house to talk to Stevie and Frankie, the encounter had been low-key, and the boys had been untroubled by it. They had chatted easily about Daisy taking them from the daycare center and leaving them near the waterfall in the darkness. The only person who had been upset by the details had been Flora.

This was the first time any of them had seen Laurie since the abduction, and Flora wasn't sure how she felt. Did she want this intrusion into their new-found peace? Or did she want to remain in ignorance about what the police had learned? Having been through a police investigation when Danny died, she knew she couldn't hide away, even if she wanted to.

"We bought homemade peach pie and iced lemon and ginger tea," Laurie said, as she approached.

"The news must be bad if you have to sweeten the blow." Leon took the pie dish and glass bottle from her. "I'll get plates and glasses."

When he returned, Flora pulled up a small table and they arranged their chairs around it.

"We can eat while we talk," Laurie said.

"You clearly don't live with twins." Leon rolled his eyes as Stevie and Frankie bounded up the porch steps. Their encounter at the bake-off hadn't spoiled their appetite for pie. They each accepted a large portion, which they shared with Tiny. Bungee, who wasn't fond of baked goods, jumped onto Cameron's lap and kneaded his thigh with sharp claws.

"They don't seem to have suffered any ill effects." Laurie observed the twins as they returned to a game of building with wooden blocks.

"They have two doctors watching them, so I guess we'll know if there are any signs of trauma. But they do appear to be fine," Flora said. "I take it this visit wasn't just about the wonderful pie?"

"Unfortunately not." Laurie's faithful notebook appeared from her tote. Flipping through it, she examined her small, neat handwriting. "Okay. One of the first things I wanted to investigate was your question about whether Daisy could have killed before all of this began."

Leon nodded. "I couldn't understand how she would pass the background checks to run a daycare center if that was the case, but she talked about killing people as though it was an everyday thing."

"How old would you say Daisy Cain was?" Laurie asked.

Flora looked at her in surprise. "Um… Early thirties?"

"That's what I'd have said." Laurie nodded. "But the Daisy Cain who registered Daisy's Daycare as a business was a forty-seven-year-old Chicago-born widow."

"I don't understand." Flora frowned as she tried to take in what Laurie was saying.

"Ten years ago, Daisy Cain made a series of complaints to the Chicago police. They were against a young woman who she claimed was harassing her. The woman, whose name was Meredith Jones, claimed to be in love with Daisy's husband, Dr. William Cain. The harassment took the form of damage to her property, theft, and even a fire. Although the police spoke to Meredith Jones, there wasn't a lot else they could do because there was no actual proof she was responsible." Laurie flipped over a page. "Then Dr. Cain was killed."

"What?" Leon sat up straighter.

"He was hit over the head, then stabbed. Details are sketchy, but no one has been convicted of his murder, and I haven't been able to discover what happened to his wife. Except, of course, that she appears to have come to Stillwater and opened a daycare center. Oh, and turned back the clock, making herself about fifteen years younger."

"Did you get a description of Meredith Jones?" Flora asked.

"Tall, dark, athletic, into running, and outdoor sports." Laurie looked up as she finished reading. "Sound familiar?"

"Very." Leon nodded. "You think Meredith Jones killed Daisy Cain's husband and stole her identity?"

"I have some more investigating to do, but I believe it's a real possibility. Meredith Jones could be another of Daisy's victims and that's a possibility I need to explore," Laurie said. "I don't have any pictures yet of Meredith Jones, but I'm fairly sure they'll bear a striking resemblance to the woman who turned up in Stillwater around the time that Dr. Cain was killed. By the way—" She looked at Leon. "Dr. Cain was described by his patients as a wonderful man, the sort of person who was loved by everyone, and who went out of his way to listen. We know the Daisy Cain who abducted the twins had a fondness for doctors who fit *that* description."

Leon shifted uncomfortably. "Are you telling me to develop a grouchy manner?"

"Don't ever change." Flora patted his hand before turning to Laurie. "What do you think happened to the real Daisy Cain?"

"I don't rate the chances that she's still alive as high. In fact, I suspect she died in the same manner, and at the same time, as her husband, but we'll keep checking," Laurie said. "As for the rest of the case, there are some things that confirm Daisy's—or probably Meredith's— involvement in each crime. We found the lid and some shards of glass from a jar of cherry pie filling in the trash at her home, together with the packaging from a ready-made pastry crust. I'm sure your technician can match them to the pie that was given to Frankie. There was a baseball bat and ski mask in the trunk of her vehicle, providing further confirmation that she was the person who attacked Dr. Laxman. We're also looking into the disappearance of the reporter who wrote the story that started all of this. There will be other things I need to discuss with you as the investigation evolves, but they can wait. I didn't come here to talk about every detail."

"You didn't?" Flora asked.

"No. *I* came with a proposition," Cameron said. "For you, Leon."

Leon raised his brows. "Go on."

"Vivien McAuley's terrible death leaves the Ryerson Center short of a doctor. Since Alan Grayson confirmed to Laurie that he has no intention of returning to Still-water, I know that means the Main Street Clinic will be closing." Cameron held out his hand. "If you want it, this is a formal job offer."

Flora caught a glimpse of the raw emotion in Leon's eyes as he took Cameron's hand. She knew what this meant to him. When Alan Grayson had taken a chance on him, the rest of the town had been skeptical. Now, he had earned his place alongside her and Raj in the prestigious center that was designed to revolutionize care in the local area.

"I accept." As Leon spoke, Flora jumped up to hug him.

His journey back from rock bottom was complete.

Twelve Months Later

"Hey, Dr. Sinclair." Flora had been standing at the sink, but she turned her head to smile at Leon as he entered the kitchen.

"Back at you, Dr. Sinclair." Leon wrapped his arms around her from behind, resting his chin on her shoulder. They stood in silence for a moment looking out at the yard before he spoke again. "Um…what happened to your flowers? Did the rabbits get into the rose garden?"

"No, Scape did. He paid us a visit and ate all the flowers."

"That's one nomadic goat." Leon shook his head. "I hope Tiny chased him?"

"Tiny hid in the shed. Bungee hissed at Scape and gave him a scare. The twins and I managed to drive him into the paddock and keep him there until Eve came to collect him." Flora laughed at the memory. "She said this isn't the farthest he's wandered. A few weeks ago, he made it all the way out to Toby Murray's ranch."

Leon whistled. "That's on the road out to Park County. Scape sure gets around."

"From what Eve said, Toby wasn't amused. Apparently, he's a perfectionist when it comes to his stables. When he caught sight of Scape cavorting around his spotless yard kicking up straw and goat droppings as he tried to head-butt one of the prize stallions...well, let's just say Eve isn't Toby's favorite person. By the way..." She turned, looping her arms around his neck. "I told Eve our news. I hope you don't mind?"

Leon dropped a kiss onto the end of her nose. "Why would I mind you sharing something so wonderful? Besides, I'm pretty sure the boys have already told everyone at the daycare center that they're getting a new sister."

"It's such a relief to know they love it there now. After everything that happened—" She broke off as he pressed a finger to her lips.

"The not-safe lady who trapped Stevie's arm and left them in the woods has gone away. That was all they ever needed to know."

"I honestly think they've forgotten all about it. And now that Tegan is running the daycare center, they bounce over the doorstep each day like they own the place." Flora frowned. "Actually, they sometimes need a reminder that they *don't* own the place."

"On the subject of Stevie and Frankie..." Leon tilted his head to one side in listening mode. "It's *way* too calm around here."

"Beth invited them over to play with Lia. Katerina's there, too. Beth will bring them back later."

He drew her closer. "So we get to enjoy an hour or two of peace and quiet?"

She smiled. "Did you have something specific in mind?"

Before he could answer, there was a crash from the direction of the family room. It was followed by a feline screech. A few seconds later, Tiny charged through the kitchen with his ears flat to his head and his tail between his legs. He looked like a dog who was being pursued by vengeful demons. Close on his heels, spitting with fury, came Bungee. They dashed through the open door and into the garden.

Flora turned back to Leon. "About that peace and quiet you mentioned?"

He laughed. "It's over-rated. Before I met you and the boys, my life was a straight, narrow road. I thought that was what I needed, that I had to be able to see exactly what was ahead of me. It was dull as all hell. Now, it has unexpected twists and turns, and I never know what's around the next corner. I love it, and I couldn't be happier."

He scooped her up into his arms and carried her into the hall.

"I'm glad you said how much you love the twists and turns," Flora said, as he stepped onto the first stair. "Because I forgot to mention that the twins found your comic book collection this morning…"

* * * * *

#2111 COLTON 911: IN HOT PURSUIT
Colton 911: Grand Rapids • by Geri Krotow
Army paralegal Vikki Colton returns to Grand Rapids to investigate a suspicious death and must work with the suspect's half brother, MP sergeant Flynn Cruz-Street. When attraction flares and they're both in a killer's sights, can she trust that Flynn isn't protecting his mad-scientist sibling?

#2112 COLTON CHRISTMAS CONSPIRACY
The Coltons of Kansas • by Lisa Childs
Neil Colton and Elise Willis were once partners in everything: a law practice and a marriage. Now Elise is the mayor of Braxville—and a one-night stand has left her pregnant with Neil's child. When someone targets both of them in an explosion, it's up to them to narrow down the long list of suspects to protect their reunited family.

#2113 THE COWBOY'S TARGETED BRIDE
Cowboys of Holiday Ranch • by Carla Cassidy
They both had ulterior motives to marry. Jerod Steen wanted a family and Lily Kidwell struggled to save her ranch. When they agree to a marriage of convenience, neither expects to find love. But after their walk down the aisle, betrayal lurks at the Holiday Ranch and it's about to turn deadly...

#2114 AGENT'S MOUNTAIN RESCUE
Wyoming Nights • by Jennifer D. Bokal
When a lead points security agency Rocky Mountain Justice in the direction of a posh resort in the hunt for a serial killer, operative and single dad Liam Alexander and child psychologist Holly Jacobs work together to hunt the huntress, eventually posing as a family to trap their prey. But as their plan backfires, Liam will do anything to save his child—and the woman he loves.

HRSCNM1020

"Look at us, we're quite the mismatched pair. Still,
we make a decent team." Reaching for her hand, Liam
stared at their joined fingers. "Plus," he added, "you're
pretty easy to talk to and to trust. I don't do either of
those things easily, but then I think you've figured that
out already. I like that about you, Holly."

She inched closer, her breath caressing his cheek.
"You're not so bad yourself."

He smiled a little. "That's better than you turning me
down."

She licked her lips. Looking away, Holly stared at
something just beyond Liam's shoulder. "I don't want to
complicate things."

"I understand," he said, even though he didn't. He wanted her. She wanted him. It all seemed pretty simple and straightforward. "I'm not going to pressure you into anything here."

"Do you really understand?" she asked. "Because I'm not sure that I know what's going on myself."

"You have your life plan. You need money to keep your school open. A relationship is a complication. Besides, you could be leaving town, which means us getting involved could be difficult for Sophie."

Holly touched her fingertips to his lips, silencing him. "If I can't get the money to keep Saplings, then I'll definitely have to leave Pleasant Pines," she said. "You said it yourself—I might not be around much longer."

"Now I'm really confused. What are you saying?"

"Kiss me," she whispered.

It was all the invitation he needed.

Don't miss
Agent's Mountain Rescue *by Jennifer D. Bokal,*
available November 2020 wherever
Harlequin Romantic Suspense
books and ebooks are sold.

Harlequin.com

HRSEXP1020

Get 4 FREE REWARDS!

We'll send you 2 FREE Books plus 2 FREE Mystery Gifts.

Harlequin Romantic Suspense books are heart-racing page-turners with unexpected plot twists and irresistible chemistry that will keep you guessing to the very end.

FREE
Value Over
$20